The Fugitive Worlds

ORBIT

An Orbit Book

Copyright © Bob Shaw 1989

First published in Great Britain in 1989
by Victor Gollancz Ltd

This edition published in 1991
by Orbit Books, a Division of
Macdonald & Co (Publishers) Ltd
London & Sydney

ISBN 0 7088 4874 5

Printed and bound in Great Britain by
Collins, Glasgow

Orbit Books
A Division of
Macdonald & Co (Publishers) Ltd
Orbit House
1 New Fetter Lane
London EC4A 1AR

A member of Maxwell Macmillan Pergamon Publishing Corporation

Contents

PART I

The Return to Land

Chapter 1

The lone astronaut had fallen from the very edge of space, down through thousands of miles of gradually thickening atmosphere, a drop which had lasted more than a day. In the later stages of the descent his body had been acted on by wind forces which had carried him far to the west of the capital city. Perhaps through inexperience, perhaps from a desire to be free of the restraints of the fallbag, he had opened his parachute too soon. It had been deployed a good ten miles above the planetary surface, and as a result was being wafted even farther into the sparsely populated regions which lay beyond the White River.

Toller Maraquine II, who had been patrolling the area for eight days, examined the creamy fleck of the parachute through powerful binoculars. It was an inconspicuous object, hardly as bright as the daytime stars, seemingly fixed in position beneath the great curving rim of the sister world which filled the centre of the sky. The movement of Toller's airship made it difficult to keep the parachute centred in his field of view, but he was able to pick out the tiny figure slung beneath it and he felt a growing sense of anticipation.

What would the astronaut have to report?

The very fact that the expedition had lasted longer than expected was a good omen in Toller's eyes, but in any case it would be a relief to pick the man up and transport him to Prad. Patrolling the near-featureless region, with nothing to do but return the companionable waves of farm workers, had been monotonous in the extreme, and Toller had a craving to get back to the city where he could at least find congenial company and a glass of decent wine. There was also some unfinished and highly pleasurable business with

9

Hariana, a blonde beauty in the Weavers' Guild. He had been in ardent pursuit of her for many days, and he sensed she had been on the verge of yielding when he had been sent away on the current irksome duty.

The airship was running easily before the easterly breeze, requiring only an occasional nudge from the jet engines to keep pace with the parachutist's lateral motion. In spite of the shade provided by the elliptical gasbag overhead, the heat on the upper deck was becoming intense, and Toller knew that the twelve men comprising his crew were as eager as he to see the mission come to an end. Their saffron airmen's blouses were dappled with sweat and their postures were as drooped as was compatible with observance of shipboard discipline.

Two hundred feet below the gondola the striated fields of the region slipped quietly by, forming patterns of stripes which flowed out to the horizon. It was now just over fifty years since the migration to Overland, and the Kolcorronian farmers had had time to impose their designs on the natural colouration of the landscape. On a planet without seasons the edible grasses and other vegetation tended to be heterogenous, each plant following its own maturation cycle, but the farmers had painstakingly sorted them into synchronous groups to achieve the six harvests a year which had been traditional on the Old World since history began. Each field of grain displayed linear variations in colour, from the delicate green of young shoots to harvest gold and the brown of shorn earth.

"There's another ship to the south of us, sir," shouted Niskodar, the helmsman. "Same altitude or a bit higher. About two miles away."

Toller located the ship—a dark sliver low on the purple-hazed horizon—and turned his glasses on it. The magnified image showed that the craft had blue-and-yellow Sky Service markings, a fact which caused Toller some surprise. Several times in the previous eight days he had glimpsed the ship which was patrolling the sector adjoining his to the south, but that had been at the mutual limit of the sweeps and the visual contacts had been fleeting. The newcomer was well inside Toller's assigned territory and, as far as he could determine, was closing with him as though also intending to intercept the returning parachutist.

"Get on the sunwriter," he said to Lieutenant Feer, who was at the rail beside him. "Give the commander of that ship my compliments and advise him to change course—I am on the Queen's business and will brook no interference or obstruction."

"Yes, sir," Feer replied eagerly, obviously pleased that the incident had come along to add a hint of savour to the foreday. He opened a locker and took out a sunwriter which was of the new lightweight design employing silvered mirror slats in place of the conventional glass sandwich construction. Feer aimed the instrument and worked the trigger, producing a busy clacking sound. For about a minute after he had finished there was no visible response, then a tiny sun began to blink rapidly on the distant ship.

Good foreday, Captain Maraquine, came the pulsed message. *The Countess Vantara returns your greeting. She has decided to take command of this operation in person. Your attendance is no longer required. You are hereby instructed to return to Prad immediately.*

Toller choked back the angry swear words the message had inspired in him. He had never met Countess Vantara, but he knew that she, as well as holding the rank of sky-captain, was a granddaughter of the Queen and that she habitually used the royal connection to enhance her authority. Many other commanders faced with a similar situation would have backed down, perhaps after a token protest, for fear of prejudicing their careers, but Toller was constitutionally unable to accept what he saw as a slur. His hand dropped to the hilt of the sword which had once belonged to his grandfather, and he scowled fiercely in the direction of the intruding ship as he composed a reply to the countess's imperious message.

"Sir, do you wish to acknowledge the signal?" Lieutenant Feer's manner was absolutely correct, but a certain brightness in his eyes showed that he relished seeing Toller faced with a tricky decision. Although of subordinate rank he was somewhat the older of the two, and he almost certainly subscribed to the general view that Toller had achieved captaincy so early through family influence. It was apparent that the prospect of witnessing a duel between the privileged and the privileged had a strong appeal to the lieutenant.

"Of course I wish to acknowledge it," Toller said, hiding his irritation. "What is that woman's family name?"

"Dervonai, sir."

"All right, forget all that countess frippery and address her as Captain Dervonai. Say: Your kind offer of assistance is noted, but in this instance the presence of another vessel is likely to be more of a hindrance than a help. Continue with your own business and do not impede me in the execution of the Queen's direct orders."

A look of gratification appeared on Feer's narrow face as he beamed Toller's words out to the other ship—he had not expected an outright confrontation to develop so quickly. There was only the briefest pause before a reply came. *Your show of discourtesy, not to say insolence, has also been noted, but I will refrain from reporting it to my grandmother if you withdraw at once. I urge you to be prudent.*

"The arrogant bitch!" Toller snatched the sunwriter out of Feer's hands, aimed it and worked the trigger. *I deem it more prudent to be reported to her Majesty for discourtesy than for treason, which would be the case were I to abandon my mission. I therefore urge you to return to your needlework.*

"Needlework!" Lieutenant Feer, who had been able to read the message from the side, gave an appreciative chuckle as Toller handed the sunwriter back to him. "The lady aviator

12

won't appreciate that one, sir. I wonder what her reply will be."

"There it is," Toller said, having raised his binoculars just in time to discern smoke pluming out from the other ship's main jets. "She's either departing the scene in a huff or going all out to reach our objective first—and if what I've heard about the Countess Vantara is true . . . Yes! We have a race on our hands!"

"Do you want full speed?"

"What else?" Toller said. "And tell the men to put on parachutes."

At the mention of parachutes Feer's gleeful expression faded and was replaced by one of wariness. "Sir, you don't think it's going to come to—"

"Anything can happen when two ships dispute a single piece of sky." Toller injected a note of joviality into his voice, subtly punishing the lieutenant for the improprieties in his attitude. "A collision could easily result in deaths, and I would prefer it that they were all on the opposition's side."

"Yes, sir." Feer turned away, already signalling to the engineer, and a moment later the main jets began a steady roar as maximum continuous power was applied. The nose of the long gondola lifted as the jet thrust tried to rotate the entire ship about its centre of gravity, but the helmsman quickly corrected its attitude by altering the angle of the engines. He was able to do so single-handed, by means of a lever and ratchets, because the engines were of the modern lightweight type consisting of riveted metal tubes.

Until quite recently each jet would have utilised the entire trunk of a young brakka tree, and consequently would have been heavy and unwieldy. The power source was still a mixture of pikon and halvell crystals, which throughout history had been extracted from the soil by the root systems of brakka trees. Now, however, the crystals were obtained directly from the earth by means of chemical refining methods developed by Toller's father, Cassyll Maraquine.

Industrial chemistry and metallurgy were the cornerstones of the Maraquine family's immense fortune and power—which in turn were the source of most of the personal difficulties Toller had with his parents. They had expected him to understudy his father in preparation for taking up the reins of the family's industrial empire—a prospect he had viewed with dread—and his relationship with them had been occasionally strained ever since he had chosen to enter the Sky Service in pursuit of excitement and adventure. Those two qualities had been less plentiful than he had hoped for, which was one of the reasons for his determination not to be elbowed aside on this particular occasion. . . .

He returned his attention to the astronaut, who was still a good mile above the surface of the undulating farmlands. There was no practical point in racing to the parachutist's estimated touchdown point, but it might strengthen Vantara's case if she could claim to have been at the site first. Toller guessed that she had by pure chance intercepted the sunwriter message he had relayed to the palace earlier in the day, and then had decided on a whim to take over at the interesting phase of what had been a tedious mission.

He was considering whether or not to send her a final warning message when he noticed that a line of dark blue had appeared on the western horizon. His binoculars confirmed that there was a substantial body of water ahead, and on consulting his charts he found that it was called Lake Amblaraate. It was more than five miles across, which meant that the astronaut had little chance of drifting himself clear of its edges, but it was traversed by a line of small, low-lying islands from which a skilful parachutist ought to be able to select a good landing site.

Toller beckoned Feer to him and showed him the chart. "I think we may be in for some sport," he said. "Those islets look scarcely big enough to accommodate a parade ground. If yonder flyaway seed manages to plant himself on one of them the task of plucking him up again will call for some fancy airmanship. I wonder if the lady aviator, as you dubbed her, will remain so anxious to claim the honour."

"The important thing is that the messenger and his dispatches are conveyed safely to the Queen," Feer replied. "Does it really matter who picks him up?"

Toller gave him a broad smile. "Oh yes, lieutenant—it matters a great deal."

He leaned on the gondola's rail, enjoying the cooling effect of the gathering slipstream, and watched the other ship draw nearer on the converging course. The range was still too great for him to be able to see any of the crew clearly, even with binoculars, but he knew they were all female. It had been Queen Daseene herself who had insisted on women being allowed to enter the Sky Service. That had been during the emergency of twenty-six years earlier, at the time of the threatened invasion from the Old World, but the tradition persisted to the present day, though for mainly practical reasons it had been decided not to use mixed crews. Toller, who had spent most of his active service on the far side of Overland, had not previously encountered any of the very few airships crewed by women, and he was interested in finding out if gender had any noticeable effect on ship-handling techniques.

As he had expected, both ships reached Lake Amblaraate while the parachutist was still high above them. Toller judged which of the islands was most likely to provide the touchdown point, ordered his ship down to a hundred feet and began cruising in a circle around the triangular patch of green. To his annoyance, Vantara adopted a similar tactic, taking up a station at the opposite side of the circle. The two ships rotated as though attached to the ends of an invisible rod, the intermittent blasts of their jets disturbing colonies of birds which nested on the low ground.

"This is a waste of good crystals," Toller grumbled.

"A criminal waste." Feer nodded, permitting himself a hint of a smile over the fact that his commander was

15

frequently reprimanded by the Service's quartermaster general for using up his stores of pikon and halvell at a greater rate than any other captain because of his impatient flying style.

"That woman should be grounded and—" Toller broke off as the parachutist, apparently having agreed with his audience on a choice of landing site, abruptly furled part of his canopy, increasing his fall-speed and steepening his angle of descent.

"Get us down there with all possible speed!" Toller ordered. "Use all four anchor guns on first contact—we must land on the first pass."

The smile returned to Toller's face as he saw that the crucial moment had come while his ship was well to the west of the island, so that a single natural manoeuvre would bring it into position for an upwind landing. It very much looked as though the aerial wheel of chance had declared against Vantara. He glanced again at the Countess's ship and was appalled to see that it was already breaking out of the flight pattern and beginning a steep descent to the island, obviously intent on making an illegal downwind landing.

"The bitch," Toller whispered. "The stupid bitch!"

He watched helplessly as the other vessel, its speed enhanced by the following breeze, speared down through the lowest levels of the air and drove towards the centre of the island. *Too fast*, he thought. *The anchors will never take the strain!* Puffs of smoke appeared on each side of the gondola as its keel touched the grass and the anchor cannon fired their barbs into the ground. The ship slowed abruptly, its gasbag distorting. For a moment it looked as though Toller's prediction would be proved wrong, then both ropes on the left side of the gondola snapped. The ship rolled and turned, hauling its rear anchor out of the soil, and would have broken free had not the crew member on the solitary remaining anchor begun paying out line at maximum possible speed, thus easing the strain on the rope. Against the odds the single line took up the load without breaking, and all at once it was impossible for Toller to bring off his intended landing manoeuvre—Vantara's ship, dipping and wallowing, lay across his line of descent.

"Abort the landing!" he shouted. "Up! Go up!"

The main jets sounded immediately and, following the emergency drill, the crewmen who were not otherwise engaged ran aft to transfer their weight and help tilt the nose of the vessel upwards. Prompt though the corrective actions had been, the inertia of the tons of gas in the envelope which strained overhead slowed down the ship's response. For nightmarishly protracted seconds it continued on its course, with the obstructing vessel expanding to fill the view directly ahead, then the horizon began to sink with nerve-abrading slowness.

From his position at the side of the bridge Toller glimpsed the long-haired figure of Countess Vantara, a momentary vision which was replaced by the swift-sliding curvatures of the other gasbag, so close that he could make out the individual stitches of the panels and load tapes. He held his breath, willing himself and his ship to rise vertically, and was beginning to hope that a collision had been averted when there came a vast groaning sound from below. The sound—low-pitched, quavering, reproachful—told him that his keel was ploughing its way across the upper surface of the other ship's gasbag.

He looked aft and saw Vantara's ship emerging from beneath his own. At least two seams had given way in the varnished linen envelope, allowing the supportive gas to spew into the atmosphere. The rents, although serious, were not bad enough to cause a catastrophe—the elliptical gasbag was slowly becoming misshapen and wrinkled, allowing the gondola beneath it to sink to the ground.

Toller gave the orders for his ship to resume normal flying and to make another circuit in preparation for landing. The manoeuvre gave him and his crew an excellent opportunity to watch the countess's ship sink down at the end of its tether, and—the final ignominy—be blotted out of sight by the collapsing gasbag. As soon as it had become apparent that nobody was going to be killed or even injured, the release of tension caused Toller to laugh. Taking their cue from him, Feer and the rest of the crew joined in and the merriment became almost hysterical when the parachutist—whose existence had virtually been forgotten—descended into the scene of action, made a comically awkward landing and ended up sitting on his backside in a patch of swamp.

"There's no hurry now, so I want a flawless showpiece landing," Toller said. "Take her in slowly."

In accordance with his instructions the ship settled down against the breeze with a stately motion and grounded with a barely perceptible shudder. As soon as the anchor cannon had secured the craft, Toller swung himself over the rail and dropped to the grass. The first of Vantara's crew were beginning to struggle out from beneath the folds of their gasbag, but Toller ignored them and walked towards the parachutist, who had risen to his feet and was gathering the sprawled canopy. He raised his head and saluted as he saw Toller approaching. He was a lean, fair-skinned youngster who looked barely old enough to have left his family home, but—and Toller was impressed by the realisation—he had completed a double crossing of the void that lay between the sister worlds.

"Good foreday, sir," he said. "Corporal Steenameert, sir. I bear urgent dispatches for her Majesty."

"I thought as much," Toller smiled. "I am under orders to transport you to Prad without delay, but I think we can take a moment to let you get out of that skysuit. It can't be very comfortable walking around with a wet arse."

Steenameert returned the smile, appreciating the way in which Toller had put the relationship on an informal footing. "It wasn't one of my best landings."

"Bad landings seem to be the order of the day," Toller said, glancing past Steenameert. Countess Vantara was striding towards him, a tall black-haired woman whose high-breasted figure was made even more impressive by the fact that she was holding herself angrily erect. Close behind her was a smaller woman, much rounder in build, wearing a lieutenant's uniform, who was labouring to keep pace with her superior. Toller returned his attention to Steenameert, his sense of wonder stirring as he thought of the magnitude of the journey the boy had completed. In spite of his youthfulness, Steenameert had seen sights and had been granted experiences Toller could scarcely imagine. Toller envied him and also was deeply curious about what had been discovered on the voyage to Land—the first since the colonisation of Overland had begun fifty years earlier.

"Tell me, corporal," he said. "What was it like on the Old World?"

Steenameert looked hesitant. "Sir, the dispatches are privy to her Majesty."

"Never mind the dispatches. Man-to-man, what did *you* see? What was it *like*?"

A gratified expression appeared on Steenameert's face as he struggled out of his one-piece skysuit, making it apparent that he had a compulsion to talk about his adventures. "Empty cities! Great cities, cities which make Prad look like a village—and all of them empty!"

"Empty? But what about the—?"

"Mister Maraquine!" The Countess Vantara was still a dozen paces away, but her voice was forceful enough to silence Toller in mid-sentence. "Pending your dismissal from the Service for wilfully damaging one of her Majesty's airships, I am taking command of your vessel. You will consider yourself under arrest!"

The arrogance and the sheer unreasonableness of Vantara's words checked Toller's breath, inspiring in him a pang of fury so intense that he knew it was vital for it to be subdued. He put on his most relaxed smile, turned slowly towards the countess, and immediately wished he had met her under different circumstances. She had one of those faces which have the effect of filling men with hopeless admiration and women with hopeless envy. It was oval, grey-eyed and perfect—flawless in a way which set its owner apart from all the other women Toller had ever seen.

"What are you grinning at?" Vantara demanded. "Did you not hear what I said?"

Putting his regrets aside, Toller said, "Don't be silly. Do you need any help with repairs to your ship?"

Vantara glanced in outrage at the lieutenant who had just arrived at her side, then triangulated her gaze on Toller's face. "Mister Maraquine, you don't seem to realise the seriousness of your situation. You are under arrest."

Toller sighed. "Listen to me, captain. You have behaved very stupidly, but fortunately no real damage has been done and there is no need for either of us to make an official report. Let us just go our separate ways and forget the whole sorry incident."

"You'd like that, wouldn't you?"

"It would be better than prolonging this lunacy of yours."

Vantara's hand moved to the butt of the pistol in her belt. "I repeat, Mister Maraquine, you are under arrest."

Scarcely able to believe what was happening, Toller instinctively gripped the haft of his sword.

Vantara's smile was icily perfect. "What do you think you could do with that ridiculous museum piece?"

"Since you ask, I'll tell you," Toller said, lightly and evenly. "Before you could even raise your pistol I could cleave your head from your body, and were your lieutenant foolhardy enough to try menacing me she would suffer the same fate. Furthermore, even if you had two others of your crew with you . . . and even if they managed to fire and put their bullets into me . . . I would nevertheless be able to run at them and cut them down.

"I hope I have made myself clear, Captain Dervonai. I

am under direct orders from her Majesty, and if *anybody* attempts to prevent me executing those orders that attempt will end in terrible bloodshed. Those are the simple facts of the matter." Keeping his expression bland, Toller waited to see what effect his words would have on Vantara. The physique he had inherited from his grandfather was a living reminder of the days when the military had comprised a separate caste in Kolcorron. He towered over the countess and had twice her weight, and yet he was not at all certain that things were going to go his way. She had the look of one who was not accustomed to being thwarted, whatever the circumstances.

There was a tense moment during which Toller was acutely aware that his entire future was trembling in the balance, and then—unexpectedly—Vantara gave a delighted laugh.

"Just *look* at him, Jerene!" she said, nudging her companion. "I do believe he's taking all this seriously." The lieutenant seemed startled for an instant, then she mustered a weak smile.

"It is a very serious—"

"Where's your sense of humour, Toller Maraquine?" Vantara cut in. "Of course, now that I think of it, you always did take yourself too seriously."

Toller was taken aback. "Are you claiming that we have met before?"

Vantara laughed again. "Don't you remember your father taking you to the Migration Day reception at the palace when you were little? Even then you went around wearing a sword . . . trying to look like your famous grandfather. . . ."

Toller was certain he was being mocked, but if this was the countess's way of backing down without too much loss of face he was prepared to be compliant. Anything was better than continuing the needless confrontation.

"I confess to not remembering you," he said, "but I suspect it is because your appearance has changed to a greater degree than mine."

Vantara shook her head, rejecting the implied compliment. "No. It's simply that you have a poor memory—what about this skyman for whose custody you were, only minutes ago, prepared to risk the safety of two ships?"

Toller turned to Steenameert, who had been listening to the exchange with interest. "Go aboard my ship and have the cook prepare you a meal. We will continue our conversation in comfort." Steenameert saluted, took hold of his parachute and dragged it away.

"I presume you asked him why the expedition lasted so much longer than expected," Vantara said casually, as though the clash of wills had never taken place.

"Yes." Toller was unsure of how to deal with the countess, but he decided to try making their relationship as informal and friendly as possible. "He said that Land was empty. He spoke of empty cities."

"Empty! But what has become of the so-called New Men?"

"The explanation, if there is one, should be in the dispatches."

"In that case I must visit her Majesty, my grandmother, as soon as possible," Vantara said. The reference to her royal family connection had been unnecessary, and Toller took it as an indication that he was expected to keep his distance.

"I, too, must return to Prad with all possible speed," he said, making his tone brisk. "Are you sure you don't want any help with repairs?"

"Positive! The seams will be sewn before littlenight, then I'll be on my way."

"There's just one more thing," Toller said as Vantara was turning away. "Strictly speaking, our ships were in collision and we are supposed to file incident reports. How do you feel about that?"

She met his gaze directly. "I find all that paperwork rather tiresome, don't you?"

"*Very* tiresome." Toller smiled and saluted. "Goodbye, captain."

He watched the countess and her junior officer walk off in the direction of their ship, then he turned and retraced his steps to his own vessel. The great disk of the sister planet was filling the sky overhead, and the shrinkage of its sunlit crescent told him there was not much more than an hour until the daily eclipse which was known as littlenight. He was acutely aware, now that they had parted company, of the extent to which he had allowed himself to be manipulated by Vantara. Had a man been guilty of such appalling behaviour in the air and arrogance on the ground, Toller would have given him a verbal blistering so fierce that it could easily have provoked a duel, and most certainly would have indicted him in an official report. As it was, he had been unmanned and bemused by the countess's incredible physical perfection, and had conducted himself like an impressionable youth. It was true that he had conclusively defeated Vantara on the main issue, but in retrospect he could almost believe that he had been as much concerned with impressing her as with carrying out his duty.

By the time he reached his ship a crewman was standing beside each of the four anchors and making ready for departure. He went up the rungs on the side of the gondola and swung himself over the rail, then paused and stared at Vantara's grounded craft. Its crew were busy detaching the gasbag and laying it out on the grass under Vantara's supervision.

Lieutenant Feer came to his side. "Continuous thrust to Prad, sir?"

If I ever get married, Toller thought, *it has to be to that woman*.

"Sir, I asked you if—"

"Of course I want continuous thrust to Prad," Toller said. "And bring Steenameert to my cabin—I want to talk to him in private."

He went to his cabin at the rear of the main deck and waited for the skyman to be shown in. The ship felt alive again, its timbers and rigging emitting occasional creaks as the structure as a whole adjusted to the tensions of flying into the wind. Toller sat at his desk and toyed abstractedly with navigation instruments, unable to put the Countess Vantara out of his thoughts. How had he managed to forget meeting her as a child? He could recall being dragged against his will to the Migration Day ceremonies, at an age when he scorned the company of girls, but surely even then he would have noticed her among the giggling, gauzy creatures at play in the palace gardens. . . .

His musings were interrupted when Steenameert tapped at the door and came into the small room, still brushing food particles from his chin. "You sent for me, sir?"

"Yes. We were interrupted at an interesting point in our conversation. Tell me more about these empty cities. Did you see no living people whatsoever?"

Steenameert shook his head. "Not one, sir! Lots of skeletons—thousands of them—but, as far as I could tell, the New Men no longer exist. Their own pestilence seems to have turned against them and wiped them out."

"How far abroad did you travel?"

"Not far—two hundred miles at the most. As you know, we only had the three skyships . . . nothing with lateral thrusters . . . and had to rely on the winds to get us about. But that was enough for me, sir. After a while I had an uncanny feeling about the place—I *knew* there was nobody there.

"I mean, we first dropped down only a couple of miles out of Ro-Atabri, the old capital. We were in the heart of ancient Kolcorron itself. If there were any people living on Land, that's where they would be found. It stands to reason that's where they would be found." Steenameert spoke fervently, as though he had a personal stake in convincing Toller that his ideas were valid.

"You're probably correct," Toller said. "Unless, of course, it is something to do with the ptertha. From what I've been taught, the worst of them infested Kolcorron, while the other side of the globe was comparatively free of them."

Steenameert became even more intense. "The second great discovery we made is that the ptertha on Land are colourless—just like those on Overland. It appears that they have already reverted to their neutral state, sir. I suppose it was because the poison they developed for use against humans had done what was required of it; and now they are in a state of readiness to war against any other type of creature which threatens brakka trees."

"That's very interesting," Toller said, but—belying his words—his attention wandered as the image of Countess Vantara's face began to swim before his mind's eye. *I wonder how I can arrange to see her again. And how long will it take?*

"It seems to me," Steenameert was saying, "that the logical thing to do now is to mount a proper expedition. Lots of ships, well-equipped and carrying settlers, to reclaim the Old World—just as King Prad predicted we would."

Toller had half-consciously noted earlier that Steenameert was unusually well-spoken for a ranker, and now it came to him that the man also seemed better educated than might have been expected. He examined Steenameert with new interest.

"You've been pondering this matter, have you?" he said. "Is it your wish to go back to Land?"

"Yes, sir!" The smooth skin of Steenameert's face grew pinker. "If Queen Daseene decides to send a fleet to Land I'll be among the first to volunteer for the journey. And if you were likewise inclined, sir, I'd consider it an honour to serve under you."

Toller considered the notion and his mind conjured up a sombre-hued picture of a handful of airships roaming over landscapes of weed-shrouded ruins wherein lay millions of human skeletons. The vision was made even more unappealing by there being no place in it for Vantara. If he went to Land, he and she would literally be worlds apart. It shocked him to find that he was already according her such a prominent place in his life scheme, and with so little justification, but it showed the extent to which she had breached his emotional defences.

"I can't help you get back to the Old World," he said to Steenameert. "I believe I have enough to keep me fully occupied right here on Overland."

Chapter 2

Lord Cassyll Maraquine breathed deeply and pleasurably as he came out to the front steps of his home on the north side of the city of Prad. There had been rain during the latter part of the night and as a result the air was sweet and invigorating, making him wish he did not have to spend the morning in the stuffy confines of the royal residence. The palace was little more than a mile away—visible as a gleam of rose-coloured marble beyond serried trees. He would have enjoyed making the journey on foot, but he never seemed to have time for such simple pleasures these days. Queen Daseene had grown highly irritable in her old age, and he dared not risk annoying her by being late for his appointment.

He went to his waiting carriage, nodding to the driver as he climbed in. The vehicle moved off immediately, drawn by the four bluehorns which were a symbol of Cassyll's elevated status in Kolcorron. Until less than five years ago it had been forbidden by law to have a carriage which required more than one bluehorn, because the animals were so necessary to the developing economy of the planet, and even now teams of four were something of a rarity.

The equipage had been a gift from the Queen and it was politic for him to use it when going to visit her, even though his wife and son sometimes bantered with him about growing soft. He always took their criticism in good part, even though he had begun to suspect that he was indeed becoming too fond of luxury and pampered ways of living. The restlessness and craving for adventure which had characterised his father seemed to have skipped a generation and manifested themselves in the young Toller. On a number of occasions he had come close to falling out with the boy over his recklessness

27

and his outmoded habit of wearing a sword, but he had never pressed matters too far. In the back of his mind there had always lurked the idea that he was acting out of jealousy of the hero worship Toller accorded his long-dead grandfather.

The thought of his son reminded Cassyll that the boy had been commander of the airship which had arrived only the previous aftday with advance dispatches from the Land expedition. In theory the contents of the dispatches were secret, but Cassyll's secretary had already been able to pass him the word that the Old World had been found to be uninhabited and free of the deadly strain of ptertha which had forced humanity to flee across the interplanetary void. Queen Daseene had been quick to call a meeting of selected advisers, and the fact that Cassyll was required to attend was an indication of the direction in which her thoughts were turning. Manufacture was his field of expertise, and in this context the concept of manufacturing led inexorably towards skyships—which implied that Daseene wanted to reclaim the Old World and thus become the first ruler in history to extend her sway to two planets.

Cassyll had an instinctive distaste for the notion of conquest, reinforced by the fact that his father had died in a monumentally futile attempt to claim the third planet of the local system, but in this case none of the usual philosophical or humanitarian restraints applied. Overland's sister world belonged to his people by right of birth, and if there was no indigenous population to be subjugated or slaughtered he could see no moral objection to a second interplanetary migration. As far as he was concerned, the only questions would relate to scale. How many skyships would Queen Daseene want, and how soon would she need them?

Toller will want to take part in the expedition, Cassyll thought. *The crossing is bound to have its dangers, but that will only serve to make him more determined to go.*

The carriage soon reached the river and turned west in the

direction of the Lord Glo Bridge, which was the principal crossing for the palace. In the few minutes that he was on the curving boulevard Cassyll saw two steam-driven carriages, neither of which had been produced by his own factory, and again he found himself wishing he had more time for practical experimentation with that form of transport. There were many improvements yet to be made, particularly with regard to power transmission, but all his time seemed to be taken up with the administration of the Maraquine industrial empire.

As the carriage was crossing the ornate bridge the palace came into view directly ahead, a rectangular block which was rendered asymmetrical by the east wing and tower which Daseene had recently built as a memorial to her husband. The guards at the main gate saluted as Cassyll passed through. Only a few vehicles were waiting in the main fore-court at this early hour, and at once he noticed the official Sky Service coach which was used by Bartan Drumme, senior technical adviser to the Chief of Aerial Defence. To his surprise, he saw that Bartan himself was loitering by the coach. At the age of fifty, Drumme still retained a lean and wiry figure, and only a slight stiffness in his left shoulder— the result of an old battle wound—prevented him from moving like a young man. A whisper of intuition told Cassyll that Bartan was waiting to see him in advance of the official meeting.

"Good foreday!" Cassyll called out as he stepped down from his carriage. "I wish *I* could afford the time to dawdle around and take the air."

"Cassyll!" Bartan smiled as he came forward to shake hands. The years had scarcely altered the boyishness of his round face. Its permanent expression of humorous irrever-ence often deceived people who were meeting him for the first time into thinking he was an intellectual lightweight, but over the years Cassyll had learned to respect him for his mental agility and toughness.

"Are you waiting to see me?" Cassyll said.

"Very good!" Bartan replied, raising his eyebrows. "How did you know?"

"You were as furtive as an urchin dallying by the bakery window. What is it, Bartan?"

"Let's walk for a minute—there is time before the meeting." Bartan led the way into an empty quarter of the forecourt where they were partially screened from view by a bed of spearblooms.

Cassyll began to chuckle. "Are we going to conspire against the throne?"

"In a way it is almost as serious as that," Bartan said, coming to a halt. "Cassyll, you know that my position is officially described as scientific adviser to the head of the Sky Service. But you also know that—simply because I survived the Farland expedition—I'm somehow expected to have a magical awareness of all that goes on in the heavens and to advise her Majesty of anything of import, anything which might constitute a threat to the realm."

"Suddenly you make me uneasy," Cassyll said. "Is this anything to do with Land?"

"No—another planet."

"Farland! Say what you've got to say, man! Out with it!" Cassyll felt a coolness on his brow as the dread thought heaved in his mind. Farland was the third planet of the local system, orbiting at roughly twice the distance from the sun as the Land-Overland pair, and throughout most of Kolcorron's history it had been nothing more than an insignificant green speck amid the splendours of the night sky. Then, twenty-six years ago, a bizarre set of circumstances had led to a single ship venturing out from Overland and crossing millions of miles of hostile vacuum to reach the outer world. The expedition had been ill-fated—Cassyll's father had not been the only one to die on that dank, rainy planet—and three of its members had returned to the home world with disturbing news.

Farland was inhabited by a race of humanoids whose technology was so advanced that they had the capability of annihilating the Overlanders' civilisation at a stroke. It was fortunate indeed for the humans that the Farlanders were an insular, inward-looking race with no interest in anything beyond the perpetual cloud-cover of their own world. That attitude of mind had been difficult for the territorially acquisitive humans to comprehend. Even after years had merged into decades with no sign of aggression from the enigmatic third planet, the fear of a sudden devastating attack from the skies had continued to lurk in some Overlanders' minds. It was, as Cassyll Maraquine had just discovered, never far beneath the surface of their thoughts. . . .

"Farland?" Bartan gave him a strange smile. "No—I'm talking of yet *another* planet. A fourth planet."

In the silence that followed, Cassyll studied his friend's face as though it were a puzzle to be solved. "This isn't some manner of jest, is it? Are you claiming to have discovered a new planet?"

Bartan nodded unhappily. "I didn't discover it personally. It wasn't even one of my technicians. It was a woman—a copyist in the records office at the Grain Quay—who pointed it out to me."

"What does it matter who actually saw it first?" Cassyll said. "The point is that you have a really interesting scientific discovery to—" He broke off as he realised he had not yet been told the whole story. "Why do you look so glum, old friend?"

"When Divare told me about the planet she said it was blue in colour, and that made me think she could have made a mistake. You know how many blue stars there are in the sky—hundreds of them. So I asked her what size of telescope was needed to see it properly, and she said a very small one would do. In fact, she said it could be seen well with the naked eye.

"And she was right, Cassyll. She pointed it out to me last

31

night . . . a blue planet . . . quite easy to see without optical aid . . . low in the west soon after sunset. . . ."

Cassyll frowned. "And you checked it with a telescope?"

"Yes. It showed an appreciable disk even with an ordinary nautical instrument. It's a planet, all right."

"But . . ." Cassyll's bafflement increased. "Why has it not been noticed before now?"

Bartan's strange smile returned. "The only answer I can think of is that it wasn't *there* to be observed before now."

"That goes against everything we know about astronomy, doesn't it? I have heard that new stars appear now and then, even if they don't last very long, but how can another *world* simply materialise in our skies?"

"Queen Daseene is bound to ask me that selfsame question," Bartan said. "She will also ask me how long it has been there, and I'll have to say I don't know; and she will then ask me what should be done about it, and I'll have to say I don't know that either; and then she will start wondering about the value of a scientific adviser who doesn't know anything. . . ."

"I think you're fretting too much on that score," Cassyll said. "The Queen is quite likely to regard it as nothing more than a mildly interesting astronomical phenomenon. What makes you think the blue planet poses any threat to us?"

Bartan blinked several times. "It's a feeling I have. An instinct. Don't tell me you're not disturbed by this thing."

"I'm deeply interested in it—and I want you to show the planet to me tonight—but why should I feel any sense of alarm?"

"Because . . ." Bartan glanced at the sky as though seeking inspiration. "Cassyll, it isn't *right!* It's unnatural . . . an omen . . . There is something afoot."

Cassyll began to laugh. "But you're the least superstitious person I know! Now you are talking as though this errant world has appeared in the firmament for the sole purpose of persecuting *you*."

"Well . . ." Bartan gave a reluctant smile, reclaiming his youthful appearance. "Perhaps you're right. I suppose I should have gone to you immediately. It wasn't until Berise died that I realised how much I depended on her to keep me on an even keel."

Cassyll nodded sympathetically, as always finding it difficult to accept that Berise Drumme had been dead for four years. Black-haired, vivacious, indomitable, Berise had given the impression that she would live for ever, but she had been swept away within hours by one of those mysterious, sourceless ailments which brought it home to medical practitioners just how little they knew.

"It was a big blow to all of us," Cassyll said. "Are you drinking?"

"Yes." Bartan detected the concern in Cassyll's eyes and touched his arm. "But not the way I was doing when I first met your father. I wouldn't betray Berise in that way. A glass or two of wryberry in the evening is enough for me these days."

"Come to my house tonight and bring a good telescope with you. We'll have a beaker of something warming and take a look at it . . . There's another job for you—we'll need a name for this mysterious world." Cassyll slapped his friend on the back and nodded towards the arched entrance of the palace, signifying that it was time to go in for their meeting with the Queen.

Once inside the shady building they went straight to the audience chamber through corridors which were almost empty. In King Chakkell's day the palace had been very much the seat of government, and it had usually been thronged with officials, but Daseene's policy had been to disperse general administration into separate buildings and to treat the palace as her private residence. Only matters such as aerial defence, in which she took a special interest, were considered important enough to merit her personal attention.

At the door to the chamber two ostiaries, sweating under

the weight of their traditional brakka armour, recognised both men and admitted them without delay. The air in the room was so hot that Cassyll had to snatch for breath. In her old age Queen Daseene continually complained of being cold, and the quarters she used were kept at a temperature which most others found unbearable.

The only person in the room was Lord Sectar, the fiscal chancellor, whose job it was to control state spending. His presence was another indication that the Queen had plans to reclaim the Old World. He was a large and top-heavy man in his sixties, with a jowled face which was florid in normal conditions and in the excessive heat of the room had turned bright crimson. He nodded at the newcomers, pointed mutely at the floor and its buried heating pipes, rolled his eyes to express consternation, dabbed perspiration from his brow and went to stand by a partially-open window.

Cassyll responded to the dumb-show with an exaggerated shrug which mimed helplessness, and sat down on one of the curved benches which faced the high-backed royal chair. At once his thoughts were drawn back to the mystery of Bartan's blue planet. It occurred to him that he had been altogether too casual in his acceptance of the reported phenomenon. How could a *world* simply materialise in the nearby regions of space? New stars had been seen to appear in the sky, and that being the case one could assume that stars sometimes disappeared, perhaps through explosion, leaving their retinues of planets behind. Cassyll could imagine such worlds blundering through the darkness of the interstellar void, but the chances of one of them joining the local system seemed vanishingly small. Perhaps the reason he did not feel the proper degree of astonishment was that in his heart he simply did not believe in the blue planet. A cloud of gas could have the semblance of solid rock, after all. . . .

Cassyll stood up as a tipstaff opened the door and pounded the floor with his metal-shod rod to announce the arrival of the Queen. Daseene came into the room, dismissed the two ladies-in-waiting who had accompanied her as far as the door, and went to her chair. She was thin and frail-looking, seemingly burdened by the weight of her green silk robes, but there was undiminished authority in the way in which she signalled for the others to be seated.

"Thank you for your attendance here this foreday," she said in a reedy but firm voice. "I know you have many demands upon your time, so we will go straight to the business of the meeting. As you are already aware, I have received an advance dispatch from the Land expedition. Its contents may be summarised as follows." Daseene went on to describe the expedition's findings in detail, doing so without hesitation or reference to notes. When she had finished she surveyed the group, eyes intent beneath the pearl-beaded coif without which she never appeared in public. As had happened before, it occurred to Cassyll that Daseene could if required have taken over the rulership of Kolcorron at any stage in her husband's career and coped well with the task. It was perhaps surprising that she had usually chosen to remain in the background, except in a few cases where women's rights had been concerned.

"I think you have already divined my purpose in calling this meeting," she went on, speaking in formal High Kolcorronian. "In view of the fact that I shall have a full report from the expedition commanders in only three days from now, you may consider my actions precipitate—but I have reached a stage in life at which I am loathe to waste so much as a single hour.

"I intend to send a fleet to Land without delay.

"It is my intention to establish Ro-Atabri as a *living* capital again before I die; therefore I require decisions from you this very foreday. I also expect the practical work of implementing those decisions to begin as soon as the coming littlenight has ended. So let us be about our work, gentlemen! My first question for you is: how large should the fleet be? You first, Lord Cassyll—what are your views?"

Cassyll blinked as he rose to his feet. This was the style of rulership developed by the late King Chakkell to suit the needs of pioneers on a new world, and he was not at all sure that it was apposite in the present situation.

"Your Majesty, as loyal subjects we all share your views about reclaiming the Old World, but may I respectfully point out that we are not in a state of dire emergency such as prevailed at the time of the Migration? As yet, we have no proof that the whole of Land is available to us, so the prudent course would be to follow up the first expedition with a primarily military force equipped with airships which could be reassembled on Land and used to circumnavigate and survey the planet."

Daseene shook her head. "That course is *too* prudent for me, and I have no time for it—your father would not have counselled me thus."

"My father's day has passed, Majesty," Cassyll said.

"Perhaps it has, perhaps it hasn't, but I take your point about the airships. I propose to send . . . four. How does that number sound to you?"

Cassyll gave a slight bow, expressing irony. "That number sounds very good to me, Majesty."

Daseene gave him a faint twisted smile to show that she had not missed the nuance, then addressed herself to Bartan Drumme. "Do you foresee any great difficulty in transporting airships to Land aboard skyships?"

"No, Majesty," Bartan said, standing up. "We could adapt small airship gondolas to serve as skyship gondolas for the single crossing. On arrival on Land it would simply be a matter of disconnecting the balloons and replacing them with airship gasbags."

"Excellent! That is the sort of positive attitude I like in my advisers." Daseene looked meaningfully at Cassyll. "Now, my lord, how many skyships can be made ready for the crossing within, say, fifty days?"

Before Cassyll could speak Bartan coughed and said,

"Forgive me, Majesty, I have something to report . . . a new development . . . something I feel should be brought to your attention at this point."

"Has it any bearing on the discussions in hand?"

Bartan shot Cassyll a worried glance. "It probably has, Majesty."

"In that case," Daseene said impatiently, "you had better speak, but do it quickly."

"Majesty, I . . . A new world has been discovered in our own planetary system."

"A new world?" Daseene frowned. "What are you prattling about, Mister Drumme? There can't be a new world."

"I have observed it with my own eyes, Majesty. A blue planet . . . a fourth world in our local system. . . ." The normally fluent Bartan was floundering as Cassyll had never seen him do before.

"How big is it?"

"We cannot decide that until we are sure how far away it is."

"Very well then." Daseene sighed. "How far away is this infant world of yours?"

Bartan looked deeply unhappy. "We cannot calculate that until we—"

"Until you know its size," the Queen cut in. "Mister Drumme! We are all indebted to you for that little excursion into the marvellously exact science of astronomy, but it is my earnest wish that you should confine your remarks to the subject already in hand. Is that clear?"

"Yes, Majesty," Bartan mumbled, sinking down on to the bench.

"Now . . ." Daseene suddenly shivered, drew her robes closer together at her throat and looked about the room. "No wonder we freeze to death in here! Who opened that window? Close it immediately before we perish from the cold."

Lord Sectar, lips moving silently, got up and closed the window. His embroidered jacket was heavily stained with sweat and he was ostentatiously mopping his brow as he returned to his place.

"You don't look well," Daseene told him tersely. "You should see a doctor." She returned her attention to Cassyll and repeated her question about the number of skyships that could be available within fifty days.

"Twenty," Cassyll said at once, deciding that an optimistic estimate was called for while the Queen was in her present mood. As head of the Sky Service Supplies Board he was in a good position to judge the quantity of ships and associated matériel which could be made ready for an interplanetary crossing as well as being spared from normal function. Ever since the discovery that Farland was inhabited a number of defensive stations had been maintained in the weightless zone midway between the two sister worlds. For some years the great wooden structures had been manned, but as public fears of an attack from Farland had gradually abated the crews had been withdrawn. Now the stations and their attendant groups of fighter jets were maintained by means of regular balloon ascents to the weightless zone. The schedule of flights was undemanding, and Cassyll estimated that about half the ships in the Sky Service fleet were available for extraordinary duties.

"Twenty ships," Daseene said, looking slightly disappointed. "Still, I suppose that's enough to be getting on with."

"Yes, Majesty—especially as we are not obliged to think in terms of an invasion fleet. One can foresee continuous traffic between Overland and Land, sparse at first, but gradually building up until—"

"It's no use, Lord Cassyll," the Queen interrupted. "Again you are advocating a sedate approach to this enterprise, and again I say to you I have no time for that. The return to Land has to be decisive, forceful, triumphant . . . a clear-cut statement which posterity cannot misread. . . .

"It may help you to gauge the strength of my feelings in the matter if I tell you that I have just given one of my granddaughters—the Countess Vantara—permission to take part in the reclamation. She is an experienced airship captain, and will be able to play a useful role in the initial survey of the planet."

Cassyll bowed in acquiescence, and there followed an intensive planning session which—in the space of a single hour—was intended to shape the future of two worlds.

On quitting the overheated atmosphere of the palace Cassyll decided against returning home immediately. A glance at the sky showed him that he had some thirty minutes in hand before the sun would slide behind the eastern rim of Land. He had time for a quiet walk in the tree-lined avenues of the city's administrative area. It would be good to get some fresh air into his system before he responded to the ever-present call of his business commitments.

Accordingly, he dismissed his coachman, strolled down to the Lord Glo Bridge and turned east along the bank of the river, a route which would take him past several governmental buildings. The streets were busy with the flurry of activity which usually preceded the littlenight meal and the daily change of tempo in human affairs. Now that the city was half-a-century old it appeared mature to Cassyll's eyes, with a permanence which was part of his life, and he wondered if he would ever make the journey to Land to view the results of millennia of civilisation. She had not said as much, but he suspected it was in Queen Daseene's heart— age-weakened though she was—to return to the world of her birth and perhaps end her days there. Cassyll could empathise with such feelings, but Overland was the only home he had ever known and he had no desire to leave it, especially as so much work remained to be done in so many different spheres. Perhaps, also, he lacked the spirit or courage to face that awesome journey.

He was drawing close to the Neldeever Plaza, which housed the headquarters of the four branches of the armed services, when he espied a familiar blond head projecting above the stream of pedestrians coming towards him. Cassyll had not seen his son for perhaps a hundred days, and he felt a pang of affection and pride as—almost with the eyes of a stranger—he noted the clear-eyed good looks, splendid physique and the easy confidence with which the young man wore his skycaptain's blue uniform.

"Toller!" he called out as their courses brought them together.

"Father!" Toller's expression had been abstracted and stern, as though something weighed heavily on his mind, but his face lit up with recognition. He extended his arms and the two men embraced while the flow of pedestrians parted around them.

"This is a happy coincidence," Cassyll said as they drew apart. "Were you on your way home?"

Toller nodded. "I'm sorry I couldn't get home last night, but it was very late before I got my ship safely berthed, and there were certain problems. . . ."

"What manner of problems?"

"Nothing to cloud a sunny day like this," Toller said with a smile. "Let's hasten homewards. I can't tell you how much I look forward to one of mother's littlenight spreads after an eternity of shipboard rations."

"You appear to thrive on those selfsame rations."

"Not as well as you on proper food," Toller said, trying to pinch a roll of fat at Cassyll's waist as they began to walk in the direction of the family home. The two men exchanged the kind of inconsequential family talk which, better than deliberated speeches, restores a relationship after a long separation. They were nearing the Square House, named after the Maraquine residence in old Ro-Atabri, before the conversation came round to weightier affairs.

"I've just been to the palace," Cassyll said, "and have

come away with news which should interest you—we are to send a twenty-strong fleet to Land."

"Yes, we're entering a truly wondrous era—two worlds, but one nation."

Cassyll glanced at his son's nearer shoulder flash, the saffron-and-blue emblem which showed that he was qualified to pilot both skyships and airships. "There'll be a deal of work for you there."

"For *me*?" Toller gave a humourless chuckle. "No thank you, father. I admit I'd like to see the Old World some day, but at present it is one great charnel house and I don't relish the prospect of clearing away millions of skeletons."

"But the journey! The adventure! I thought you'd jump at the chance."

"I have quite enough to occupy me right here on Overland for the time being," Toller said, and for a moment the sombre expression Cassyll had noted earlier returned to his face.

"Something is troubling you," he said. "Are you going to keep it to yourself?"

"Have I that option?"

"No."

Toller shook his head in mock despair. "I thought not. You know, of course, that it was I who picked up the advance messenger from Land. Well, another ship appeared on the scene at the last moment—unwarranted—and tried to scoop up the prize from under my very nose. Naturally I refused to give way. . . ."

"Naturally!"

". . . and there was a minor collision. As there was no damage to my ship I forbore making an official entry in the log—even though the other commander was entirely to blame—but this morning I was informed that an incident report had been filed against me. I have to face Sky-commodore Tresse tomorrow."

"There's no cause for you to worry," Cassyll said, relieved

to hear that nothing more serious was afoot. "I will speak to Tresse this aftday and acquaint him with the real facts."

"Thanks, but I think I am obliged to deal with this kind of thing by myself. I should have covered my flank by making an entry in the flight log, but I can call on enough witnesses to prove my case. The whole thing is really very trivial. A flea-bite. . . ."

"But one you continue to scratch!"

"It's the sheer deceitfulness involved," Toller said angrily. "I trusted that woman, father. I *trusted* her, and this is how she repays me."

"Aha!" Cassyll almost smiled as he began to plumb beneath the surface of what he had heard. "You didn't say that this unprincipled commander was a woman."

"Didn't I?" Toller replied, his voice now casual. "It has no relevance to anything, but it so happens that she was one of the Queen's brood of granddaughters—the Countess Vantara."

"Handsome woman, is she?"

"It is possible that some men might . . . What are you trying to say, father?"

"Nothing, nothing at all. Perhaps I'm a little curious about the lady because this is the second time within the span of a couple of hours that her name has been mentioned to me." From the corner of his eye Cassyll saw Toller give him a surprised glance, but—unable to resist tantalising his son— he volunteered no further information. He walked in silence, shading his eyes from the sun in order to get a better view of a large group of ptertha which were following the course of the river. The near-invisible spheres were swooping and bounding just above the surface of the water, buoyed up by a slight breeze.

"That's quite a coincidence," Toller finally said. "What was said to you?"

"About what?"

"About Vantara. Who spoke of her?"

"No less a person than the Queen," Cassyll said, watching his son carefully. "It appears that Vantara has volunteered to serve with the fleet we are sending to Land, and it is an indication of the strength of the Queen's feelings towards the enterprise that she is giving the young woman her blessing."

There was another protracted silence from Toller before he said, "Vantara is an airship pilot—what work is there for her on the Old World?"

"Rather a lot, I'd say. We're sending four airships whose task it will be to circle the entire globe and prove there are no disputants to Queen Daseene's sovereignty. It sounds quite an adventure to me, but of course there will be all the privations of shipboard life—and you've had your fill of service rations."

"I don't care about that," Toller exclaimed. "I want to go!"

"To Land! But only a moment ago. . . ."

Toller halted Cassyll by catching his arm and turning to face him. "No more play-acting, father, please! I want to take a ship to Land. You will see to it that my application is successful, won't you?"

"I'm not at all sure that I can," Cassyll said, suddenly uneasy at the prospect of his only son—who was still a boy in spite of all his pretensions to manhood—setting off across the perilous bridge of thin air which linked the two worlds.

Toller produced a broad smile. "Don't be so modest, father of mine. You're on so many committees, boards, tribunals, councils and panels that—in your own quiet way, of course—you practically run Kolcorron. Now, tell me that I'm going to Land."

"You're going to Land," Cassyll said compliantly.

That night, while he was waiting for Bartan Drumme to arrive with a telescope, Cassyll thought he could identify the

43

true cause of his misgivings about Toller's proposed flight to the Old World. Toller and he had a harmonious and satisfying relationship, but there was no denying the fact that the boy had always been unduly influenced by the stories and legends surrounding his paternal grandfather. Apart from the striking physical resemblance, the two had many mental attributes in common—impatience, courage, idealism and quickness of temper among them—but Cassyll suspected that the similarities were not as great as the younger Toller pretended. His grandfather had been much *harder*, capable of total ruthlessness when he deemed it necessary, possessed of an obduracy which would lead him to choose certain death rather than betray a principle.

Cassyll was glad that Kolcorronian society was gentler and safer than it had been even a few decades ago, that the world in general offered fewer chances for young Toller to get himself into the kind of situation where—simply through trying to live up to self-imposed standards—he might forfeit his life. But now that he was committing himself to fly to the Old World those chances were bound to increase, and it seemed to Cassyll that the ghost of the long-dead Toller was stirring into life, stimulated by the scent of dangerous adventure, preparing to exert its influence on a vulnerable young man. And even though he was thinking about his own father, Cassyll Maraquine devoutly wished that that restless spirit would confine itself to the grave, and to the past. . . .

The welcome sounds of Bartan Drumme being admitted by a servant at the front entrance roused Cassyll from his chair. He went down the broad staircase and greeted his friend, who was carrying a wooden-tubed telescope and tripod. The servant offered to take the telescope, but Cassyll dismissed him, and he and Bartan carried the heavy instrument up to a balcony which afforded a good view to the west. The light reflected from Land was strong enough for reading, but nevertheless the dome of the sky was thronged with countless bright stars and hundreds of spirals of varying sizes and shapes, ranging from circular whirlpools to the narrowest of ellipses. No less than six major comets were visible that night, splaying fingers of radiance across the heavens, and meteors darted almost continuously, briefly linking one celestial feature to another.

"You surprised me this foreday, you know," Cassyll said. "Nobody I know can talk like you, regardless of the audience and circumstances, but you seemed flummoxed for some reason. What was the matter with you?"

"Guilt," Bartan said simply, raising his head from the task of setting up the tripod.

"Guilt!"

"Yes. It's this damned fourth planet, Cassyll. Every instinct I have tells me that it does not bode well for us. It shouldn't *be* there. Its presence is an affront to our understanding of nature, a sign that something is going terribly amiss, and yet I am unable to convince anyone—not even you—that we have cause for alarm. I feel that I have betrayed my Queen and country through my sheer ineptness with words, and I don't know what to do about it."

Cassyll gave a reassuring chuckle. "Let me see for myself this harbinger which troubles you so much—anything which stills the famous Drumme tongue must be worthy of careful perusal."

He was still in a mood of comparative levity when, having prepared and aligned the telescope for him, Bartan stepped aside and invited him to look into the eyepiece. The first thing to meet Cassyll's gaze was a fuzzy disk of bluish brilliance which resembled a soap bubble filled with sparkling gas, but one touch on the focusing lever achieved a remarkable result.

There before him, suddenly, swimming in the indigo depths of the universe, was a *world*—complete with polar snow caps, oceans, land masses and the white curlicues of weather systems.

It had no right to exist, but it did exist, and in that moment of visual and intellectual confrontation Cassyll's first thought —with no justification he could understand—was for the future safety of his son.

Chapter 3

The height gauge consisted of a vertical scale from the top of which a small weight was suspended by a delicate coiled spring. Its operating principle was so simple and effective— as a ship rose higher and gravity lessened the weight moved upwards on the scale—that only one modification had been introduced in fifty years. The spring, which would once have been a hair-like shaving of brakka wood, was now made of fine-drawn steel. Metallurgy had made great strides in Kolcorron in recent decades, and the guaranteed consistency of steel springs made gauges easy to calibrate.

Toller studied the instrument carefully, making sure it indicated zero gravity, then floated himself out of the cabin and over to the ship's rail. The fleet had reached the weightless zone in the middle of a daylight period, which meant that the sun's rays were washing across him in a direction parallel with the deck. In one direction the universe appeared its normal dark blue, plentifully scattered with stars and silver spirals, but in the other there was a surfeit of light which made viewing difficult. Below his feet, Overland was a huge disk exactly bisected into night and day, the latter half making its own contribution to the general luminance; and over his head, although occulted by the ship's balloon, the Old World was similarly adding to the confusion of radiance.

On a level with Toller, starkly floodlit by the sun, were the three other balloons which supported airship gondolas in place of the lightweight box structures normally used by skyships. The smooth outline of each gondola had been marred by the addition of a vertically mounted engine, the exhaust cone of which projected well below the keel. Further down the sky, ranged in groups of four against the glowing complexities of Overland, were the sixteen ships making up the main part of the fleet. Seen from above, their balloons looked perfectly spherical and had the apparent solidity of planets, with load tapes and lines of stitching to represent meridians. The roar of jet exhausts filled the sky, occasionally reaching an accidental climax as a number of ships fired their pulsed bursts in unison.

Toller was using binoculars to search for the circular group of permanent defence stations, and wishing for a speedy method of finding them regardless of the disposition of sun and planets. The nub of the problem was that he had no real idea which direction was most likely to yield results. His reading of the height gauge could be out by tens of miles, and the convection currents which helped make the air bridge between the world so cold often gave ascents lateral dispersions of the same order. Large though they were on the human scale, the stations were insignificant in the chill reaches of the central blue.

"Have you lost something, young Maraquine?" The voice was that of Commissioner Trye Kettoran, official leader of the expedition, who had chosen to fly in one of the modified ships. He was subject to low-gravity sickness and had hoped that the comfort of an enclosed cabin would lessen the severity of his attacks. His expectations had been in vain, but he was enduring his illness with great fortitude in spite of his age. At seventy-one, he was by far the oldest member of the expedition. He had been appointed by Queen Daseene precisely because he had clear recollections of the old capital of Ro-Atabri and therefore was well qualified to report on present conditions there.

"I have orders to inspect the Inner Defence Group," Toller said. "The Service was hard pressed to loft twenty ships for this expedition, and as a result we are forced to omit a fifty-day inspection—but if I see anything going seriously wrong I am empowered to divert one of the expedition's ships for as long as it takes to put things right."

"Quite a burden of responsibility for a young captain," Kettoran said, his long pale face showing faint signs of animation. "But—even with the aid of those splendid glasses —what kind of inspection can you carry out at a range of several miles?"

"A superficial one," Toller admitted. "But in truth all we have to concern ourselves with at this early stage is the general alignment of the stations. If one is seen to have separated from the others, and to be drifting towards Overland or Land, it is simply a matter of nudging it back into the datum plane."

"If one begins to fall, won't they all follow suit?"

Toller shook his head. "We are not dealing with inert pieces of rock. The stations contain many kinds of chemicals —pikon, halvell, firesalt, and so on—and a slight change in conditions can lead to the production of gases which could leak through a hull if a seal weakens. The thrust produced may have no more force than a maiden's sigh, but let it go on for a long time—then augment it with the growing attraction of gravity—and, all at once, one is confronted with an unruly leviathan which is determined to dash itself upon one world or the other. In the Sky Service we consider it prudent to take corrective action long before that stage is reached."

"You have quite a way with words, young Maraquine," Kettoran said, his breath pluming whitely through the scarf which was protecting his face from the intense cold of the weightless zone. "Have you ever considered diplomacy as a career?"

"No, but I may have to if I fail to locate these accursed wooden sausage skins before long."

"I will help you—anything to take my mind off the fact that my stomach wants to rise into my mouth." Kettoran knuckled his watery eyes with a gloved hand, began surveying the sky and within a few seconds—to Toller's surprise—gave a satisfied exclamation.

"Is that what we're in search of?" he said, pointing horizontally to the east, past the three modified skyships. "That line of purple lights. . . ."

"Purple lights? Where?" Toller tried in vain to see something unusual in the indicated part of the sky.

"There! *There!* Why can't you. . . ?" Kettoran's words faded into a sigh of disappointment. "You're too late—they have gone now."

Toller gave a snort of combined amusement and exasperation. "Sir, there are no lights—purple or otherwise—on the stations. They have reflectors which shine with a steady white glow, if you happen to catch them at the right angle. Perhaps you saw a meteor."

"I know what a meteor looks like, so don't try to—" Kettoran broke off again and pointed at another part of the heavens. "There's your precious Defence Group over there. Don't try to tell me it isn't, because I can see a line of white specks. Am I right? I *am* right!"

"You're right," Toller agreed, training his binoculars on the stations and marvelling at the speed with which luck had directed the old man's gaze to the correct portion of the sky. "Well done, sir!"

"Call yourself a pilot! Why, if it hadn't been for this unruly stomach of mine I would have. . . ." Kettoran gave a violent sneeze, retreated into the cabin and closed the door.

Toller smiled as he heard further sneezes punctuated by muffled swearing. In the five days of the ascent to the weightless zone he had grown to like the commissioner for his humorous grumpiness, and to respect him for his stoicism in the face of the severe discomforts of the flight. Most men of his age would have found some means of evading the responsibility thrust upon him by Queen Daseene, but Kettoran had accepted the charge with good grace and seemed determined to treat it as yet another in a lifetime of routine chores undertaken on behalf of the ruler.

Toller returned his attention to the defence stations and was relieved to see that they formed a perfectly straight line. When he had first qualified as a skyship pilot he had enjoyed the occasional maintenance ascents to the stations. Entering the dark and claustrophobic hulls had been a near-mystical experience which had seemed to conjure up the spirit of his grandfather and his heroic times, but the futility of the so-called Inner Defensive Group's very existence had quickly dominated his thoughts. If there was no threat from Farland the stations were unnecessary; if the enigmatic Farlanders ever *were* to invade their technological superiority would render the stations irrelevant. The wooden shells were merely a token defence which had in some measure eased the late King Chakkell's mind, and to Toller their principal value was that maintaining them was a way of preserving the nation's interplanetary capabilities.

Having satisfied himself that there was no need to make a diversion from the vertical course, he lowered the binoculars and gazed thoughtfully at the furthermost of the other three ships making up his echelon. It was the one commanded by Vantara. Ever since the foreday he had learned that the Countess was taking part in the expedition he had been undecided about which approach to use in future dealings with her. Would an air of aloofness and dignified reproval wring an apology from her and thus bring them together? Or would it be better to appear cheerful and unaffected, treating the incident of her report as the sort of boisterous skirmish which is bound to occur when two free spirits collide?

The fact that he, the injured party, was the one who planned reconciliation had occasioned him some unease, but all his scheming had proved redundant. Throughout the preparations for the flight Vantara had managed to keep her distance from him, and had done so with an effortless grace

51

which denied him the consolation of feeling that he was important enough to be evaded.

One hour after the fleet had passed through the datum plane the group of defence stations had shrunk to virtual invisibility, and the pull of Land's gravity was imperceptibly adding to the ships' speed. A sunwriter message from General Ode, the fleet commander, was flashed back from the flagship instructing all pilots to carry out the inversion manoeuvre.

Glad of the break in the shipboard routine, Toller drew himself along a safety line to the midsection, to where Lieutenant Correvalte was at the engine controls. Correvalte, who was newly qualified, looked relieved when he heard that he was not expected to handle the inversion. He relinquished the controls and positioned himself a short distance away as Toller began the delicate task. The ship had four slim acceleration struts which joined the gondola to the balloon's equatorial load tape, and which gave the whole assemblage the modest degree of stiffness required for flying in the jet propulsion mode. Although the balloon itself was very light, a flimsy envelope of varnished linen, the gas within it had a mass of many tons, with inertia to match, and had to be coaxed with infinite care when any change of direction was called for. A pilot who was too enthusiastic in his use of the ship's lateral jets would soon find that he had driven the top end of a strut through the envelope. While not necessarily serious in low-gravity conditions, that kind of damage was difficult and time-consuming to put right—and the offender was always given good cause to regret his error.

For what seemed a long time after Toller had begun firing one of the tiny cross-mounted jets it seemed that its thrust was having no effect, then with grudging slowness the great disk of Overland made its way up the sky. As it showed itself above the ship's rail, hanging before the crew in all its painted vastness, the immense convexity that was the Old World emerged from behind the balloon and drifted downwards.

There was a moment during which, simply by turning his head from side to side, Toller could see two worlds laid out in their entirety for his inspection—the twin arenas in which his kind had fought all the battles of evolution and history.

Superimposed on each planet, and similarly lit from the side, were the other ships of the fleet. They were in varying attitudes—each pilot inverting at his own pace—arcs of white condensation from their lateral jets complementing the global cloud patterns thousands of miles below. And embracing the spectacle was the frozen luminous panoply of the universe—the circles and spirals and streamers of silver radiance, the fields of brilliant stars with blue and white predominant, the silent-hovering comets and the darting meteors.

It was a sight which both thrilled and chilled Toller, making him proud of his people's courage in daring to cross the interplanetary void in frail constructs of cloth and wood, and at the same time reminding him that—for all their ambitions and dreams—men were little more than microbes labouring from one grain of sand to another.

He would not have cared to admit as much to any of his peers, but it was a comfort to him when the inversion manoeuvre had been completed and the ship was sinking back into humanity's natural domain. From now on the air would grow thicker and warmer, less inimical to life, and all his preoccupations would begin to resume their normal importance.

"That's how it's done," he said, returning control of the vessel to Correvalte. "Get the mechanic to convert the engine back to burner mode, and tell him to make sure that the heaters are working properly."

Toller emphasised the final point because, although the aerial environment would indeed grow less harsh as the ship lost height, the direction of the airflow over the ship would be reversed. The considerable amount of heat lost from the balloon's surface would be borne upwards and away in the slipstream instead of bathing the gondola with an invisible balm which helped protect its occupants from the deadly coldness of the mid-passage.

The engine had to be shut down while being converted from a thrust creator to a producer of hot gas for conventional aerostatic flight, and Toller took advantage of the period of quietude to go into the forward cabin in search of nourishment. Nobody had ever explained the baffling sensation of falling which men experienced in and close to the weightless zone, but it had been spoiling his appetite for more than a day and as a result he was in the ambivalent position of needing food while not actually wanting it. The selection of fare he found in the provision nets—strips of dried meat and fish, cereals and puckered fruit and berries—was less than seductive. He rummaged through what was available and finally settled for a slab of grain cake which he chewed upon without enthusiasm.

"Don't despair, young Maraquine!" Commissioner Kettoran, who had wedged himself into a seat at the captain's table, was feigning cheerfulness. "We'll soon be in Ro-At-abri, and once we're there I'll take you to some of the best eating places in the world. Mind you, they'll be in ruins—but I'll take you to them anyway." Kettoran winked at his secretary, Parlo Wotoorb—who was across the table from him—and both old men hunched their thin shoulders in amusement, looking strangely alike.

Still chewing, Toller nodded gravely to acknowledge the witticism. Kettoran and Wotoorb had been contemporaries of his grandfather. They had actually known him—a privilege he envied—and both had survived to quite an advanced age with no apparent erosion of their faculties. Toller doubted that he would reach his seventies with the same degree of fortitude and resilience. It had always seemed to him that there was a special quality about the men and women who had lived through the great events of recent history—the ptertha plague, the Migration, the conquest of Overland, the war between the sister worlds. It was as though their characters and spirits had been tempered in the crucible of their times, whereas he was destined to live through a fallow period, never knowing for sure if he had it within him to respond to, and as a consequence be ennobled by, a great challenge. Try as he might, he could not imagine the tamed and stable circumstances of his day yielding up adventures which were in any way comparable with those which had earned Toller the Kingslayer his place in legend. Even the journey between the worlds, which had once been the dangerous limit of men's experience, had become a routine matter. . . .

A sudden brightness washed in through the portholes on the left side of the room—momentarily rivalling the prisms of sunlight which slanted across the table from the opposite wall—and somebody outside on the open deck gave a howl of fright.

"What was *that*?" Toller was starting for the door, hindered by the lack of gravity, when there came an appalling burst of sound, akin to the loudest thunderclap he had ever heard. The room tilted and small objects chattered noisily in their brackets.

Echoes of the thunder were still booming and surging when Toller got the door open and was able to propel himself out of the cabin. The ship was twisting in violent air currents which drew groans and creaks from the rigging. Lieutenant Correvalte and the mechanic were clinging to lines by the engine, their shocked faces turned towards the north-west. Toller looked in the same direction and saw a restless, swirling core of fiery brilliance which quickly dwindled into nothingness. All at once the sky was placid again, the silence complete except for faint cries coming from men on other ships.

"Was it a meteor?" Toller called out, aware of the question's superfluity.

Correvalte nodded. "A big one, sir. It missed us by about

a mile, perhaps more, but for a moment I thought our time had come. I never want to see anything like that again."

"You probably never will," Toller said reassuringly. "Get the rigger to check the envelope for damage, particularly around the strut attachments. What is the fellow's name?"

"Getchert, sir."

"Well, tell Getchert to look lively—it's time he did something to earn his salt on this trip."

As Correvalte moved away towards the aft superstructure, where the ordinary crew members were housed, Toller gripped a transverse line and drew himself to the rail. Now that the inversion had been carried out he could see only the ships of his own echelon and, below him, the balloons of the four leading vessels, but all seemed well with the fleet in general. He had made many ascents to the weightless zone and as a result had become inured to the thought of a meteor actually striking a ship. It was one of the rare cases in which he could draw comfort from thinking about man's insignificance in the scale of cosmic events. His ships were so small and the universe so large that it would be quite unreasonable for one of the blazing cosmic bullets to find a human mark.

It was ironic that only minutes earlier he had been privately bemoaning the humdrum nature of interplanetary flight, but if there were to be dangers he wanted them to be of a type which could be challenged and overcome. There was precious little glory to be wrung from casual extermination by a blind instrument of nature, a commonplace fragment of rock speeding through the void from. . . .

Toller raised his head, directing his gaze to the south-east, to the part of the sky where the meteor must have originated, and was intrigued when he picked out what looked like a tiny cloud of golden fireflies. The cloud was roughly circular and was expanding rapidly, its individual components brightening with each passing second. He stared at it, bemused, unable to recall having seen anything similar amid the sky's sparkling treasures, and then—like the abrupt clarification of an image in an optical system—his sense of scale and perspective returned, and there came a terrible realisation.

He was looking at a swarm of meteors which appeared to be heading directly towards the fleet!

His understanding of the spectacle transformed it, seeming to increase the tempo of events. The shower opened radially like a carnivorous blossom, silently encompassing his field of vision, and he knew then that it could be hundreds of miles across. Unable to move or even to cry out, he gripped the ship's rail and watched the blazing entities fan ever outwards, racing towards the peripheries of his vision, still in utter silence despite the awesome energies being expended.

I'm safe, Toller told himself. *I'm safe for the simple reason that I'm too small a prey for these fire-monsters. Even the ships are too small. . . .*

But something new was happening. A radical change was taking place. The obsidian horsemen from the far side of the cosmos, who had pursued their courses through total vacuum for millions of years, had at last encountered a denser medium, and they were destroying themselves against barriers of air, the gaseous fortifications which protected the twin planets from cosmic intruders.

Favourable though the encounter was for any creature living on the surface of Land or Overland, it boded ill for travellers taken by surprise at the narrowest point of the bridge of air between the two worlds. The meteors, racked by intolerable stresses, began to explode, and as they shattered into thousands of diverging splinters they were bound to become less discriminatory in their choice of targets.

Toller flinched as, with a wash of light and overlapping peals of thunder, the disintegrating meteors momentarily filled the whole sky. Suddenly they were behind him. He turned and saw the entire phenomenon in reverse, the great disk of radiance contracting as it raced into the remoteness of space. The main difference in its appearance was that there was less corpuscularity—the circle was a nearly uniform area of swirling flame. On leaving the last tenuous fringes of the twin worlds' atmosphere, the fiery bullets were deprived of fuel and quickly faded from sight. A numb silence engulfed the tower of ships.

How did we survive? Toller thought. *How in the name of. . . ?*

He became aware of shouting from somewhere not far above him. There came a blurry explosion, typical of the pikon-halvell reaction, and he knew that at least one of the ships had been less fortunate than his own.

"Put us on our side," he shouted to Lieutenant Correvalte, who was frozen at the control station. Toller clung to the rail, impatiently straining to see upwards past the curvatures of the balloon, while Correvalte began the regulated intermittent firing of one of the lateral jets.

A few seconds later Toller's eyes were greeted by the bizarre spectacle of a bluehorn drifting downwards in the sunlit air, against the background of daytime stars. The explosion must have hurled it clear of the gondola in which it was being transported. It was barking in terror and lashing out with hooved feet as it imperceptibly fell towards Land.

Toller turned his attention to the stricken ship, now coming into view. Its balloon had been reduced to a formless canopy of fabric panels. All four sides of the gondola had been blasted away from the base, and were still spinning slowly as part of an irregular ring which was made up of the figures of men, boxes of stores, coils of rope and general debris. Here and there among the floating confusion were flashes and fizzlings which emitted billows of white condensation as small quantities of pikon and halvell encountered each other and, not being confined, burned harmlessly against the pastel background of Overland.

Crew members from the other three ships of the same echelon were already launching themselves out from the sides of their vessels to begin rescue work. Toller scanned the struggling human figures which were part of the central chaos, and felt a pang of relief as he reached the unexpected conclusion that none of them was dead. He guessed that the gondola had received a glancing blow from a tiny meteor fragment and had turned on its side, thereby causing some of the green and purple power crystals to mingle and ignite, perhaps in the engine hoppers.

"Are we under attack? Are we to die?" The quavering words came from Commissioner Kettoran, his long pale face appearing at the door of the cabin.

Toller was about to explain what had happened when he noticed a movement at the rail of Vantara's ship. She had come to the side, accompanied by the smaller and less impressive figure of the lieutenant who had been with her at the time of their inauspicious meeting. Even at a distance the sight of the princess was enough to disturb Toller's composure. He saw that Vantara and her officer seemed to be concentrating their attention on the still-struggling bluehorn. The animal had lost all the momentum imparted to it by the explosion, and was apparently in a fixed position roughly midway between Vantara's ship and Toller's.

He knew, however, that the permanence of the spatial relationship was an illusion. The bluehorn and the ships were all in the grip of Land's gravity, and all were falling towards the surface thousands of miles below. The all-important difference was that the ships were receiving some degree of support from their hot air balloons, whereas the bluehorn was falling freely. This close to the weightless zone the discrepancy in speeds was hard to detect, but it was there nevertheless, and in accordance with the laws of physics was steadily increasing. Unless corrective action was taken quite quickly the bluehorn—a valuable animal—would be condemned to that fatal plunge, lasting more than a day and a night, which every skyman had experienced in bad dreams.

Vantara and the lieutenant, whose name Toller had forgotten, were busy with their hands and within seconds he realised why. They propelled themselves over the rail with weightless ease, and he saw they had donned their personal flight packs. The units, powered by miglign gas, were a far cry from the old pneumatic systems hastily invented at the time of the interplanetary war, but in spite of their advanced design they were tricky enough for the unpractised operator.

Evidence of that fact came almost immediately when Vantara, failing to keep the thrust in line with her centre of gravity, went into a slow tumble and had to be righted and steadied by her companion. It occurred to Toller at once that the two women, obviously intent on retrieving the bluehorn, could be getting themselves into real danger. The terrified beast was still lashing out with its plate-sized hooves, one blow from which would be sufficient to pulp a human skull.

"We had a close call," he shouted over his shoulder to Kettoran as he snatched a flight unit from a nearby rack. "Ask Correvalte about it!"

He went over the rail and sprang out into the sunlit air with the unit still in his hand. The twin worlds with all their intricate detail filled most of the sky on each side of him, and the space between was largely occupied by ranks of bulbous ships, plus wreaths of smoke and condensation through which miniature humanoid figures could be seen going about their enigmatic errands. Daytime stars and the brightest of the nebulae and comets effectively completed a full sphere of visual phenomena.

Toller, who had made a point of mastering the standard flight unit, used his drift time to strap the pack securely around his torso. He brought himself into a good alignment and fired a long burst which took him directly towards the bluehorn. The fierce chill of the midworld region, enhanced by slipstream, clawed at his eyes and mouth.

Vantara and her lieutenant were now close to the bluehorn, which was still barking and crowing in terror. They edged nearer to it and were beginning to uncoil the rope they had brought when Toller used his retro jet to bring himself to a halt close by. It was a long time since he had been within speaking distance of Vantara, and—in spite of the bizarre circumstances—he felt a tingling awareness of her physical presence. The very molecules of his body seemed to be reacting to an invisible aura which surrounded her. Her oval face, partially shaded by the cowl of her skysuit, was as lovely as he remembered it—enigmatic, utterly feminine, unnerving in its perfection.

"Why can't we meet in ordinary places, the way other people do?" Toller said.

The countess eyed him briefly, turned away with no change of expression and spoke to her lieutenant. "We'll bind the back legs first—it would be easier that way."

"I would like to try calming the beast down first," the lieutenant replied. "It's too risky to go behind it while it's so fretful."

"Nonsense!" Vantara spoke with the brisk confidence of one who had had extensive stables at her disposal since childhood. Forming a wide noose with the rope, she sailed closer to the bluehorn on a plume of miglign condensation. Toller was about to call out a warning when the animal, which was continually twisting its head around and had a full view of its surroundings, struck out with both hind legs. One of its enormous hooves grazed Vantara's hip, catching the material of her suit without impacting on her body. The imparted force put her into a spin which was checked almost at once by the cold-stiffened rope she was still holding. Had the bluehorn's hoof connected with her pelvis she would have been seriously injured, and it was apparent that she understood the fact because her face was pale when she regained a stable attitude.

"Why did you pull on the line?" she demanded of her lieutenant, her voice stinging with anger. "You drew me in! I could have been killed!"

The lieutenant's jaw sagged and she shot a scandalised

glance at Toller, tacitly enlisting him as a witness. "My lady, I did no such—"

"Don't argue, lieutenant."

"I *said* we should calm the beast down before—"

"Let's not set up a court of enquiry," Vantara interrupted, her breath forming white wreaths of condensation in front of her face. "If you have suddenly become expert in animal husbandry *you* may retrieve this foul-tempered sack of bones. It's of pretty poor stock, anyway." She twisted in the air and propelled herself back towards her ship.

The lieutenant watched her depart, then looked at Toller, an unexpected smile plumping her already rounded cheeks. "The theory is that if this poor dumb creature had good breeding it would have known not to kick a member of the royal family."

Toller felt that the levity was misplaced. "The countess had a narrow escape."

"The countess brings these things down on herself," the lieutenant said. "The reason she took it on herself to retrieve the bluehorn—rather than leave the job to common hands —was that she wanted to demonstrate her natural control over bloodstock. She firmly believes in all the aristocracy's most cherished myths—that their males are born with an instinctive mastery of generalship; that the females are gifted in every branch of the arts and—"

"Lieutenant!" Toller's annoyance had been growing throughout the discourse and suddenly could no longer be contained. "How dare you speak thuswise to me about a superior officer! Don't you realise I could have you severely punished for that kind of talk?"

The lieutenant's eyes widened in surprise, then her expression became one of disappointment and resignation. "Not you, too. Not another one!"

"What are you talking about?"

"Every man who meets her. . . ." The lieutenant paused, shaking her head. "I would have thought that after that business of the collision report . . . Do you know that the beautiful Countess Vantara did her utmost to have you deprived of your command?"

"Do you know that you are supposed to use the proper form of address when speaking to a senior officer?" Toller was vaguely aware that there was something ludicrous about his manner—especially when the two of them were poised in blue emptiness between the swirled disks of planets—but he was unable to listen passively while Vantara was subjected to such acidulous criticism.

"I'm sorry, sir." The lieutenant's face had lost all expression and her voice was neutral. "Do you want me to see what I can do about the bluehorn?"

"What's your name, anyway?"

"Jerene Pertree, sir."

Toller now felt pompous, but could see no way out of the web he had woven around himself. "There's no scarcity of experienced handlers on this flight—are you sure you won't get yourself sent flying?"

"I grew up on a farm, sir." Jerene opened the valve of her propulsion unit a short distance, producing just enough thrust to drift her towards the bluehorn's head. The animal's bulging eyes rolled as she drew near and shining strands of saliva gathered in the air around its mouth. Toller felt a stab of concern—those massive jaws could easily rend human flesh beneath the stoutest garment—but Jerene was making gentle, wordless sounds which seemed to have an immediate soothing effect on the bluehorn. She slipped one arm around its neck and began stroking the animal's brow with her free hand. It submitted to her touch, visibly becoming docile, and in a few seconds she was able to slide its eyelids down over the staring amber eyes. Jerene nodded towards Toller, signalling for him to come in with the rope.

He jetted forward, bound the bluehorn's back feet together, paid out a short length of line and repeated the process with the forelegs. He was not accustomed to that kind of work, and all the while was half-expecting a violent response from the captive animal, but it allowed him to complete the operation without mishap.

By that time the chaos above was being brought under control. The stricken ship was being abandoned. Overland's surface was almost completely occulted by condensation trails as crewmen from other vessels began the work of salvaging supplies. They were shouting to each other, sounding almost cheerful as they realised how slight was the damage to the fleet as a whole, compared to what it could have been. It occurred to Toller that the expedition had been lucky in another respect—if the encounter with the meteor swarm had not happened so close to the weightless zone recovery from it would have been much more difficult, if not impossible. Every object he could see was falling towards Land, but the rate of descent was so leisurely that in practice it could be disregarded for the time being.

Men were also jetting upwards from the four ships of the first echelon, among them Sky-commodore Sholdde, chief executive officer for the expedition. Sholdde was a tough and laconic fifty-year-old, much favoured by the Queen because of the relish with which he tackled difficult assignments. The fact that he had lost a ship, although no blame could be laid at his door, was going to make him edgy and difficult to deal with for the rest of the flight.

"Maraquine!" he shouted at Toller. "What do you think you're doing there? Get back to your ship and see what extra stores you can take on board. You shouldn't be concerning yourself with that miserable flea-bag."

"How dare you call me a flea-bag!" Jerene murmured in Sholdde's direction, feigning indignation. "Flea-bag, yourself!"

"Look, I've already warned you about. . . ." Toller, who had been about to admonish the lieutenant on her disrespect for senior officers, met the humorous glint in her brown eyes and his resolve foundered. He liked people who could make jokes at times of stress, and he had to admit that he would have had trouble summoning up the nerve to go as close to the frightened bluehorn's head as Jerene had done.

"You may rejoin your ship now," he said stiffly. "The farmers can collect their bluehorn when they're ready."

"Yes, sir." Jerene pushed herself clear of the quiescent animal and reached for the controls of her propulsion unit.

Toller now felt that he had been unfair. "By the way, lieutenant. . . ."

"Sir?"

"You did well with the bluehorn."

"Why thank you, sir," Jerene said, smiling demurely in a way which left Toller almost certain that he was being mocked. He watched her jet away from him, trailing a cone of rolling white condensation, and his thoughts turned immediately to Vantara. She had narrowly escaped injury from the bluehorn's hoof and had done the right thing in retiring to her ship at once. It was unfortunate, though, that her doing so had deprived him of the opportunity to establish a better relationship between them.

But I've got time in hand, he thought, deciding to be philosophical. *There'll be all the time in the world when we get to Land.*

Chapter 4

Divivvidiv was awakened from mid-brain-sleep by a tele-pathic whisper from the Xa.

Look about you, Beloved Creator, the Xa said, using the mind-colour green to show that it considered the matter to be of some urgency.

What is happening? Divivvidiv responded, still not fully restored to every level of consciousness. He had been dream-ing of simpler and happier times, in particular about his early childhood on Dussarra, and his high-brain had just begun devising the scenario for a fulfilling day, one which would have been fed in every detail into slumbering mid-brain and which he would have lived in full while asleep. He would, of course, be able to recreate it during his next inert period, but inevitably there would be some minor differences, and he could not help but experience a slight sense of loss. The vanished dream-day had promised to be well-nigh perfect. Nostalgia compounded. . . .

The Primitives ascending from the surface of their planet have passed through the datum plane, the Xa went on. *They have inverted their vessels and—*

Which shows they are on their way to the sister planet, Divivvidiv interrupted. *Why did you disturb me?*

I have been able to perceive them with greater clarity, Beloved Creator, and I must inform you that their organs of sight are much superior to yours. Also, they have developed instruments which efficiently magnify optical images.

Telescopes! The idea of a primitive species having been able to devise ways of manipulating a medium as intractable as light startled Divivvidiv into full wakefulness. He sat up on the smooth, spongy block which was his bed and switched off its artificial gravity field, without which he would have been unable to enter any but the most superficial level of sleep.

Tell me, he said to the Xa, *will the Primitives be able to see us?* He had to ask the question, to rely for the moment on the Xa's senses, because his own radius of direct perception was severely curtailed by the metal walls of the habitat.

Yes, Beloved Creator. Two of them are already scanning the general area of the visual sphere in which we are located —one of them with the aid of a double telescope—and there is a strong possibility of our being detected. The heaters of the protein synthesising station are the most likely to draw attention—they leak radiation which is well within that part of the spectrum spanned by the Primitives' eyes. 'Purple' is the word they use for it.

I will shut down the heaters immediately. Divivvidiv floated himself out of the habitat's living quarters and into the principal operations hall. His trajectory carried him through the air to the control matrix which governed nutrient production, and he used a pencil-slim grey finger to divert the flow of power away from the row of exterior heaters.

I have done it, he said to the Xa. *Have the Primitives seen anything?*

There was a brief pause before the Xa replied. *Yes—one of them has commented on seeing 'a line of purple lights', but there is no associated emotional reaction. The event has been dismissed as insignificant, and is already being forgotten.*

I am glad of that, Divivvidiv said, using the mind-colour appropriate to relief.

Why do you experience relief, Beloved Creator? Surely a species at such an early stage of its development can pose no threat to you.

I was not concerned about my own safety, Divivvidiv said. *If the Primitives had been curious about us, and had decided to investigate, I would have been forced to destroy them.*

There was another pause before the Xa spoke. *You are reluctant to kill any of the Primitives.*

Naturally.

Because it is immoral to deprive any being of its life?

Yes.

In that case, Beloved Creator, the Xa said, *why have you decided to kill me?*

I have told you many times that nobody has decided to kill you—it is simply a matter of . . . The talk of killing reminded Divivvidiv of why he was there, of the awesome crime against nature being perpetrated by his own kind, and a pang of anguish and guilt stilled his thoughts.

Chapter 5

The ancient city of Ro-Atabri was *immense*.

Toller had been standing at the rail of his gondola for more than an hour, staring down at the slowly expanding patch of intricate line and colour patterns which differentiated the city from the surrounding terrain. He had been conditioned to regard Prad, Overland's capital, as an imposing metropolis, and had visualised Ro-Atabri as much larger but essentially the same. The reality of the historic seat of Kolcorronian power, however, was something for which he could not have prepared himself.

He sensed that such a huge difference in size somehow led to a difference in kind, but there was more to it than that. All the cities, towns and villages on Overland had been planned, and therefore their chief characteristics sprang from the will of their architects and builders, but from high in the air Ro-Atabri resembled a natural growth, a living organism.

It was all there, just as in the sketches his maternal grand-mother—Gesalla Maraquine—used to make for him when he was a child. There was the Borann River winding into Arle Bay, which in turn opened out upon the Gulf of Tronom, and to the east was the snow-capped Mount Opelmer. Cupped in and shaped by those natural features, the city and its suburbs sprawled across the land, a vast lichen of masonry, concrete, brakka wood and clay which represented centuries of endeavour by multitudes of human beings. The great fires which had raged on the day the Migration had begun had left a still-visible discoloration in some areas, but the durable stonework had survived intact and would serve humanity again in some future era. Flecks of orange-red and orange-brown showed where the ill-fated New Men had begun capping the shells of buildings with new tiled roofs.

"What do you think of it, young Maraquine?" Commissioner Kettoran said, appearing at Toller's side. Now that gravity was back to normal he was feeling much better and was taking a lively interest in all aspects of the ship's affairs.

"It's big," Toller said simply. "I can't take it in. It makes history . . . real."

Kettoran laughed. "Did you think we'd made it up?"

"You could have done, as far as most of the present generation are concerned, but this . . . It hurts my brain, if you know what I mean."

"I know exactly what you mean—think how *I* feel." Kettoran leaned further across the rail and his long face became animated. "Do you see that square patch of green just to the west of the city? That's the old Skyship Quarter—the exact spot we took off from fifty years ago! Will we be able to land there?"

"It seems as good a place as any," Toller said. "The lateral dispersions on this flight have been remarkably slight, and those that did occur have cancelled each other out. The decision rests with the Sky-commodore, of course, but I'd say that's where we'll put down."

"That would make it perfect. The perfect full circle."

"Indeed yes," Toller agreed, no longer really listening, his attention captured by the realisation that the ten-day flight between the worlds was all but over, and that very soon he would have unlimited opportunities to court Vantara. He had not even glimpsed her since the incident with the blue-horn, and the lack of contact had fuelled his obsession to the point where the prospect of seeing another world for the first time seemed no more of an adventure than being able to speak to the countess face to face and perhaps win her over.

"I envy you, young Maraquine," Kettoran said, gazing wistfully downwards at the natural stage upon which the

half-remembered scenes of his youth had been enacted.
"Everything lies before you."

"Perhaps." Toller smiled, savouring his own interpretation
of the commissioner's words. "Perhaps you're right."

The village of Sty-vee contained no more than a hundred or
so buildings, and even in its heyday would have housed only
a few hundred people. Toller was tempted to cross it off his
list and proceed on his way without even landing, but it
would then have become necessary to falsify an inspection
report and he could not allow himself to sink to petty dis-
honesty. He studied the layout of the village for a moment,
noting that its central square was very small, even for such
an out-of-the-way place.

"What do you think, corporal?" he said, testing the
younger man's judgment. "Is it worth trying to put the ship
down on those few yards of turf?"

Steenameert leaned over the rail to assess the prospects.
"I wouldn't take the risk, sir—there's very little leeway and
there's no telling what the eddy currents are like around that
group of tall warehouses."

"That's what I was thinking—we'll make a pilot of you
yet," Toller said jovially. "Head for those pastures to the
east, beside the river, and drop us there."

Steenameert nodded, his naturally pink face growing even
more roseate with gratification. Toller had taken a liking to
Steenameert on the occasion of their first meeting, when he
had parachuted down from the interplanetary void, and had
put in a special request to have him in his crew for the flight
to Land. Now he was personally grooming Steenameert for
a field promotion, somewhat to the annoyance of Lieutenant
Correvalte, who had spent the customary year in a training
squadron.

Toller turned to Correvalte, who officially should have
been conducting the landing manoeuvre and was showing his
discomfiture by lounging in a seat in a posture of exaggerated

boredom. "Lieutenant, detail one man to guard the ship and get the others ready to inspect the village—the walk will do them good."

Correvalte saluted, very correctly, and left the bridge. Toller maintained a carefully neutral expression as he watched the lieutenant go down the short stair to the gondola's main deck. He had already decided to recompense Correvalte by recommending him for a full captaincy earlier than usual, but had decided not to let him know until the current mission had been completed.

It was the middle of foreday, and already in the equatorial region of Land the sun's heat was baking the ground. Most of the gondola was in the shadow of the ship's gasbag, a fact which made the environment beyond seem preternaturally bright and vivid. As the vessel performed a slow half-circle to face the slight breeze, sinking all the while, Toller saw that the fields surrounding the village had almost returned to their natural uniform shade of green.

With no seasons to orchestrate the cycle of maturation, individual plants in the wild state tended to follow their own timetables, with a proportion in the earliest stages of growth while others were at their peak or in the process of withering and returning their constituents to the soil. From time immemorial, Kolcorronian farmers had sorted the seeds of useful vegetables into synchronous batches—typically creating six harvests a year—and as a result areas of cultivated land presented patterns of stripes of varying colours.

Here, after decades of neglect, those patterns had all but disappeared as the edible grasses and other crop vegetables had slowly returned to botanic anarchy. The advanced stage of the reversal led Toller to suspect that the village of Sty-vee was not one of those which the New Men had reclaimed after the ptertha plague had wiped out the normal human population. If that were the case, the inspection of the village promised to be yet another in a series of unpleasant and highly depressing experiences.

The final stages of racial extinction—half a century ago—had come so swiftly that there had been no time for the dying to bury the dead. . . .

The thought cast a pall over Toller's mood, reminding him of how wrong he had been in his supposition that the fleet's arrival on Land would give him endless opportunity to keep company with the Countess Vantara. At the heart of his mistake had been a single historical fact.

The migration from Land to Overland had been a carefully planned affair, one which should have been carried out in orderly stages, but in the event it had been essayed in circumstances of panic and chaos. With the city of Ro-Atabri burning, with mobs on the rampage and the army's discipline gone, the evacuation had been forced through with only minutes of notice for the refugees—and in that extreme *not one book* had been taken on the journey between the worlds. Jewellery and useless bundles of currency notes had been carried in plenty, but not one painting, not one written poem, not one sheet of music.

While men and women of culture were later to complain that the race had left its soul behind, King Chakkell and his heirs were to fret about a more irksome oversight. In all the turmoil and confusion nobody had thought of bringing any maps of Kolcorron, of the empire, or of Land itself. From the time of the Migration until the present day—although the Kolcorronian royal family still claimed sovereignty over the Old World—the lack of charts had proved an annoyance more than anything else, but the situation had changed entirely.

Prince Oldo, Daseene's sole remaining offspring, was now in his late fifties and had been thwarted all his life by the Queen's refusal to step down from the throne. And, just as his mother's frailty was promising to clear the way for him, he had been given an extra frustration to contend with in that he was about to become heir to a kingdom whose actual and potential wealth were almost a total mystery.

Unknown to Toller, he had prevailed on Daseene to put off the circumnavigation of Land until a detailed survey of Kolcorron itself had been carried out. Thus it was that, instead of pacing Vantara's ship on a challenging round-the-world flight, Toller had found himself committed to a seemingly endless series of aerial hops from one deserted village or town to another. He had been on Land for almost twenty days and in all that time had not even seen Vantara, who was engaged on similar duties in a different quarter of the country.

Just as the city of Ro-Atabri had impressed him with its sheer size, Kolcorron was overwhelming him with the multiplicity of centres, large and medium and small, which had once been necessary to house its population. Having lived all his life on Overland, where it was possible to fly for hours without seeing a single habitation, Toller felt oppressed, suffocated, by the extent of men's interference with the natural landscape. He had begun to visualise the old kingdom as one vast, seething hive in which any individual would have counted for very little. Even the knowledge that it was the birthplace of his grandfather did little to counteract his negative feelings about Kolcorron's tamed and overworked countryside.

He gazed moodily at the cluster of dwellings and larger buildings, apparently tilting with the airship's movements, which made up Sty-vee. The old maps and gazetteers which had been found in Ro-Atabri showed that its chief importance arose from the fact that the village contained a pumping station which had been vital to the irrigation of a considerable area of farming land north of the local river and canal system. It was required of Toller that he should inspect the station and report on its condition.

Still keeping a watchful eye on Steenameert and his handling of the airship, Toller consulted his list and confirmed that after Sty-vee had been crossed off there would be only three further locations to check. If there were no complications he could be on his way back to base camp in the capital before littlenight of the following day. Vantara might also have returned to Ro-Atabri by that time. The thought helped to dispel some of Toller's forebodings about the task in hand, and he began to whistle as he took his sword from a locker. The steel weapon—which had once belonged to his grandfather—was too awkward to wear in the close confines of a ship, but he never ventured abroad without it strapped to his side. It enhanced his sense of kinship with that other Toller Maraquine, the one whose exploits he would never have the chance to emulate.

A minute later—to the accompaniment of short bursts from the secondary jets—the gondola's keel made contact with the ground and the four anchor cannon fired their barbs into the grassy earth. Crewmen leapt over the side immediately with extra lines and began doubly securing the ship against the possibility of the heat vortices which commonly roamed the land close to the equator.

"Closing down the engines, sir," Steenameert said, his eyes seeking Toller's as he vented the pneumatic reservoir which fed power crystals to the jets. "How was the landing?"

"Passable, passable." Toller used a tone of voice which showed that he was more pleased with the corporal's performance than his choice of words implied. "But don't stand there all day congratulating yourself—we have business in yonder metropolis. Over the side with you!"

As had happened before, during the short walk to the edge of the village Toller felt oddly self-conscious, as though hidden observers were watching every step he took. He knew how absurd the notion was, but yet he was unable to forget what easy targets he and his men would be if defenders with muskets were to appear at the blank upper windows of the nearest houses. His uneasiness, he decided, sprang from a feeling that he had no right to be doing what he was doing, that the last resting places of so many people should be left undisturbed. . . .

An outburst of swearing from one of the crewmen a dozen paces to his left caused him to look in that direction. The man was gingerly skirting something which Toller could not see because of the long grass.

"What is it, Renko?" he said, knowing in his heart what the answer would be.

"A couple of skeletons, sir." Renko's saffron airman's shirt was already darkened with sweat in several places and he was showily limping. "I nearly fell over them, sir. Nearly broke my ankle."

"If it doesn't mend soon I'll have the incident noted in your service record," Toller said drily. "Clashed with two skeletons—came off second best." His comment brought a round of laughter from the other men and Renko's limp rapidly disappeared.

On reaching the village the group fanned out in what had become a routine procedure, with the crewmen entering houses and reporting on their condition to Lieutenant Correvalte, who was making copious notes in a dispatch book. Toller took the opportunity to find some comparative solitude, wandering separately through narrow passageways and the remains of gardens. The derelict condition of the buildings convinced him that Sty-vee had not been occupied by the New Men, that half a century had passed since human families had enlivened the crumbling stonework with their presence.

There were no skeletons visible out of doors, but that was not unusual in Toller's experience. In the final and most virulent phase of the ptertha plague victims had survived for only two hours after infection, but some instinct seemed to have prompted them to seek out places of seclusion in which to die. It was as if some lingering sense of propriety had been outraged at the thought of defiling their communities with decaying corpses. A few had made their way to favourite beauty spots or vantage points, but in general the citizens of old Kolcorron had chosen to die in the privacy of their homes, very often in bed.

Toller had lost count of the number of times he had seen pathetic family tableaux consisting of male and female skeletons still locked in a last embrace, sometimes with smaller bony frames lying between them. The sight of so many reminders of the ultimate futility of existence in such a short span had contaminated his spirit with a deep melancholia which at times overcame his natural ebullience, and now—unashamedly—he avoided entering the silent dwelling places whenever he could.

His meandering course through the village eventually brought him to a large windowless building which had been built on the bank of the river. Part of it extended down into the slow-moving water. Identifying the structure as the pumping station which was the chief item of interest in the area, he walked around it until he came to a large door in the north wall. The door had been constructed from close-grained wood well reinforced with brakka straps and appeared to have been quite unaffected by fifty years of neglect. It was locked and, as he expected, barely quivered when he threw his considerable weight against it.

Muttering with annoyance, Toller turned away, shaded his eyes from the sun and scanned the village. More than a minute went by before he spotted the burly figure of Gabbleronn, the sergeant-artificer, who was responsible for maintenance of the airship. Gabbleronn had just emerged from what had once been a store of some kind, and was cramming a small object into his pouch. He looked startled when Toller called him, and responded to the summons with an evident lack of enthusiasm.

"I wasn't looting, sir," he protested as he drew near. "I just picked up a little candle holder fashioned from that black wood. It's of no value, sir . . . a souvenir to take home to Prad for my wife . . . I'll put it back if you—"

"Never mind that," Toller interrupted. "I want this door opened. Fetch whatever tools you need from the ship. Blow it off its hinges if that's what it takes."

"Yes, *sir*!" Looking relieved, Gabbleronn studied the door for a moment, then saluted and hurried away.

Toller sat down on the stone doorsteps and made himself as comfortable as he could while he waited for the sergeant to return. The heat was increasing as the sun climbed higher, and the sky was so bright that only a few of the normal daytime stars were visible. Directly above him, the great disk of Overland occupied the centre of the heavens, looking fresh and unsullied in his eyes, and he felt a sudden pang of homesickness for its dew-fresh open spaces. The entire planet of Land was one vast charnel house—exhausted, ghost-ridden, dusty and sad—and even the presence of Vantara somewhere over the horizon scarcely compensated for the gloominess which had begun to impose itself on his mind. It would be different if he could actually be in her company, but this business of being near to her and yet completely cut off from her was much worse than. . . .

What am I doing to myself? he thought suddenly. *What kind of man am I becoming? Would that other Toller Maraquine have mooned around in such a manner—lovesick and homesick—like a sallow-faced adolescent?*

The questions propelled Toller to his feet and he was pacing in impatient circles, a hand on the hilt of his sword, when he saw Correvalte approaching with the rest of the crew in his wake. The lieutenant was checking his notes as he walked, looking businesslike, competent and very much at ease with himself and his surroundings. Toller felt a twinge of envy coupled with a momentary suspicion that Correvalte had the potential to be the better officer of the two.

"The report is almost complete, sir—except for an inspection of the pumping station," Correvalte said. "Have you been inside the building?"

"How could I enter the building when the accursed door is barred?" Toller snapped. "Do I look like a wraith which can insinuate itself through cracks in the woodwork?"

The lieutenant's eyes widened and then became opaquely impersonal. "I'm sorry, sir—I didn't realise. . . ."

"I have sent Gabbleronn for some tools," Toller cut in, already ashamed of his display of peevishness. "See if he needs any help in carrying them—I have no wish to linger in this cemetery any longer than necessary."

He turned away as Correvalte was performing one of his ultra-correct salutes and walked along the bank of the river until he came to a narrow wooden bridge. From a distance the bridge had appeared quite sound, but on close examination he saw that its structure had a grey-white spongy texture which signalled that it had been ravaged by wood-boring insects. He drew his sword and struck at one of the handrail stanchions. It severed with very little resistance to the blade and toppled into the river, taking a section of the rail with it. Half a dozen further blows were sufficient to cut through the two main beams of the bridge, sending the whole rotten edifice plunging down into the water amid puffs of powdered wood and a buzzing of minute winged creatures which had been disturbed in their appointed task.

"You have had a good meal," Toller said, whimsically addressing the multitudes of insects and their grubs which must have been still inside the fallen timbers, "now you can enjoy a drink."

The little flurry of physical activity, frivolous though it had been, helped ease the tensions in his mind and he was in a better mood as he retraced his steps to the village. He reached the pumping station just as Gabbleronn and two of his helpers had succeeded in prising the door open with the aid of large crowbars.

"Good work," Toller said. "Now let us see what marvels of engineering lie within."

Before arriving on Land he had known from his history tuition that the planet had no metals, and that brakka wood had always been employed for applications where, on Overland, the designer would have chosen iron, steel or some other suitable metal. Nevertheless, machinery whose gear-wheels and other highly stressed components were carved from the black wood seemed cumbersome and quaint to his eye, relics of a primitive era.

He led the way along a short passage to a large, vaulted chamber which contained massive pumping machinery. The windows in the roof were heavily encrusted with grime, but there was enough light filtering down from them to show that the machinery, although coated with dust, was complete and in a good state of repair. Those parts not made of brakka—beams and struts—were of the same close-grained wood as the station's door, a material which evidently resisted wood-boring insects or was not to their taste. Toller tested one of the beams with his thumbnail and was impressed by its hardness, even after fifty years without maintenance.

"I believe it's called rafter wood, sir," Steenameert said, coming to his side. "You can see why it was favoured by builders."

"How do you know what it's called?"

Steenameert blushed. "I have read descriptions of it many times in the—"

"Oh, *no!*" The voice was that of Lieutenant Correvalte, who had been walking around the perimeter of the chamber, opening the doors into side rooms as he came to them. He was backing off from a doorway, shaking his head, and Toller knew at once that he had witnessed a great obscenity. *This*, Toller told himself, *is what I have been expecting since we entered the village. I knew something bad was in store for us, and I have no wish to set eyes on it.*

He knew, also, that he could not avoid personally inspecting the find lest the word get about among the crewmen that he had become soft. The most he could do was to delay the grim moment. He stooped over a control lever and ratchet and brushed the dust away from them, pretending to take a special interest in the precise carving, and while doing so watched his men. Their curiosity aroused by Correvalte's reaction, they were taking turns at venturing into *the* room. None stayed longer than a few seconds, and—professionally callous though they were—each looked subdued and thoughtful as he returned to the main chamber.

I have an appointment in that room, Toller thought, *and it would be unseemly to delay any longer.*

He straightened up, hand unconsciously falling to the hilt of his sword, and walked to the waiting doorway. The room beyond resembled a prison cell. It was devoid of furniture, and was cheerlessly illuminated by a broken skylight in the sloping roof far above. Ranged around the walls, in the seated position, were perhaps twenty skeletons. The wispy remnants of dresses and skirts, plus the presence of necklaces and ceramic bangles, informed Toller that the skeletons were the remains of women.

It isn't all that bad, he thought. *It was a fact of life, a fact of death, that the plague was impartial. It struck down women just as readily as men, and since arriving on this unhappy world I have seen many, many. . . .*

His mind seized up, chilled, as he absorbed a fact which had not been readily apparent at first glance. Curled up in the pelvic basin of each of the skeletons was another skeleton —a tiny armature of fragile bones which was all that remained of a baby whose life had ended before it had properly begun.

Yes, the plague had been very *impartial.*

Toller longed to turn and flee from the room, but the deadly coldness in his mind had percolated down through his body, immobilising his limbs. Time had become distorted, stretching seconds into aeons, and he knew that he was destined to spend the rest of his life frozen to the same spot, on that threshold of pessimism and pure despair.

"The villagers must have put all their pregnant women in here, hoping these walls would protect them," Lieutenant Correvalte said from close behind Toller. "Look! One of them was having twins."

Toller chose not to seek out that refinement of horror.

Breaking free of his paralysis, he turned and walked away from the room, acutely aware of being closely scrutinised by every member of his crew.

"Make a note," he said over his shoulder to Correvalte. "Say that we inspected the pumping machinery and found it to be in good condition and capable of being restored to working order in a short time."

"Is that all, sir?"

"I haven't noticed anything else that our sovereign would regard as important," Toller said in casual tones, walking slowly towards the station's entrance, disguising the anxiousness he felt, the pressing need to reassure himself that the sanity of sunshine could still be found in the outside world.

The Migration Day celebrations had taken Toller completely by surprise.

He had completed his survey mission and arrived back at the base camp in Ro-Atabri less than an hour before nightfall, having lost track of the date. Unusually for him, he felt deeply tired. The news that it was Day 226, the anniversary of the first touch-downs on Overland, had failed to strike any spark within him, and he had gone straight to bed after signing his ship over to Fleet Master Codell. Even the word that Vantara had returned to base earlier in the day had not roused him from the pervasive lethargy, the weariness of spirit which was taking the light out of everything.

Now he was lying in darkness in his room, which was part of the quarters which had once housed the guard of the Great Palace, and was quite unable to sleep. He had never been given over to introspection and soul-searching, but he understood very well that his tiredness was not physical in its origins. It was a mental tiredness, a psychic fatigue induced by a long period of doing that for which he had no taste, of going against his own nature.

Before leaving home he had visualised Land as one vast charnel house, and the reality of it had more than conformed to his expectations, culminating in the grisly find at the Sty-vee pumping station. Perhaps he was being self-indulgent. Perhaps—as one born into a privileged position in society—he was having his first taste of what life must be like for a common man who was forced to spend all his days in a kind of toil he detested and which had been forced on him from above. Toller tried reminding himself that his grandfather, that other Toller Maraquine, would not have allowed his composure to be so quickly disturbed. No matter what fearful sights and experiences the *real* Toller Maraquine had had to contend with he would have deflected the force of them with his shield of toughness and self-sufficiency. But . . . but. . . .

How do I find room inside my head for twenty skeletons neatly ranged against a wall, with another twenty skeletons curled up inside them in the pelvic cradles? Another twenty-one skeletons, I should have said. Didn't you notice that one of the women was having twins? What are you supposed to do about two little mannikins, with whitened twigs in place of bones, who kept each other company in death instead of life?

An extra-loud burst of laughter from somewhere in the palace grounds brought Toller to his feet, swearing in exasperation. Men and women were getting drunk out there, getting themselves into a state in which they could exchange handshakes with skeletons, return the grins of skeletons, and pat unborn babies on their still-bifurcated craniums. It came to Toller that his only prospect of sleep that night lay in dosing himself with large quantities of alcohol.

Welcoming the positive decision, his inner tiredness abating slightly, Toller pulled on some clothes and left the room. Finding his way through unfamiliar corridors with some difficulty, he reached the garden on the north side of the grounds which was the centre of the festivities. It had been chosen because it was mostly paved and therefore had stood up to decades of neglect better than the others. Even the parade ground at the rear of the palace was waist-high in grass and weeds. Several small fires had been lit in the garden, their orange-and-yellow rays partially obscured and softly reflected by ornamental fountains, statues and shrubs, making the place look much larger than it did in daylight.

Couples and small groups strolled through the spangled dimness, while others stood near the long table which had been set up for refreshments. Males outnumbered females by about three to one on the expedition, which meant that women who were in the apposite mood that night were enjoying a surfeit of romantic attention, while males who were redundant in such respects were concentrating on food, drink, song and the telling of bawdy stories.

Toller found Commissioner Kettoran and his secretary, Parlo Wotoorb, standing behind the table serving food and drink. The two old men were obviously enjoying the menial task, proving to all of the company that in spite of their exalted rank they still possessed the common touch.

"Welcome, welcome, welcome," Kettoran called out when he espied Toller approaching. "Come and have a drink with us, young Maraquine."

Toller thought that the commissioner was slightly overplaying his role—perhaps afraid of somebody missing the point —but it was a harmless enough foible, not one he found objectionable. "Thank you—I'll have a very large beaker of Kailian black."

Kettoran shook his head. "No wine. No ale either, for that matter. A question of useful payload on the ships, you see —you will have to settle for brandy."

"Brandy it is then."

"I'll let you have some of the good stuff, in one of my best glasses."

The commissioner sank down to his knees behind the table and a moment later stood up with a glittering crystal filled to the brim. He was handing the glass over when the jovial expression abruptly departed his face and was replaced by one of mingled surprise and pain. Toller took the glass quickly and watched with some concern as Kettoran pressed both forearms against his lower ribcage.

"Trye, are you unwell?" Wotoorb said anxiously. "I *told* you you should take more rest."

Kettoran inclined his head briefly towards the secretary, then winked knowingly at Toller. "This old fool thinks he is going to live longer than I am." He smiled, apparently no longer in distress, picked up his own glass and raised it to Toller. "I bid you good health, young Maraquine."

"Good health to you, sir," Toller said, unable to muster a reciprocal smile.

Kettoran studied his face closely. "Son—I trust you will not think me impertinent—but you no longer seem the young game-cock who captained my ship on the voyage to Land. Something seems to have taken the starch out of you."

"Out of *me!*" Toller laughed incredulously. "Put your mind at ease, sir—I don't soften up so readily. And now, if you will excuse me. . . ."

He turned and walked away from the table, privately disturbed by the commissioner's comments. If the effects of his malaise could be discerned so quickly by one who scarcely knew him, what chance had he of keeping the respect of his own crewmen? Maintaining discipline was difficult enough at times without having the men begin to regard him as a hothouse plant who was likely to wilt at adversity's first cold breath. He sipped some brandy and walked around the garden close to the perimeter, keeping away from noisier centres of activity, until he found an unoccupied marble bench. Grateful for the solitude, he sat down.

Above him the narrowing crescent of Overland was nested near the centre of the Great Wheel, that enormous whirlpool of silver luminance which dominated the night sky in the latter part of the year. Several comets were splaying their tails across the heavens, and myriads of stars—some of them like coloured coachlamps—added to the splendour, burning with an unwinking permanence which contrasted with the brief dartings of meteors.

Toller addressed himself to his outsized goblet, which must have contained close on a third of a bottle of brandy, downing the warming liquor in patient, regular sips. It was a night on which it would have been good to have female companionship, but even the thought that Vantara might be only a few dozen paces away in the scented gloaming failed to elicit any response from within him. It was also a night for facing up to truths, for discarding illusions, and the plain facts of the matter were that he had made an enemy of the countess on their first meeting as adults, that she despised him now and would go on doing so for as long as he stayed in her memory.

Besides, came the slithering thought, *how can you even think of courting a woman when there are twenty-one miniature skeletons watching you?*

Toller kept on with his methodical drinking until the goblet was empty, then assessed his condition. In spite of the tiredness he had not yet succeeded in stunning himself with alcohol. There was a perverse wakefulness at the core of his mind which told him that at least one more brimming crystal would be necessary if he were to escape the reproachful gaze of the twenty-one bone-babies and sink into unconsciousness before deepnight engulfed the world.

He stood up, as steady as a well-rooted tree, and was starting in the direction of the table to avail himself of Kettoran's generosity when he saw a woman approaching him. She was slim and dark-haired, and he knew before being able to see her face properly that she was Vantara. She was wearing full uniform—no doubt her way of distancing herself from those officers who were prepared to forget about rank for the sake of the revel—and Toller braced himself for a verbal skirmish. He did not have long to wait.

"What's this?" she said lightly. "No sword? Of course! How silly of me to forget—there aren't any kings ripe for skewering at this little gathering."

Toller nodded, acknowledging the reference to his grand-father, who had been dubbed Kingslayer by the populace of his day. "That's very funny, captain." He made to move past her, but she halted him by placing a hand on his arm.

"Is that all you have to say?"

"No." Toller was disconcerted by the unexpected physical contact. "I would add that I'm going to replenish my glass."

Vantara looked up into his face, frowning slightly as she scanned his features. "What's the matter with you?"

"I fail to understand the question."

"Where is the great warrior, Toller Maraquine the Second, who is immune to bullets? Is he off duty tonight?"

"I was never one for riddles, captain," Toller said stonily. "Now, if I may be excused—I'm ready for another of the commissioner's sleeping potions."

Vantara transferred her grip to the hand in which he held his glass—the warmth of her touch like ambersparks playing on his flesh—and briefly bowed her head over it. "Brandy? Bring one for me, please. But not on such a gigantic scale."

"You want me to bring you a drink?" Toller said, aware of sounding slow-witted.

"Yes—if you don't mind." Vantara sat down and made herself comfortable on the bench. "I'll wait here for you."

Feeling slightly bemused, Toller made his way back to the refreshments table and obtained another huge bumper of brandy for himself and a normal-sized one for Vantara, to the accompaniment of much nodding and winking from Kettoran and Wotoorb. While he was on his way back to the bench a ptertha came drifting across the garden, its bubble-like structure glinting but scarcely visible in the uncertain light. It was ascending in the updraught from one of the fires when it was noticed by a group of the revellers. Whooping with glee, they began throwing large twigs and pebbles at it. One of the sticks flailed through the ptertha and it abruptly ceased to exist. A cheer went up from the on-lookers.

"Did you see that?" Vantara said as Toller approached her. "Just listen to them! Overjoyed because they managed to kill something."

"The ptertha killed many of us in their day," Toller replied, unmoved. *Including twenty-one unborn babies.*

"So you approve of killing them for sport?"

"No, no," Toller said, sensing a return of Vantara's old antagonism and feeling unable to cope with it. "I don't approve of killing anything, for sport or any other reason. I've seen enough of the butchers' handiwork to last me a lifetime." He sat down, handed Vantara her glass and took a sip from his own.

"Is that what's wrong with you?"

"There is nothing wrong with me."

"I know—that's what is wrong with you. Having something wrong is a natural state with. . . ." Vantara paused. "I'm sorry. As well as being too involuted, that was uncalled for."

"Did you ask for that drink merely to occupy your hands?" Toller took a gulp of his brandy, suppressing a grimace as the excessive quantity of the fiery liquid washed into his throat.

"Why are you so determined to get drunk tonight?"

"In the name of. . . !" Toller gave an exasperated sigh. "Is this your normal mode of conversation? If it is I'd be grateful if you would go and sit elsewhere."

"Again, I apologise." Vantara gave him a placatory smile and sipped from her glass. "Why don't *you* lead the conversation, Toller?"

The informal and quite intimate use of his given name surprised Toller, adding to the mystery of her change of attitude towards him. He gazed thoughtfully at Vantara and found that in the half-light her face was impossibly beautiful, a concordance of perfect features which might have existed only in the mind of an inspired artist. It occurred to him that one of his fantasies had suddenly and unexpectedly been

translated into reality—*she*, with all of her incredible woman-
liness, was close beside him. And it was a night for romance.
And there was a thrilling softness in her voice. And it was
the *duty* of every human to seize what happiness he could
whenever he could—no matter how many tiny skeletons
he had looked upon—because nature produced millions of
beings of every species for the precise reason that some of
them were bound to be unfortunate, and if a member of the
lucky majority failed to savour life to the full that would be
a betrayal of the few who had been sacrificed on his behalf.
It was now up to him to make the maximum effort to win
the object of all his desires by attracting her to him with
his qualities of strength, courage, consideration, fortitude,
knowledge, humour, generosity. Perhaps a well-turned compliment would be the best way to begin.

"Vantara, you look so. . . ." He paused, aware of the
scrutiny of eyes that no longer existed in twenty-one fist-sized
skulls, and listened like a bystander to the words which were
issuing from his mouth. "What is happening here? Usually
when we meet you behave like an arrogant bitch, and now
—all of a sudden—we're on first-name terms and the very
air is suffused with warmth and friendliness. What private
scheme are you about?"

Vantara laughed and gasped at the same time. "Arrogance! You talk to me about *arrogance*! You who always
approach a woman with your male armour clanking and your
phallic sword swinging through the air!"

"That is the most twisted and. . . ."

Vantara silenced him by raising one hand, fingers spread
out, as a barrier between their eyes and mouths. "Say no
more, Toller, I beg you! Neither of us is wearing armour on
this night and therefore either of us could easily be wounded.
Let us accept things the way they are for this single hour; let
us have this drink together; and let us *talk* to each other.
Will you agree to that?"

Toller smiled. "How could any reasonable man refuse?"

"Very well! Now, tell me why you are no longer the Toller Maraquine I have always known."

"We've returned to the same subject!"

"We never left it."

"But. . . ." Toller gazed at her in perplexity for a moment, and then the unthinkable happened—he began to speak freely about what was in his mind, to confess his newly discovered weaknesses, to admit his growing belief that he would never be able to live up to the example set for him by his grandfather. At one point, while he was describing the tragic find at the pumping station in Sty-vee, his voice faltered and he experienced a terrible fear that he would be unable to continue. When he had finished he took another drink of his brandy, but found it was no longer to his taste. He set the glass aside and sat staring down at his hands, wondering why he felt as shaky as a man who had just emerged from the most harrowing ordeal of his life.

"Poor Toller," Vantara said gently. "What has life done to you that you should be ashamed of having finer feelings?"

"You mean, of being weak."

"It isn't weakness to feel compassion, or to experience doubt, or to need human contact."

Toller thought he glimpsed a way of repairing some of the cracks in his personal façade. "I could do with *lots* of human contact," he said wryly. "Provided it's the right sort."

"Don't talk like that, Toller—there is no need for it." Vantara set her own glass down and swung one leg over the bench so that she was sitting facing him. "Very well, you may touch me if you want to."

"This is not the way I. . . ." Toller fell silent as Vantara took his hands and guided them on to her breasts. They felt warm and firm, even through the thickly embroidered material of her captain's jupon. He moved closer.

"Pray do not misunderstand," Vantara whispered. "I am not going to share your bed—this degree of human contact is sufficient for the needs of the hour." Her lips parted slightly, inviting him to kiss, and he accepted the invitation as in a dream, scarcely able to believe what was happening. The utter femininity of her swamped his senses, reducing the sounds in the garden to a remote murmur. Vantara and he held the same position for a long but indeterminate time, perhaps ten minutes, perhaps twenty, repeating the kiss over and over again, tirelessly, feeling no need to vary or advance the act of physical communion. And when finally they separated Toller felt replenished, restored to completeness. He smiled at Vantara and she responded, his smile grew wider and suddenly they were laughing. Toller was aware of a sense of relief and relaxation akin to that which followed sexual congress, but it was more pervasive and had a component which hinted at greater permanence.

"I don't know what you did to me," he said. "An apothecary could grow rich if he could put such a remedy in a jar."

"I didn't do anything."

"But you did! I had become so weary of this old planet that even the circumnavigation flight was beginning to pall on me. Now, all at once, I'm looking forward to it again. We will not actually be together when we take to the skies, but I'll be continuously in sight of your ship, day after day, and at night there'll be no landing in graveyard cities. I'll see to that. We can. . . ."

"Toller!" Vantara looked oddly wary. "I told you not to misinterpret what has taken place between us."

"I am presuming nothing, I assure you," Toller said quickly and easily, knowing he was lying, filled with an exulting new certainty that in this respect he knew Vantara better than she knew herself. "All I am saying is—"

"Forgive me for interrupting," Vantara cut in, "but you *are* making one rather large presumption."

"And that is. . . ?"

"That I will be taking part in the flight."

Toller was jolted. "How can you *not* take part? You're

here because you're an air captain, and the round-the-globe flight is the most important part of the entire mission. Sky-commodore Sholdde will not excuse you from it."

Vantara smiled in a way that was almost shame-faced. "I confess that I was anticipating some difficulty in that direction, but it transpires that my beloved grandmother—the Queen—had foreseen this kind of thing happening, and had given the commodore instructions that my requests were not to be denied." She smiled again. "I have a feeling he will shed very few tears when I leave."

"Leave?" Toller understood exactly what Vantara was saying, but his lips framed the question nevertheless. "Where do you intend to go?"

"Home, of course. I despise this tired and gloomy world even more than you do, Toller—so tomorrow I will escape from it by flying to Overland, and I doubt if anything will ever persuade me to come back here." Vantara stood up, symbolically breaking the bonds of Land's gravity, putting the interplanetary chasm between herself and Toller, and when she spoke again her voice contained a note of casual insincerity which he felt like a blow to the face.

"Perhaps we will meet again in Prad—in some future year."

Chapter 6

Divivvidiv floated near the viewing post of an electronic telescope and waited until the Xa had completed all adjustments in the aim-and-focus circuits. When the image on the screen had steadied a comparatively small area of the planet below remained as background, the rest having flowed outwards and vanished. He seemed to be looking vertically downwards through a window, the view from which was crossed by swirls of cloud superimposed on ochreous land patterns.

In the exact centre of that view was a small silvery crescent, resembling a miniature moon which had somehow been frozen in place. Closer examination of the object revealed that it was a brownish sphere illuminated on one side by the sun. It appeared solid enough to be a rocky asteroid, but Divivvidiv knew he was looking at one of the fabric balloons used by the Primitives for travel between their worlds. As it was still ascending towards the weightless zone the ship's gondola was optically invisible, but the Xa could "see" the crew very well by other means.

They are five in number, Beloved Creator, the Xa said. *All are female, which is unusual if our limited experience of this race is anything to go by.*

Are they aware of the station? Or of you?

There was a short pause. *No, Beloved Creator. The ship, which is one of the group we saw previously, is returning to its home world for reasons which, although they are not clear to me, are obviously connected with the emotional well-being of its commander. There is no thought of observing or investigating our activities.*

The communication from the Xa was correctly and courteously formed, but it contained shadings of mind-colours which seemed inappropriate. Divivvidiv associated them with malice and gloating, and he had little trouble in identifying the most likely source.

Do you predict that we will be observed?

It is almost inevitable, the Xa replied. *In fact, it is almost inevitable that there will be a collision. The Primitive ship is experiencing virtually no lateral drift, and—as you know— my body is now expanding at its maximum rate.*

Divivvidiv withdrew at once into the high-brain mode so that he could ponder the problem without being overheard by the Xa. The extermination of five uncultured bipeds would be an utterly trivial occurrence—especially when one considered the events which were soon to overtake this entire region of space—but he would have to take the decision in person. And the deaths would be *close*.

Those facts, coupled with his direct involvement, would forge a mental link between him and the five whose lives were to be brought to a close and, inescapably, he would be caught up in each reflux. The reflux was the brief, incredibly fierce and inexplicable burst of psychic activity which always occurred one or two seconds after the death of an intelligent being. Even when the physical form was instantaneously vaporised, and in theory no further mental interaction with the living could possibly take place, there always came that searing pang—excruciating, chastening, ineffable, *poignant* —that momentary spiritual refulgence which had a profoundly disturbing effect on those who felt it.

The fact that the reflux happened at all was taken by many as proof of the continuance of the personality after death. Some component of the mind-body complex was migrating to a new existence, it was claimed. Others of a more materialistic nature seized on the way in which the strength of the reflux faded with distance as an indication that there were realms of physics which Dussarran science had yet to explore.

Divivvidiv did not adhere to either school of thought, but he had been close to reflux epicentres twice in his life—when his parents had died—and he had no wish to repeat the experience if it could be avoided. Morality was powerfully reinforced by self-interest, leaving him in a dilemma which he would have to resolve quickly if he were to meet his obligations to the all-important Xa.

Part crystal, part computer, part sentient being—the Xa could only grow to the size necessary for its eventual purpose in a region where there was a complete absence of gravity, coupled with an abundance of oxygen. The Dussarrans had been fortunate in finding such an environment within reach of their original home, but the existence of a burgeoning technical society on the twin worlds was an unwelcome complication to their plans, mainly because the Xa's structure —in spite of being so huge—was comparatively fragile. The Primitives were capable of damaging it, with or without malicious intent, and therefore had to be controlled like vermin if they came near.

Divivvidiv considered the problem for a short time, then arrived at a solution which satisfied his fondness for the creative compromise. It would involve his going outside the station's pressurised living quarters so that he could communicate privately and efficiently with Director Zunnu-nun on the home world, Dussarra. Luckily, the series of relocations had been successfully completed and Dussarra was now part of the local system, visible as a bright blue mote against the rich stellar background. At a range of only a few million miles it would be easy to establish mind-to-mind contact with Zunnunun with no risk of others intercepting the communication. Divivvidiv reverted to mid-brain mode and, with his eyes fixed on the image of the ship which was labouring up from the alien planet, contacted the Xa.

You have already told me that the Primitives are unaware of our presence, he said. *Does that mean they are totally without means of direct communication?*

There was a brief hesitation while the Xa carried out the necessary investigation. *Yes, Beloved Creator, the Primitives are completely passive in that respect.*

Divivvidiv felt a surge of mingled revulsion and pity—how could any creature endure going through its entire existence in a condition of mind-blindness? The Primitives' lack of higher sense organs made them easier to deal with in this instance, but the cautious and meticulous side of Divivvidiv's nature prompted him to ask further questions.

Are they a belligerent race?

Yes, Beloved Creator.

Do they carry weapons?

Yes, Beloved Creator.

Extract a description of the weapons for me.

Another pause followed before the Xa spoke. *Their weapons employ solid lead projectiles expelled through tubes by the force of gases compressed in metal containers.* Simultaneously the Xa conveyed to Divivvidiv exact details of the dimensions and energy transference capabilities of the types of weapons the Primitives carried both on their persons and aboard their slow-moving craft.

Divivvidiv felt a growing sense of satisfaction as he became certain there was no obstacle to the plan he had conceived for dealing with the approaching ship and its crew.

You are well pleased, Beloved Creator, the Xa said.

Yes—I shall now return to my dream and await the arrival of the Primitives in comfort.

You are pleased because it will not be necessary for you to terminate the Primitives' lives.

Yes.

In that case, Beloved Creator, why does it not trouble you that soon you will kill me?

You do not understand these things. Divivvidiv felt a sudden impatience with the Xa and its obsession with preserving its own pseudo-life. Each time it returned to the subject his own mind was clouded with dark thoughts of genocide, and—in spite of the mental disciplines at which he was adept—the echoes of those thoughts disturbed his dreams.

Chapter 7

Toller knew it was only his imagination, but an abnormal quietness seemed to have descended over the Five Palaces area of Ro-Atabri. It was not the sort of quietness which comes when human activity is in abeyance—it was more as if an invisible blanket of soundproof material had been pressed down over everything in his vicinity. When he looked about him he could see evidence that carpenters and stone-masons were busy with their restoration work; bluehorns and wagons were sending up clouds of dust which added scumbles of yellow to the blue of the foreday sky; ground crew and airmen were going about their business of getting the ships ready for the round-the-world flight. Everywhere he looked there was purposeful movement, but the noises of it seemed to be reaching him through the filters of distance, attenuated, lacking in relevance.

The flight was due to begin within the hour, and it was *that* fact—Toller knew—which was numbing his reactions, separating him from the perceived world of the senses. Nine days had passed since Vantara's departure for Overland, and during that time he had sunk into a mood of depression and apathy which had defied all efforts to overcome it.

When he should have been preparing his men and his ship for the circumnavigation he had been lost in thought, living and reliving that strange hour with Vantara at the Migration Day festivity. What had prompted her to behave as she had? Knowing that she was on the eve of quitting the planet altogether, she had raised him to the heights—he could still *feel* her lips against his, her breasts cupped in his hands— only to dash him down again with her sudden callous aloofness. Had she been playing cat-and-mouse on a whim, passing a dull hour with a trivial game?

There were moments in which Toller believed that to be the case, and at those times he plumbed new depths of misery, hating the countess with a passion which could whiten his knuckles and rob him of speech in mid-sentence. At other times he saw clearly that she had exerted herself to break down barriers between them, that she considered him a person of value, and that she would indeed be waiting to receive him when next he set foot on Overland. In those periods of optimism Toller felt even worse, because he and his love—the finest and most desirable woman who had ever lived—were literally worlds apart, and he was unable to imagine how he could endure the coming years without seeing her.

He would stare up at the great disk of Overland, its convex vastness crossed again and again by streamers of cloud, and wish for some means of instantaneous communication between the sister planets. There had been fanciful talk of some day building huge sunwriters, with tilting mirrors as large as rooftops, which would have been capable of sending messages between Land and Overland. If such a device had existed Toller would have used it, not so much to talk to Vantara—bridging the interworld gulf in that unsatisfactory way might have made his yearnings even more insupportable —but to get in touch with his father.

Cassyll Maraquine had the power and influence to obtain his son a special release from the Land mission. In the past, before he had been touched by the madness of love, Toller had scorned such uses of privilege, but in his present state of mind he would have seized on the favour with unashamed greed. And now, to make matters worse, he was on the point of setting out on a voyage which would take him through the Land of the Long Days, that distant side of the planet where he would not even have the spare consolation of being able to see Overland and in his mind's eye watch over Vantara while she went about her oh-so-special life. . . .

"This will never do, young Maraquine," said Commissioner Kettoran, who had approached Toller unnoticed, making his way among piles of lumber and other supplies. He was wearing the grey robe of his office, but without the official emblems of brakka and enamel. Another man of his rank might have sequestered himself in imposing quarters or only ventured abroad with an entourage, but Kettoran liked to wander unobtrusively and alone through the various sections of the base.

"Instead of mooning around here like a maiden with the colic," he continued, "you should be checking the loading and balance of your ship."

"Lieutenant Correvalte is dealing with all that," Toller replied indifferently. "And probably making a better fist of it than I would."

Kettoran pulled the brim of his hat down over his eyes, creating a prism of shade from which he regarded Toller with concern. "Listen, my boy, I know it is none of my business, but this infatuation with the Countess Vantara bodes ill for your career."

"Thank you for the advice." Toller deeply resented the elderly man's words, but he had too much respect for Kettoran to hint at his anger other than by mild sarcasm. "I'll keep your good counsel in mind."

Kettoran gave him a small, sad smile. "Believe me, son, before you know it, these days which seem so interminable and so full of pain will be nothing more than faint memories. Not only that—they will seem joyous in comparison to what is to come. You are foolish not to make the most of them."

Something in Kettoran's voice affected Toller, drawing his thoughts away from his own circumstances. "This hardly seems credible," he said, claiming the right to intimacy he had earned on the interplanetary crossing. "I never expected to hear Trye Kettoran talk like an old man."

"And I never expected to *be* an old man—that was a fate exclusively reserved for others. Ponder on what I am telling you, son. And don't be a fool." Commissioner Kettoran squeezed Toller's shoulder with a thin hand, then turned and walked away towards the eastern flank of the Great Palace. His gait seemed to lack something of its usual jauntiness.

Toller stared after the commissioner for a moment, frowning. "Sir," he called out, prompted by a sudden unease, "is all well with you?"

Appearing not to hear, Kettoran continued on his way and was soon lost to view. Toller, now troubled by premonitions about the commissioner's well-being, somehow felt obliged to pay more heed to the advice he had just been given. He began making conscientious efforts to follow what was undoubtedly good philosophical counsel—after all, he was young and healthy and all his life lay before him—but each time he ordered himself to feel cheerful the only result was an obstinate upsurge of his misery. Something within him was antagonistic to reason.

He returned to his ship and went on board, supervising the departure arrangements with a gloomy inattentiveness which he knew was bound to communicate itself to the crew. Lieutenant Correvalte responded by becoming even more wooden and correct in his manner. The voyage was expected to take about sixty days, assuming no mishaps were to occur, and the gondola was a very small space for eight men to be cooped in for that length of time. The psychological strain would be considerable even under ideal conditions, and with a commander who was making it clear from the outset that he had no stomach for the mission there could be problems with morale and discipline.

Eventually all the formalities were completed, and the signal for departure came when a trumpet sounded on board the lead ship. The four vessels took off in unison, their jets sending flat billows of sound rolling out across the parks which surrounded the Five Palaces and into the sunlit environs of Ro-Atabri. Toller stood at the rail, hand on the hilt of his sword, leaving the control of the ship to Correvalte, and stared out at the sprawling expanse of the old city. The sun was high in the sky, nearing Overland, and the gondola was completely contained within the shadow of its elliptical gasbag, making the scenery beyond look exceptionally bright and sharply defined. Traditional Kolcorronian architectural styles made extensive use of orange and yellow bricks laid in complex diamond patterns, with dressings of red sandstone at corners and edges, and from a low altitude the city was a glittering mosaic which shimmered confusingly on the eye. Trees at different stages of their lives provided islands of extra colour which ranged from pale green to copper and brown.

The ships made a partial circuit of the base and took a north-eastern course, seeking the trade winds which would help conserve power crystals during the voyage. Local surveys had indicated that there would be no shortage of mature brakka trees along the route, but broaching their combustion chambers to obtain the green and purple crystals would have been a time-consuming business, and it was intended that the little fleet should complete the circumnavigation using only its on-board supplies.

Toller gave an involuntary sigh as Ro-Atabri began to slide into the distance aft of his ship, its various features flattening into horizontal bands. The voyage, with all its promised tedium and privation, had begun in earnest, and it was time for him to face up to that fact. He became aware of Baten Steenameert, newly promoted to the rank of air-sergeant, eyeing him as he passed on his way to the lower deck. Steenameert's pink face was carefully impassive, but Toller knew his recent moodiness had had its effect on the youngster, who had developed an intense loyalty to him since they had left their home world. Toller halted him by raising a hand.

"There is no need for you to fret," he said. "I have no intention of hurling myself over the side."

Steenameert looked puzzled. "Sir?"

"Don't play the innocent with me, young fellow." Toller was only two years older than the sergeant, but he spoke in the same kind of fatherly tones that Trye Kettoran often used to him, consciously trying to borrow some of the commissioner's steadiness and stoicism. "I've become the butt of quite a few jests around the base, haven't I? The word has gone about that I'm so besotted with a certain lady that I scarcely know night from day."

The bloom on Steenameert's smooth cheeks deepened and he lowered his voice so as not to be overheard by Correvalte who was nearby at the airship's controls. "Sir, if anybody dared speak ill of you in my presence I would. . . ."

"You will not be required to do battle on my behalf," Toller said firmly, addressing his wayward inner self as much as anybody else, then saw that Steenameert's attention had been drawn elsewhere.

The sergeant spoke quickly, before Toller could frame a question. "Sir, I think we are receiving a message."

Toller looked aft in the direction of Ro-Atabri and saw that a point of intense brilliance was winking amid the complex layered bands of the city. He immediately began deciphering the sunwriter code and felt a peculiar thrill, an icy mingling of excitement and apprehension, as he realised that the beamed message concerned him.

By the time Toller got back to base the balloon of the skyship was fully inflated and the craft was straining at its anchor link, ready to depart for Overland. It was swaying a little within the three timber walls of the towering enclosure, like a vast sentient creature which was becoming impatient with its enforced inactivity. A further indication of the urgency of the situation was that Sky-commodore Sholdde was waiting for Toller by the enclosure instead of in his office.

He nodded ungraciously, obviously in a foul temper, as Toller—flanked by Correvalte and Steenameert—approached him at a quick march and saluted. He ran his fingers through his cropped iron-grey hair and scowled at Toller.

"Captain Maraquine," he said, "this is a cursed inconvenience. I've already been deprived of one airship captain —and now I have to find another."

"Lieutenant Correvalte is perfectly capable of taking my place on the round-the-world flight, sir," Toller replied. "I have no hesitation in recommending him for an immediate field promotion."

"Is that so?" Sholdde turned a hard-eyed, critical gaze on Correvalte and the look of gratification which had appeared on the lieutenant's face quickly faded.

"Sir," Toller said, "is Commissioner Kettoran *very* ill?"

"He looks to me like he's already dead," Sholdde said indifferently. "Why did he particularly ask for you to fly him home?"

"I don't know, sir."

"I can't understand it either. It seems a strange choice to me. You haven't exactly distinguished yourself on this mission, Maraquine. I kept waiting for you to trip over that antiquated piece of iron you insist on wearing."

Toller unconsciously touched the haft of his sword and he felt his face grow warm. The commodore was subjecting him to unnecessary ignominy by giving him a dressing down in the presence of lesser ranks. The most Toller could do to register a protest was to hint that he viewed Sholdde's remarks as a waste of valuable time.

"Sir, if the commissioner looks as poorly as you say. . . ."

"All right, all right, begone with you." Sholdde glanced briefly at Steenameert. "Has this man become a Maraquine family retainer, part of your personal entourage?"

"Sir, Corporal Steenameert is a first-class skyman and his services would be invaluable to me on—"

"Take him!" Sholdde turned and strode away without any kind of salute, an action which could only be interpreted as another direct insult.

So that's it, Toller thought, alerted by the commodore's reference to the "Maraquine family". *My grandfather was the most famed warrior in Kolcorronian history; my father is one of the most brilliant and most powerful men alive—and even the likes of Sholdde resent me for it. Is that because they believe I secretly make use of family influence? Or is it because, by overtly not making use of it, I proclaim a special kind of egotism? Or can it be that I shame or annoy them by refusing to grasp opportunities for which they would give. . . ?*

A prolonged blast on the skyship's burner, echoing in the huge cavity of the balloon, interrupted Toller's reverie. He touched Correvalte's shoulder in farewell, ran with Steenameert to the gondola and climbed over the side. The ground crew sergeant who was at the burner controls, keeping the ship in readiness, saluted and nodded towards the passenger compartment.

Toller went to the chest-high cane partition and looked over it. Commissioner Kettoran was lying on a pallet and, in spite of the heat, was covered with a quilt. His long face was extremely pale, with lines of age and weariness graven into it, but his eyes were alert. He winked when he saw Toller and twitched a thin hand in an attempted greeting.

"Are you travelling alone, sir?" Toller said with concern. "No physician?"

A scornful expression briefly animated Kettoran's features. "Those blood-letters will never get their hands on me."

"But if you are ill. . . ."

"The doctor who could cure my complaint has yet to be born," Kettoran said, almost with satisfaction. "I suffer from nothing less than a dearth of time. Speaking of which, young Maraquine, I was under the impression you also were anxious to make a speedy return to Overland."

Toller mumbled an apology and turned to the sergeant, who immediately moved away from the burner controls and clambered over the gondola's side. Pausing for a few seconds on the outside ledge, he explained to Steenameert where all necessary provisions, including skysuits, had been stored. As soon as he had dropped out of sight Toller fed a plentiful charge of hot gas into the pliable dome of the balloon above him and pulled the anchor link.

The skyship surged upwards, its acceleration enhanced by the lift created as the curved upper surface of the balloon moved into the current of air flowing over the enclosure. Well aware that the extra buoyancy would be cancelled as soon as the balloon fully entered the westerly airstream and began to move with it, Toller kept the burner going. The skyship—in spite of being so much below its maximum operating weight—performed a queasy slow-motion shimmy as it adapted to the changing aerial environment, causing Steenameert to clutch theatrically at his stomach. From Commissioner Kettoran, hidden behind his wicker partition, came a moan of complaint.

For the second time in less than an hour the sprawling panorama of Ro-Atabri began to recede from Toller, but now it was retreating downwards. *I can scarcely believe that all this is happening to me*, he thought dreamily, almost stupefied by the flux of circumstance. Only minutes earlier he had been racked by fears that he would never see Vantara Dervonai again—now he was on his way to her, keeping an appointment which had been specially arranged for him by the forces of destiny.

Soon I will be able to see Vantara again, he told himself. *For once, things are working out in my favour.*

Toller had not eaten anything for a day, and had taken only a few sips of water, barely enough to replace the bodily moisture lost by exhaling into the arid air of the middle passage. Toilet facilities on a skyship were necessarily primitive and unpleasant to use at the best of times, but in weightless conditions the disadvantages—including the sheer indignity—were so great that most people chose to suspend their natural functions as completely as possible for a day on either side of turnover. The system worked reasonably well for a healthy adult, but Commissioner Kettoran had begun the voyage in a severely weakened state, and now—much to Toller's concern—appeared to be using up the last dregs of his strength merely to stay alive.

"You can take those slops away from me," Kettoran said in a grouchy whisper. "I refuse to be suckled like a babe at my time of life—especially from a revolting dug like that."

Toller unhappily fingered the conical bag of luke-warm soup he had been proffering. "This will do you good."

"You sound just like my mother."

"Is that a reason for not taking sustenance?"

"Don't try to be clever, young Maraquine." Kettoran's breath issued in white clouds from a small opening in the mound of quilts in which he had ensconced himself.

"I was only trying to—"

"My mother could make much better food than any of the cooks we ever employed," Kettoran mused, paying no heed to Toller. "We had a house on the west side of Greenmount —not far from where your grandfather lived, incidentally— and I can still remember riding up the hill, going into our precinct and knowing immediately, just by the aromas, whether or not my mother had chosen to prepare the evening meal. I went back there a few days after we landed in Ro-Atabri, but the entire district had been burnt out a long time ago ... during the riots ... gutted ... hardly a building left intact. It was a mistake for me to go there—I should have preserved my memories."

At the mention of his namesake Toller's interest picked up. "Did you ever see my grandfather in those days?"

"Occasionally. It would have been hard *not* to see him— a fine figure of a man, he was—but I more often saw his brother, Lain ... going back and forth between his house and the Lord Philosopher's official residence in Greenmount Peel."

107

"What did my grand—?" Toller broke off, alarms clamouring silently in his mind, as there was a subtle but abrupt change in his environment. He rose to his feet, holding a transverse line to keep himself from drifting clear of the deck, and looked all about him. Steenameert, muffled in his skysuit, was strapped into his seat at the control station. He was firing the main jet in the steady rhythm needed to maintain the ship's ascent, and he appeared completely unperturbed. Everything seemed absolutely as normal in the square microcosm of the gondola, and beyond its rim the familiar patterns of stars and luminous whirls shone steadily in the dark blue sky.

"Sir?" The swaddled, anonymous bulk of Steenameert moved slightly. "Is there something wrong?"

Toller had to survey his surroundings again before he was able to identify the source of his unease. "The light! There was a change in the light! Didn't you notice?"

"I must have had my eyes closed. But I still don't. . . ."

"There was a drop in brightness—I'm sure of it—and yet we have more than an hour till nightfall." Baffled and disturbed, wishing he could have a direct view of the sun, Toller drew himself closer to the control station and looked up through the mouth of the balloon. The varnished linen of the envelope was dyed dark brown so that it would absorb heat from the sun, but it was to some extent translucent and he could see a geometrical design of panel seams and load tapes radiating from the crown, emphasising the vastness of the flimsy dome. It was a sight he had seen many times, and on this occasion it looked exactly as it had always done. Steenameert also looked into the balloon, then lowered his gaze without comment.

"I tell you something happened," Toller said, trying to keep any hint of uncertainty out of his voice. "Something happened. There was a change in the light . . . a shadow . . . *something*."

"According to the height gauge we are somewhere close

THE RETURN TO LAND

to the datum plane, sir," Steenameert said, obviously striving to be helpful. "Perhaps we have come up directly beneath the permanent stations and have touched their shadows."

"That is virtually impossible—there is always a certain amount of drift." Toller frowned for a moment, coming to a decision. "Rotate the ship."

"I . . . I don't think I'm ready to handle an inversion."

"I don't want it turned over yet. Just make a quarter-rotation so that we can see what's above us." Realising he was still holding the food bag he tossed it towards the passenger compartment on a descending curve. It fouled a safety line, swung round it and floated out over the gondola's side, slowly tumbling as it went.

Toller pulled himself to the rail, straining to see upwards, and waited impatiently while Steenameert fired one of the tiny lateral jets on the opposite side of the gondola. At first the jet appeared to be having no effect, except that the slim acceleration struts on each side of Toller emitted faint creaks; then, after what seemed an interminable wait, the whole universe began a ponderous downwards slide. The whorled disk of Land moved out of sight beneath Toller's feet, and above him—stealthily uncovered by the ship's balloon—there came into view a spectacle unlike anything he had ever seen.

Half the sky was occupied by a vast circular sheet of white fire.

The sun was slipping out of sight behind the eastern edge, and at that point the brilliance was intolerable, a locus of blinding radiance which sprayed billions of prismatic needles across the rest of the circle.

There was a slight falling off in the intensity of light across the disk, but even at the side farthest from the sun it was enough to sting the eyes. To Toller the effect was akin to looking upwards from the depths of a sunlit frozen lake. He had expected to see Overland filling a large area of the heavens, but the planet was hidden behind the beautiful, inexplicable, *impossible* sheet of diamond-white light, through which rainbow colours raced and danced in clashing zigzag lines.

As he stood at the rail, transfixed, he became aware that the incredible spectacle was drifting down the sky at undiminished speed. He turned and saw that Steenameert was staring out past him, jaw sagging, with eyes which had become reflective white disks—miniature versions of the phenomenon which was mesmerising him.

"A *quarter* turn I told you," Toller bellowed. "Check the rotation."

"Sorry, sir." Steenameert stirred into action and the lateral jet mounted low down on Toller's side of the gondola began to spew miglign gas. Rings of condensation rolled away from it through the gelid air. The sound of the jet was puny, quickly absorbed by the surrounding void, but it gradually achieved the intended effect and the skyship came to rest with its vertical axis parallel to the sea of white fire.

"What's going on out there?" The querulous voice of Trye Kettoran issuing from the passenger compartment helped bring Toller out of his own tranced condition.

"Have a look over the side," he called out for the commissioner's benefit, then turned to Steenameert. "What do you think yonder thing is? Ice?"

Steenameert nodded slowly. "Ice is the only explanation I can imagine, but. . . ."

"But where did the water come from? There is the usual supply of drinking water in the defence stations, but that amounts to no more than a few barrels. . . ." Toller paused as a new thought struck him. "Where are the stations, anyway? We must try to locate them. Are they embedded in the. . . ?" His voice failed altogether as related questions geysered through his mind. How thick was the ice? How far away from the ship was it? How wide was the enormous circular sheet?

How wide is the circle?

The last question suddenly reverberated in his consciousness, excluding all others. Until that instant Toller had been overawed by the brilliant spectacle confronting him, but it had inspired no sense of danger. There had been a feeling of wonder—but no threat. Now, however, certain facts of aerial physics were beginning to assume importance. A disturbing importance. A potentially *lethal* importance. . . .

He knew that the atmosphere which enveloped the sister planets was shaped like an hourglass, the waist of which formed a narrow bridge of air through which skyships had to pass. Old experiments had established that ships had to keep near the centre of the bridge—otherwise the air became so attenuated that the crews were bound to asphyxiate. Largely because of the difficulty of taking measurements in the region, there was some uncertainty about the thickness of that core of breathable air, but the best estimates were that it was no more than a hundred miles in diameter.

The enigmatic sea of sun-blazing ice was rendered featureless by its brilliance, and in the absence of spatial referents it could have been hovering "beside" the skyship at a distance of ten miles, or twenty, or forty, or . . . Toller could think of no way to ascertain its distance, but he could see that it spanned almost one third of the visual hemisphere, and that gave him enough information to perform an elementary calculation.

Lips moving silently, he stared at the radiant disk while he dealt with the relevant figures, and a coldness which had nothing to do with the harsh environment entered his system as he reached a conclusion. If the disk proved to be as much as sixty miles away—which it could quite easily be—then, by the immutable laws of mathematics, it was sufficiently wide to block the air bridge between Land and Overland. . . .

"Sir?" Steenameert's voice seemed to come from another universe. "How far would you say we are from the ice?"

"That is an excellent question," Toller said grimly, taking the ship's binoculars from the control station locker. He

111

aimed them at the disk, striving to pick out detail, but could see only a shimmering field of brightness. The sun was now fully occulted, spreading its light more evenly over the vast circle, making an estimate of its distance more difficult than before. Toller turned away from the rail, knuckling round green after-images from his eyes, and examined the height gauge. Its pointer was perhaps a hair's breadth below the zero-gravity mark.

"You can't rely much on those devices, sir," Steenameert commented, unable to resist showing off his knowledge. "They are calibrated in a workshop, with no allowance for the effect of low temperatures on the springs, and—"

"Spare me," Toller cut in. "This is a serious matter—I need to know the size of that . . . *thing* out there."

"Fly towards it and take note of how it expands."

Toller shook his head. "I have a better idea. I have no intention of turning back unless all other options are denied me—therefore we will fly towards the edge of the circle. Its exact diameter in miles is not all that significant. The truly important thing is to ascertain whether or not we can fly our ship around the obstacle.

"Do you wish to remain at the controls?"

"I would value the experience, sir," Steenameert replied. "What burner rhythm do you require?"

Toller hesitated, frowning, frustrated by the fact that no practicable air speed indicator had ever been developed for use on skyships. An experienced pilot could get some idea of his speed from the slackening of the rip line as the crown of the balloon was depressed by air resistance, but the abundance of variables made accuracy impossible. It would not have been beyond Kolcorronian ingenuity to devise a reliable instrument, but the motivation had never been present. A skyship's job was to crawl up and down between the planetary surface and the weightless zone—a journey which always took roughly five days on each leg—and a difference of a few miles an hour was neither here nor there.

"Give it two and six," Toller said. "We shall pretend to ourselves that we are making twenty miles in the hour and base all our estimates accordingly."

"But what is the *nature* of the barrier?" Commissioner Kettoran said from close behind Toller. He was in an upright position, holding the edge of the cane partition with one hand and keeping a quilt around him with the other.

Toller's first impulse was to request him to lie down again to achieve the complete rest which had been prescribed by the base physician, then it occurred to him that in the absence of weight it made no difference which attitude was adopted by a person with a heart condition. Allowing his thoughts to be diverted into irrelevancies, he visualised a new use for the pathetic little group of defence stations in the weightless zone. Properly heated and supplied with good air, they could best serve as rest centres for those with certain kinds of ailment. Even a cripple would be. . . .

"I'm addressing you, young Maraquine," Kettoran said peevishly. "What is your opinion of that curious object?"

"I think it might be made of ice."

"But where would such a vast quantity of water come from?"

Toller shrugged. "We have had rocks and even pieces of metal descend on us from the stars—perhaps the void also contains water."

"A likely story," Kettoran grumbled. He gave a theatrical shrug and his long, solemn face—now purple with the cold —slowly sank from view as he returned to his cocoon of downy quilts.

"It's an omen," he added, his voice muffled and indistinct from behind the partition. "I know an omen when I see one."

Toller nodded, smiling thinly in scepticism, and returned to his vigil at the gondola's rail. By calling out the firing times for the various lateral jets he helped Steenameert guide the ship into a course which closed with the fire-sheet at an unknown angle, aiming it for the westernmost edge. The main jet was roaring in a steady two-six rhythm and Toller knew that the ship's speed could easily be as much as his putative twenty miles an hour—but the aspect of the sheet did not alter noticeably with the passing of the minutes.

"Our friend, the omen, appears to be a veritable giant," he said to Steenameert. "We may have some trouble in getting around him."

Wishing he had the simple navigational instruments available on the humblest airship, Toller kept his gaze on the eastern rim of the great circle, willing it to descend and thus prove that the ship was making significant progress. He was just beginning to convince himself that he could indeed see a change in the vital angle, when the glowing sheet was swept by waves of prismatic colour. They moved at breathtaking orbital speed, crossing the entire disk in mere seconds and stilling Toller's heart with their message that cosmic events were taking place, reminding him of how unimportant the affairs of mankind were when measured against the grandeur of the universe. The sun, already hidden from his view by the icy screen, was being further occulted by Overland. As soon as the bands of colour—engendered by the refraction of the sun's light in Overland's atmosphere—had fled into infinity the disk's overall luminosity began to decrease. Night was falling in the weightless zone.

Here, so close to the datum plane, the terms "night" and "littlenight" no longer had any relevance. Each diurnal cycle was punctuated by two periods of darkness approximately equal in length, and Toller knew it would be some four hours before the sun reappeared. The hiatus could hardly have come at a more inconvenient time.

"Sir?" Steenameert, a sentient pyramid of swaddling in the fading light, had no need to voice the full question.

"Keep going, but reduce thrust to one and six," Toller ordered. "We can shut down the jet altogether if we find we

114

can't keep a check on our course. And be sure to keep the balloon well inflated."

Grateful for Steenameert's competence, Toller remained at the rail and studied the disk. Sunlight was still being reflected from Land—which was now directly behind him—so the icy wall remained visible, and with the change in illumination he began to see hints of an internal structure. There was a tracery of the palest violet, arranged like rivers which divided and kept on dividing until they faded from the sight, lost in distant shimmers.

They're like veins, Toller thought. *Veins in a giant eye.* . . .

As Land was gradually enveloped in Overland's shadow the disk steadily darkened to near-blackness, but its edge was still clearly defined against the cosmic background. The rest of the sky was now ablaze with its customary extravagance of galaxies—glowing whirlpools ranging from circles to slim ellipses—plus formless ribbons of light, myriads of stars, comets and darting meteors. Against that luminous richness the disk was more mysterious than ever—a featureless well of night which had no right to exist in a rational universe.

By occasionally ordering a slight pendulum movement of the ship Toller was able to look ahead and satisfy himself that it was on course for the disk's western edge. As the hours of darkness dragged by the air became progressively thinner and less satisfying to the lungs, evidence that the skyship was far from the centre of the invisible bridge that linked the two worlds. Although Commissioner Kettoran did not voice any complaint, his breathing became clearly audible. He had mixed some firesalt with water in a vellum bag and could be heard sniffing from it at frequent intervals.

When at last daylight returned, heralded by a brightening of the disk's western rim, Toller found he could see the rim without having to tilt the ship. Perspective returned; geometry again became a useful tool.

"We're only a mile or so from the edge," he announced

for the benefit of Steenameert and Kettoran. "In a few minutes we should be able to work around it and head back into the good air."

"It's about time!" Kettoran's cowled face appeared above the passenger compartment partition. "How far to the side have we travelled?"

"Perpendicular to the ideal course, we must have done in the region of thirty miles—" Toller glanced at Steenameert and received a nod of confirmation—"which means we are dealing with a lake, a *sea*, of ice some sixty miles across. I find it hard to credit what I'm saying, even though I am looking straight at the thing. Nobody in Prad is going to believe what we say."

"We may have corroboration."

"By telescope?"

"By your lady friend—Countess Vantara." Kettoran dabbed a drop of moisture from the end of his nose. "Her ship departed not so many days before ours."

"You're right, of course." Toller was dully surprised to realise he had forgotten about Vantara for several hours. "The ice . . . the barrier . . . whatever it is . . . may have been in place when she made the crossing. It is something we will have to confer over in detail."

Having derived an unexpected grain of comfort from the discussion—a readymade reason to seek out Vantara, wherever she might be—Toller gave his attention to the task of steering his ship around the edge of the disk. The manoeuvre was not a difficult one in theory. All he had to do was pass the western rim by a short distance, carry out a simple inversion and begin flying back into the thicker air at the core of the atmospheric bridge.

Leaving Steenameert at the controls, he remained by the rail in order to obtain the most advantageous viewpoint and started giving detailed handling instructions. The ship was moving very slowly as it drew level with the rim, probably at no more than walking pace, but after some minutes had passed it came to Toller that it was taking longer than he had expected to reach the limit of the ice wall. Suddenly suspicious, he trained his binoculars on the rim. The sun was close to his aiming point, hurling billions of needles of radiance into his eyes and making the viewing difficult, but he managed to get a clear look at the icy boundary. It was now less than a furlong away in reality, and the image in his glasses brought it much closer.

Toller grunted in surprise as he discovered that the rim of the ice sheet was *alive*.

In place of what he had expected—the inertness of frozen water—there was a kind of crystalline seething. Glassy prisms and spikes and branches, each as tall as a man, were sprouting outwards on the rim with unnatural rapidity. They were extending the boundary of the sheet with the speed of billowing smoke—each thrusting into the gelid air and glistening in the sunlight for a moment before being overtaken and assimilated by others in the racing, sparkling vitreous foment.

Toller stared at the phenomenon, tranced, his mind awash with the unexpected and incredible beauty of it, and it seemed a long time before the first coherent thought came to him: *The rim of the barrier is moving outwards at almost the same speed as the ship!*

"Increase speed," he shouted to Steenameert, his voice strained by the bitter coldness and the inimical nature of the thinning air. "Otherwise you'll never see home again!"

Commissioner Kettoran, who had seemed almost a well man during the passage through the weightless zone, had been struck by a fresh seizure when the ship was only a few thousand feet above the surface of Overland. In one second he had been standing with Toller at the gondola's rail and pointing out familiar features in the landscape below; in the next he was lying on his back, unable to move, eyes alert and afraid, beaconing an intelligence trapped inside a

117

machine which no longer responded to its master's bidding. Toller had carried him to his nest of quilts, wiped the frothy saliva from the corners of his mouth, and had gone immediately for the sunwriter in its leather case.

The lateral drift had been greater than usual, bringing the ship down some twelve miles to the east of the city of Prad, but the sunwriter message had been picked up in good time. A sizeable group of coaches and mounted men—plus a sleek airboat in grey-and-blue royal livery—had been waiting in the touchdown area. Within five minutes of the landing the commissioner had been transferred to the airboat and sent on his way to an emergency audition with Queen Daseene, who was waiting in the overheated confines of her palace.

There had been no opportunity for Toller to pass on any words of reassurance or farewell to Kettoran, a man he had come to regard as a good friend in spite of the disparity in age and status. As he watched the airboat dwindle into the yellow western sky he became aware of a sense of guilt and it took him some time to identify its source. He was, of course, deeply concerned about the commissioner's health, but at the same time—and there was no getting around the fact—one part of him was thankful that the older man's misfortune had come along, like the answer to a prayer, exactly when he had needed it. No other circumstance that he could readily think of could have placed him back on Overland and within reach of Vantara in such a short time.

What sort of monster am I? he thought, shocked by his own selfishness. *I must be the worst. . . .*

Toller's bout of introspection was interrupted by the sight of his father and Bartan Drumme descending from a coach which had just arrived at the landing site. Both men were attired in grey trews and three-quarter-length tabards gored with blue silk, a formal style of dress which suggested they had come straight from an important meeting in the city. Toller strode eagerly to meet his father, embraced him and then shook hands with Bartan Drumme.

"This is truly an unexpected pleasure," Cassyll Maraquine said, a smile rejuvenating his pale triangular face. "It is a great shame about the commissioner, of course, but we must assume that the royal physicians—a plentiful breed in these times—will quickly put him to rights. How have you been, son?"

"I am well." Toller looked at his father for a moment in that unique gratification which springs from an harmonious relationship with a parent, and then—as extraneous matters crowded into his mind—he shifted his gaze to include Bartan Drumme in what had to follow. The latter was the only surviving member of a fabled voyage to Farland, the local system's outermost planet, and was acknowledged as Kolcorron's leading expert on astronomical matters.

"Father, Bartan," Toller said, "have you been observing the skies within the last ten or twenty days? Have you noticed anything unusual?"

The older men exchanged cautiously surprised glances. "Are you speaking of the blue planet?" Bartan said.

Toller frowned. "Blue planet? No, I'm talking about a barrier . . . a wall . . . a lake of ice . . . call it what you will . . . which has appeared at the midpoint. It is at least sixty miles across and growing wider by the hour. Has it not been observed from the ground?"

"Nothing out of the ordinary has been observed, but I'm not even sure that the Glo telescope has been in use since—" Bartan broke off and gave Toller a quizzical stare. "Toller . . . Toller, you can't *have* an accretion of ice at the midpoint—there simply isn't the water. The air is too dry."

"Ice! Or crystal of some kind. I *saw* it!" The fact that he was being disbelieved did not surprise or unduly disturb Toller, but it caused an uneasy stirring in the lower levels of his consciousness. There was something wrong with the *pattern* of the conversation. It was not going as it should have gone, but some factor—perhaps a deep-seated unwillingness

119

to face reality—was for the moment paralysing vital mental processes.

Bartan gave him a patient smile. "Perhaps there has been a major failure in one of the permanent stations, perhaps an explosion which has scattered power crystals over a wide area. They might be drifting and combining and forming large clouds of condensation, and we both know that condensation can give the appearance of being very substantial . . . like banks of snow or—"

"The Countess Vantara," Toller interrupted with a numb smile, keeping his voice steady to hide the fear that had been unleashed in him as certain doors swung open. "She made the crossing only nine days ago—had she nothing unusual to report?"

"I don't know what you mean, son," Cassyll Maraquine said, speaking the words which Toller had already prepared for him on a parchment of the mind. "Yours is the first and only ship to have returned from Land. Countess Vantara has not been seen since the expedition departed."

PART II

Strategies of Despair

Chapter 8

Divivvidiv had had a very good dream, one in which he had savoured every diamond-sharp second of a day in his childhood. The day chosen had been the eighty-first of the Clear Sky Cycle. His high-brain had taken his memories of the actual day as the basis of the dream, then had discarded those which were less than perfect and replaced them with invented sequences. The content of the fabricated sections had been excellent, as had been the merging of their boundaries with the rest of the dreamscape, and Divivvidiv had awakened with intense feelings of happiness and fulfilment. For once there had been no undertones, no stains of guilt seeping in from the present, and he knew he would return to the dream—perhaps with minor variations—many times in the years to come.

He lay for a moment in the weak artificial gravity field of his bed, enjoying a mental afterglow, then became aware that the Xa was waiting to communicate with him. *What is it?* he said, raising himself to an upright position.

Nothing of great urgency, Beloved Creator—that is why I waited until you had achieved a natural return to consciousness, the Xa replied at once, using a mind-colour similar to yellow for reassurance.

That was very considerate of you. Divivvidiv massaged the muscles of his arms in preparation for a return to activity. *I sense you have good news for me. What is it?*

The Primitives' ship is returning, with two males on board, and this time they will not pass beyond my perimeter.

Divivvidiv was immediately on the alert. *You are quite positive about this?*

Yes, Beloved Creator. One of the males is emotionally

linked to one of the females. He believes that she and her companions have damaged their ship in a collision with my body during the hours of darkness, and that they have taken refuge in one of the habitats we found in the datum plane. It is his intention to find and retrieve the female.

How interesting! Divivvidiv said. *These beings must have an unusually strong inclination towards single-partner reproduction. First we learn of their mind-blindness, and now this —how many handicaps can a race endure and yet remain viable?*

Stated in those terms, Beloved Creator, the question is meaningless.

I expect so. Divivvidiv turned his attention to matters of a more practical nature. *Tell me, are the male Primitives becoming aware that you belong to a class of object totally outside their previous experience?*

Object? Object?

Being. I should have referred to you as a being, of course. How do they perceive you?

As a natural phenomenon, the Xa said. *An accretion of ice or some other crystalline form of matter.*

That is good—it reduces their potential for causing damage and at the same time makes them easier for us to capture. Divivvidiv shifted his thinking to the high-brain mode to exclude the Xa from his deliberations. Obtaining specimens of the Primitives for Director Zunnunun's personal study was in a way a frivolity, something quite extraneous to the great project, and if the Xa were to be damaged in the course of it the penalties would be dire. He, Divivvidiv, would almost certainly be subjected to personality modification as a punishment for allowing himself to be diverted from his duties. After all, the project was the single most important undertaking in the history of his people. The future of the entire race. . . .

Beloved Creator! The Xa's call was an unexpected intrusion. *I have a question for you.*

What is it? Divivvidiv demanded, hoping the Xa was not about to make more of the increasingly tiresome enquiries about its own future. The Xa would not have been able to build itself had it not been provided with a powerful artificial intelligence, but its designers—in the remote high floors of the Palace of Numbers—had not anticipated the development of self-awareness.

Tell me, Beloved Creator, the Xa said, *what is a Rope?*

The shock of the question was so sudden, so forceful, that Divivvidiv experienced a momentary giddiness and a dangerous weakening of mental control. For one perilous instant he almost gave the Xa access to all high-brain networks, and the effort of closing off hundreds of neural highways left him feeling chilled and sick.

Practising eye-of-the-hurricane rituals to induce a state of calmness, he said, *Who told you about Ropes?*

There was a slight delay before the Xa responded. *Not you, Beloved Creator. Not anybody. The word has lately begun to exist all around me. It must be continually in the minds of millions of intelligent beings, but the concepts behind it are too elusive to be captured. All I know is that the word is associated with fear . . . a terrible fear of ceasing to exist. . . .*

It is nothing for you to be concerned about, Divivvidiv said, using every mental reinforcement technique he knew to give strength to the lie. *The word is little more than a sound. Its origins lie in certain aberrations of the human mind— logical lesions, you might say—metaphysics, religion, superstition. . . .*

But why has it begun to impinge on my consciousness?

For no particular reason. A tide, a current, an eddy. You trouble yourself with things that do not concern you. I command you to be at peace and concentrate on your given task.

Yes, Beloved Creator.

Grateful for the Xa's compliant attitude, Divivvidiv

severed the telepathic link and floated to the airlock which was closest to his living quarters. As he pulled on the suit which would enable him to survive the outer cold he pondered, with some disquiet, on the Xa's acquisition of the term "Rope". Did it simply mean that the Xa's direct communication capability had increased? Or was there a new degree of alarm on the home world, a heightening of fear which had driven telepathic ripples through the surrounding regions of space?

Divivvidiv entered the airlock and completed the inner seal. As soon as he opened the outer door the bitter coldness stung his face and eyes, and breathing became so painful that he almost gasped aloud. The metallic plazas of the station stretched away before him, flat and bare in some places, replete with engineered complexities in others. The antennae of the teleportation unit projected into the sunlit air—slim and delicately curved sculptures—and occasional flickers of green fire at their tips showed that a consignment of the Xa's nutrients was currently being received. Beyond the angular boundaries of the station the Xa's body, now grown huge, formed a sea of white crystalline brilliance stretching into remoteness on all sides.

Divivvidiv's eyes were not able to focus on infinity without artificial aid, and so the universe beyond the white horizon was simplified into a vision of the sun and one of the local planets on a background washed and speckled with blurs of luminance. He was, nevertheless, able to gaze directly at the mote of blue light which was his home world of Dussarra, and within seconds was in contact with Director Zunnunun.

What is it? Zunnunun said. *Why do you interrupt my work?*

I have good news, Divivvidiv replied. *It was an unfortunate and freakish circumstance that the sampling of Primitives I supplied to you consisted entirely of females. Also, we were unlucky in that the second ship—containing Primitive males —became aware of the Xa in time to guide their ship successfully past its perimeter.*

You said you had good news. Zunnunun tinted the words with the mind-colours of growing irritability.

Yes! The same Primitive ship is now ascending towards the datum plane, and those on board believe—or hope—that the lost females have taken refuge within the habitats I found here. This time, Director, there is no doubt at all that I will be able to send them to you, because—as a simple consequence of previous physical contact—the sole purpose of the males in making the new ascent is to retrieve the females. They will come directly to me.

This is quite incredible, Zunnunun said. *Are you sure of your facts?*

Absolutely.

You bring me good news indeed—I had no idea that such powerful bonding could exist between individuals of any species. I look forward to receiving the Primitive males and to carrying out appropriate experiments.

It is my pleasure to serve you, Divivvidiv said, pleased that he had regained the Director's approval. *While we are in private discourse, may I raise another matter?*

Proceed.

The Xa's consciousness continues to reach new levels, and it has just made an initial enquiry about the Ropes.

Does it have any understanding? Any insight?

No. Divivvidiv paused, qualifying the statement. *But I sensed undertones . . . Has there been a new development?*

I have to say—yes. There was a brief silence, and when Director Zunnunun spoke again his words were clouded with strange colours indicative of doubt and apprehension. *As you know, a powerful faction in society has forced those in the Palace of Numbers to carry out a new assessment of the local situation, and the latest data have strengthened the opinion that the Ropes really do exist. It also seems highly probable that as many as twelve Ropes once intersected near our galaxy—compared with the original estimate of seven.*

And if that is truly the case, not only will our own galaxy cease to exist—as many as a hundred other galaxies in the cosmic region will be annihilated.

I see. The surrounding cold seemed to invade Divivvidiv's clothing with relentless force as he broke the mental contact. *This is strange*, he thought. *Why should a force which promises to annihilate a million other galaxies be feared more than a force which threatens to destroy only this one—when my personal fate will be exactly the same in either case? And why should I trouble myself over my people's plan to obliterate a pair of undeveloped and sparsely populated minor worlds when the cosmos itself is bent on such monstrous feats of destruction?*

Chapter 9

During the last fifty miles of the ascent Toller and Steena-meert had turned the ship on its side at frequent intervals. The purpose had been to get an early view of the small line of wooden stations and spaceships so that they could steer directly towards them by countering lateral drift. Even in good viewing conditions the artifacts would have been hard to find, but with a sea of crystal spanning the sky and diffusing the sunlight into a uniform white brilliance Toller had expected his task to be doubly difficult. He had therefore been surprised when, at a range of some thirty miles, he had begun discerning a mote of solid darkness at the centre of the translucent disk. As the ship crept closer to it, binoculars revealed that the object—although irregular in its general outline—was bounded by straight lines and square corners. Its silhouette resembled the plan of a very large building to which numerous extensions had been added in quite a haphazard manner.

For a time Toller was able to reject the implication—there simply was no room for it in his scheme of reality—but eventually the painful mental *shift* took place. . . .

"Whatever that thing is," he said to Steenameert, "I cannot visualise it growing there by itself like a crystal of ice. It has to be a midpoint station of some kind, but. . . ."

"Not built by the likes of us," Steenameert supplied.

"You speak truly. The size . . . We could be looking at a palace in the sky."

"Or a fortress." Steenameert's voice was low, almost furtive, in spite of the fact that he and Toller were alone on the ship in the vast reaches of the weightless zone. "Could it be that the Farlanders have at last decided on conquest?"

"They are going about it in an odd way, if they have," Toller replied, frowning, instinctively rejecting the idea of a military invasion from the third planet. Bartan Drumme was one of the two men still alive who had been on the single epic voyage to Farland many years ago, and Toller had often heard him declare that its inhabitants were insular in their outlook, totally lacking in the colonial urge. Besides, the enigmatic sea of living crystal and the gigantic midpoint station were obviously connected in some respect, and what military commander—no matter how alien his mind—would set about an invasion in such a pointless manner?

"No, this is something new to us," Toller went on. "We know there are many other worlds circling distant stars, and we also know that on some of those worlds there are civilisations much further advanced than ours. Perhaps, my friend Baten, what we see above us is . . . is . . . but one of many far-flung palaces belonging to some unimaginable king of kings. Perhaps those reaches of ice are his hunting grounds . . . his deerparks. . . ." Toller paused, lost for the moment in the exotic grandeur of his vision, but was recalled when Steenameert posed a crucial question.

"Sir, do we go on?"

"Of course!" Toller pulled his scarf down from over his nose and mouth so that his words could be heard with perfect clarity. "I continue to assume that the Countess and her crew have taken refuge in one of our stations, but if we fail to find them there . . . Why, we now have one other place to look!"

"Yes, sir."

Steenameert's eyes, peering from the horizontal slit between his scarf and the edge of his hood, gave no indication that anything out of the ordinary was happening, but Toller was suddenly struck by the fantastic import of his own words. His hand dropped of its own accord to the hilt of his sword as he realised that his entire being was awash with dread.

Even as he was first hearing of Vantara's disappearance there had been born in him the sickening fear that she was

130

dead. He had refused to acknowledge that fear, driving it out of his mind with manufactured optimism and the demanding activities of the hurriedly-mounted rescue expedition. But new elements had been added to the situation —bizarre, monstrous and inexplicable new elements—and it was impossible to see how they could bode anything but ill.

The six wooden structures were known collectively as the Inner Defence Group—a name which had clung to them since the days of the interplanetary war although it had long since lost all relevance.

Toller and Steenameert had located the group on the Overland side of the ice barrier and about two miles out from the alien station. Taking his ship in a wide curve, Toller had approached the wooden cylinders very cautiously from an outer direction, keeping them between him and the mysterious angular outline. He had chosen the course with a tenuous hope of avoiding detection by alien eyes, although it was purely an assumption that the metallic construct housed living beings. It appeared to be embedded in the crystalline barrier, and when viewed through his powerful glasses had something of the look of a vast and lifeless machine— an incomprehensible engine which had been placed in the weightless zone to carry out some incomprehensible task on behalf of equally incomprehensible builders.

And now, as his ship nudged to within a furlong of the cylinders, Toller was developing the conviction that they were empty. They were nestling against the underside of the frozen sea, apparently held in place by slim girdles of crystal which had grown around them. Four of the cylinders were habitats and stores, and two longer versions were functional copies of the spaceship which had once flown to Farland, but they all had one thing in common—the appearance of lifelessness.

If Vantara and her crew had been waiting within any of

the wooden shells they would surely have been maintaining a watch and by this time would have signalled to the approaching skyship. But there was no sign of activity. All the portholes remained uniformly dark, and the hulls obstinately remained what they had been since Toller first saw them—inert relics of years long gone.

"Are we going to go inside?" Steenameert said.

Toller nodded. "We have to—it is expected of us—but. . . ." His throat closed up painfully, forcing him to pause for a moment. "You can see for yourself that nobody is there."

"I'm sorry, sir."

"Thanks." Toller glanced at the strange alien edifice which projected from the icecap far to his left. "If that had been an aerial palace—as I so foolishly surmised—or even a fortress, I could have clung to some shred of hope that they had taken refuge in it. I would even have preferred to imagine them as the captives of invaders from another star—but the thing looks like nothing more than a great block of iron . . . an *engine* . . . Vantara could have seen no prospect of a haven there."

"Except. . . ."

"Go on, Baten."

"Except in a case of the utmost desperation." Steenameert had begun to speak quickly, as though fearful of having his ideas dismissed. "We don't know how wide the ice barrier was when the Countess reached it, but if she did so in the hours of darkness—and there was a collision which disabled her ship—she would have been on the Land side of the barrier. The *wrong* side, sir. It would have been impossible to locate or reach our own vessels, and under those circumstances the . . . engine could have seemed a likely place to shelter. After all, sir, it is certainly large enough, and there may be hatches or doors leading to its interior, and—"

"That's good!" Toller cut in as the darkness in his mind suddenly began to abate. "And I'll tell you something else!

I have been treating this whole affair as though the Countess were an ordinary woman, but nothing could be further from the truth. We have been talking about an accidental collision, but there may not have been one. If Vantara had chanced to see the alien engine from afar she would have taken it upon herself to investigate it!

"She and her crew could be watching us through some vent at this very minute. Or . . . they might have spent some days exploring the machine and then have decided to return to Land. They could have passed us unseen as we were ascending with the commissioner—such things can easily happen. Don't you agree that such things can easily happen?"

The tentative way in which Steenameert nodded in assent told Toller something he already knew—that he was allowing the pendulum of his emotions to swing too far—but the black despair he had begun to feel had to be staved off as long as possible, and by any means available. In the unexpected upsurge of hope it mattered little to him that his reactions were immature, that the *real* Toller Maraquine would have acted differently—he had been restored to the universe of light and was determined to remain in it as long as possible.

Now keyed up to a state in which he had to undertake some physical action, his system thrumming with emotional energy, Toller grinned fiercely at Steenameert. "Don't just sit there fiddling with the controls—we have work to do!"

They fully inverted the ship and shut down the jet, letting the vessel coast to a gentle halt only fifty yards from the nearest of the wooden cylinders. The gondola's landing legs actually came in contact with the barrier's glowing surface, which at close range proved to be highly uneven—a haphazard mass of man-sized crystals. Most of them appeared to be hexagonal in cross-section, but others were circular or square, and many displayed feathery interior patterns of pale violet. The overall effect was visually stunning—a seemingly endless vista of unearthly beauty and brilliance.

Toller and Steenameert strapped on their personal propulsion units and made an inspection tour of the six cylinders. As expected, they were empty except for the provisions which had been stored against an emergency which had never come. The shells, with their varnished timbers and reinforcement bands of black iron, were colder and more silent than tombs. Toller was glad he had satisfied himself in advance that Vantara and her crew were elsewhere, otherwise the opening and investigating of each darkly brooding hull would have been an unbearable experience.

Towards the end of the tour he was struck by the fact that, although the crystals of the barrier had indeed extended themselves downwards to encompass the cylinders, they had done so in a very sparing fashion. Instead of completely engulfing the wooden hulls, as would have seemed natural to Toller, they had encircled each with only a narrow and spiky growth. It was something he might have puzzled over had his thoughts not been fully occupied with what lay ahead.

When the formal search had been completed, he and Steenameert—riding on plumes of white condensation—returned to their ship and collected from it seven parachutes and seven fallbags, which they stored in the nearest of the habitats. Toller had insisted on bringing the survival equipment in case something catastrophic should happen to the skyship's balloon while manoeuvring close to the crystalline spikes of the barrier.

With the bags and parachutes at hand he and Steenameert, and any others they might rescue, were rendered independent of their skyship as far as descending to Overland was concerned. Protected from slipstream's deadly chill by the fleecy wombs of the fallbags, they could drop for more than a day and a night towards the planetary surface, only deploying the parachutes for the last few thousand feet of the descent. Daunting though the prospect might seem to the uninitiated, in all the years it had been in use the system had resulted in only one death—that of an experienced messenger who, it was thought, had fallen so deeply asleep that he had not roused himself in time to emerge from the fallbag and open his parachute.

Leaving their ship hanging in the inverted position, Toller and Steenameert began the strange two-mile flight to the huge alien artifact. Their jet units carried them at walking pace below a fantastic, glittering ceiling of giant crystals which appeared to have grown at random, except that at widely spaced intervals there were flatter areas in which the crystals were packed in what looked like orderly ranks, and in which the faint violet patterns within were more evident.

As the structure ahead expanded to fill more of his vision Toller began to revise his opinion that it was merely a lifeless engine. Here and there on the metallic surface he could see what seemed to be portholes, and there were hatches which had the size and proportions of doorways. The thought that Vantara might be at one of the portholes and watching his approach added to the heady excitement which suffused his system. At last, after a lifetime of waiting, he was taking part in an adventure which could stand comparison with the exploits which had studded his grandfather's career.

On reaching the nearest edge of the artifact he saw that it was rimmed with a single metal rail supported by slim posts which could easily have been made in a foundry on Overland. The sea of crystals abutted the perimeter of the artifact with no discernible gap. Toller shut down his jet and brought himself to a halt by gripping the rail. Steenameert arrived at his side a moment later.

"This is obviously a handrail," Toller said. "I fancy we are about to meet travellers from another star."

Steenameert's face was all but hidden by his scarf, but his eyes were wide with wonder. "I hope they bear no ill will towards trespassers. Anybody who can loft a redoubt like this into the sky. . . ."

Toller nodded thoughtfully as he surveyed the structure and saw that it was at least half a mile across. He and Steenameert were perched at the edge of a flat area the size of a large parade ground, beyond which a central tower-like extrusion projected a hundred feet or more into the chilled air. As Toller studied it his senses made an adjustment and suddenly he was no longer "beneath" a fantastic landscape. In his new orientation he was looking across a plain towards a strange castle, and the great disk of Overland was directly overhead. Far off to his right was a cluster of curved, tapering poles—like giant reeds sculpted in steel—and as he watched a cold green fire began to flicker around their tips. The phenomenon served as a reminder that he was venturing far beyond the limits of his people's understanding.

"We have nothing to gain by waiting here," he said briskly, fending off an unwelcome surge of doubt and timidity. "Are you ready to. . . ?"

He broke off, shocked into silence, as from behind him came a sudden and unexpected sound. It was a hissing noise and a continuous crackling noise merged into one, like dried leaves and twigs being consumed in a fierce blaze. Toller tried to spin around, but panic and the absence of gravity combined to thwart his intention. He only succeeded in thrashing helplessly for a few seconds, and by the time he had used the handrail to steady himself it was too late—the trap had been sprung.

A sparkling globe composed of fist-sized crystals had grown up around him and his companion with breath-stopping speed, enclosing them in a spherical prison some six paces in diameter.

It had extruded itself from the greater crystals of the frozen sea and part of its lower edge was moulded and attached to the metal of the alien station. The glittering material of it encompassed a section of the handrail to which the two men were clinging. Toller and Steenameert gaped at each other for a moment, faces contorted with shock, then Toller pulled off one of his gloves and touched the inner surface of the sphere. It was as cold as ice, and yet remained dry under his fingertips.

"Glass!" He pointed at the pistol slung on Steenameert's equipment belt. "Blow a few holes in it and we'll soon be out of here."

"Yes, yes. . . ." Steenameert unclipped the weapon and at the same time removed a pressure sphere from his carrier net. He was feverishly screwing it to the pistol's underside when a silent voice—cool, all-knowing and totally convincing —reverberated inside Toller's head.

I advise you not to fire the weapon. The material with which you are surrounded is protected by a reciprocal energy layer. The layer's prime function is to deflect meteors away from the parent construction, but it is effective against any kind of projectile. If the weapon is fired the bullet will ricochet around the interior of the sphere with undiminished velocity until its energy is absorbed by one of your bodies. If the weapon is discharged the sphere will not be weakened in any way, but one of you may be killed.

Toller knew at once, without being able to explain why, that both he and Steenameert had been party to the same communication. The non-voice, modulations of silence, had addressed itself directly to their inner selves . . . mind had spoken to mind . . . which meant that. . . .

He glanced to his left and flinched as he saw that there was a figure just outside the sphere. The glass honeycomb surface of the sphere was distorting and fragmenting the outline, but the figure was man-sized, human in its general appearance, and was holding itself in place by gripping the handrail as any man would have done. Toller had no doubt that it was the source of the mentally-heard voice, but he was unable to understand how the alien newcomer had crossed the metallic plain so quickly and without being seen.

He also felt afraid. His fear was unlike anything he had experienced before—a compound of xenophobia, shock and simple concern for his own safety which rendered him speech-less and almost unable to move. He saw that Steenameert was equally stricken, equally immobilised, and had stopped attaching the pressure sphere to his pistol. The voiceless communication had not merely been a statement—it had passed on pure knowledge and now both men *understood* that a bullet striking the inside of the sphere would be repelled by a force whose magnitude was directly influenced by its speed.

There is no reason for you to be alarmed. The non-voice conveyed assurance and something which might have been mistaken for kindliness but for its underlying condescension and lack of warmth.

We are not afraid . . . of. . . . Toller's unspoken challenge was lost in the chaos of his mind as he began to wonder if he could communicate with his captor.

Speaking in your normal way will organise your thoughts sufficiently for us to exchange ideas, the alien told him. *But do not waste time on untruths, empty boasts or threats. You were about to assert that you are not afraid of me, and that is manifestly untrue. What you must do now is compose yourselves and avoid the mistake of trying to offer me any form of resistance.*

The utter confidence with which the alien spoke, the sheer smugness of the assumption of superiority, triggered in Toller a response—inherited from his grandfather—which he had never been able to control. A surge of red-clouded anger erupted through his system, freeing him from the stasis which had affected his mind and body.

"*You* are the one in danger of making a mistake," he cried out. "I don't know what your design is, but I will resist it to the death—and the death I have in mind is *yours!*"

This is quite interesting. The alien's thought was tinged with amusement. *One of your females reacted with exactly the same kind of irrational belligerence, Toller Maraquine— and I am almost certain she was the one to which you are emotionally bonded.*

The reply jolted Toller into a wider frame of awareness. "Have you taken our women?" he bellowed, suddenly forgetful of his own situation. "Where are they? If they have come to any harm. . . ."

They have not been harmed in any way. I have simply transported them to a place of safety far from here—as I am about to do with you. I shall now inject a sedative gas into the confine. Do not be alarmed by it. The gas will cause you to enter a deep sleep, and when you recover consciousness you will be in comfortable surroundings. And although it will be necessary to detain you there indefinitely, you will be adequately provisioned.

"We are not animals to be penned and provisioned," Toller snapped, his anger further fuelled. "We will go with you to the place to where the women are imprisoned, but of our own free will and with our eyes wide open. Those are my terms, and if you consent to them I give you my word that neither of us will cause you any injury."

Your arrogance is quite astonishing—and equalled only by your ignorance, came the reply, calm and amused. *Beings at your primitive stage of development could never injure me, but I will sedate you, nevertheless, to prevent your causing any minor inconvenience while you are being transported.*

The figure beyond the crystal wall made a slight movement —which was translated into flowing colour transformations of icy facets—and then a particular darkening of one of the hexagonals showed that something was being placed against its outer surface. Steenameert completed his arming of the pistol, raised it and aimed at the focus of activity.

Suicide, Baten Steenameert? The non-voice held something of the detached pity of a naturalist watching a delicate fly drift closer to a spider's web. *Surely not!*

Steenameert glanced at Toller, his eyes unfathomable in the narrow space between scarf and cowl, and lowered the pistol. Toller nodded to him in evident approval of his prudence and—with a deliberate abandonment of conscious intention—drew his sword and in a single swift movement drove the point of it into the crystal wall. He had clamped his left forearm around the handrail, turning his body into a closed system of forces, and the tip of the steel blade buried itself in the shining cells with a power which sent vitreous fragments spinning outwards from the point of impact.

The crystal sphere screamed.

The scream was noiseless, but had no other resemblance to the type of precisely shaped and controlled mental communication employed by the alien. Toller knew, without understanding how, that it was emanating from the walls of the sphere and also from the frozen lake beyond—a multiplied shriek of agony in which chance harmonics and discordant echoes clashed again and again until they faded away and a strange, whimpering non-voice made itself heard. . . .

I have been hurt, Beloved Creator! You did not tell me that the Primitives would be able to damage my body.

Toller, obeying warrior's instinct, did not allow the unexpected voice to inhibit him or blunt his attack. He had hurt an enemy and that was the signal to press forward with renewed vigour, to go for a kill. His sword seemed to be meeting a peculiar resistance, as though passing through a layer of invisible sponge, but his repeated thrusts were retaining enough force to damage and dislodge glassy cells. In only a few seconds he had shattered an adjacent pair and created a small hole in the sphere.

Changing the style of attack, he used the haft of his sword to strike the damaged area, and in spite of the unseen resistance he succeeded in dislodging the two cells entirely, sending them tumbling away into the outer void. Feverishly inspired, he transferred the sword to his other hand and punched the same area of wall with his gauntleted fist. This time there was no magical barrier to soften the blow and several more of the hexagonal cells, their structural unity weakened, went spinning out of sight, greatly enlarging the hole in the sphere.

The silent, inhuman screaming began again.

Steenameert followed Toller's example and—bracing himself against the handrail—began raining blows on the irregular edge of the hole, adding to the destructive effect.

In the roaring furnace of Toller's mind virtually no time passed until the way ahead of him had been cleared and he was outside the sphere and, in weightless flight, closing on a silver-suited figure which was turning to flee. His left arm clamped around the alien's neck in the instant of collision, and he whipped the sword—which seemed to have returned to his right hand of its own accord—into position for a thrust into the alien's side.

How did you achieve this? The alien's words were tinged with revulsion because of the physical contact, but Toller was unable to feel any fear.

You had fully coordinated control of all your muscles, the voice went on, *but there was no coherent mental activity that I could detect. It was impossible for me to anticipate your actions. How was it done?*

"Be silent," Toller snarled, hooking a leg around the handrail to prevent himself and his captive drifting free of the metal surface of the station. "Where are the women?"

All you need to know, the alien said imperturbably, *is that they are in a place of safety*. Again, and to Toller's bafflement, the mental contact revealed no shadings of alarm.

"*Listen* to me!" Toller gripped the alien by the shoulder and thrust him to arm's length, a movement which brought them face to face for the first time. In one searching, wondering, dismayed moment Toller took in every detail of a face which was surprisingly human in the disposition of its features. The principal differences were that the skin was grey; the eyes, lacking pupils, were white orbs drilled with black holes; and the small upturned nose had no central division. Toller could see far back into the nasal cavity, where red-veined orange membranes fluttered back and forth or clung together in tune with the alien's breathing.

"You haven't been *listening*." Toller, repressing an urge to push himself away from the hideous caricature of a human being, leaned harder on his sword and forced it deep into the reflective material of the other's suit. "You will tell me what I need to know—*immediately*—or I will kill you."

The alien's charcoal lips slackened into what could have been a smile. *At this range? So close? While we are in actual physical contact? No member of a humanoid species could possibly. . . .*

Toller's head filled with crimson thunder. His mind blurred, became a montage of smeared visions of Vantara and death-hued alien predators; and the rage, a special rage —beguiling and repugnant, shameful and joyous—took hold of his being. He pulled the alien towards him, at the same time going in hard with the sword, and it was only a startled cry from Steenameert which returned him to sanity.

You hurt *me!* The alien's silent words were shaded with astonishment and the beginnings of fearful comprehension. *You* could *have done it! You were prepared to kill me!*

"That's what I have been telling you, greyface," Toller ground out.

My name is Divivvidiv.

"You resemble a corpse to begin with, greyface," Toller went on, "and it would occasion me not the slightest qualm of conscience were I forced to reconcile appearance with reality. I repeat, if you do not tell me—"

He broke off, disconcerted, as the alien's face rippled with muscular convulsions, and the frail shoulder gripped in his left hand began to vibrate in tune with internal tremors. The black-rimmed mouth underwent asymmetrical changes, flowing in one direction and then another like a sea anemone pulled by conflicting currents, sending threads of discharged saliva snaking weightlessly through the air. Blurred mental echoes picked up by Toller told him that his captive had never been directly threatened with death before. At first it had been impossible for Divivvidiv even to believe that his life was in danger, and now he was undergoing an extremely violent emotional reaction.

Toller, receiving his first insight into a culture totally dissimilar to his own, responded by renewing the pressure of his sword point. "The women, greyface . . . the *women*! Where are they?"

They have been transported to my home world. Divivvidiv was regaining some physical control, but his words reeked with fear, revulsion and barely contained hysteria. *They are in a secure place—millions of miles from here—in the capital city of the most advanced civilisation in this galaxy. I can assure you that it is far beyond the abilities of a Primitive like you to alter those circumstances in any way, therefore the logical thing for you to do is—*

"Your logic is not my logic," Toller cut in, hardening his voice in the hope of concealing the dismay which was washing through him. "If the women are not brought back unharmed, I will send *you* to another world—one from which no man has ever returned. I trust my meaning is clear. . . ."

Chapter 10

The room was large and almost bare, its principal item of furniture being a blue oblong which looked like a bed except that it lacked restraint nets. Ranged around the walls were rectangular and circular panels which continuously changed colour, slowly in some cases, rapidly in others. The floor was of a grey-green seamless material closely perforated with small holes. Toller noticed that his feet tended to stick to the floor, obviating the need for zero-gravity lines, and he guessed the holes formed part of a vacuum system.

He was, however, giving little thought to his surroundings —his attention being concentrated on Divivvidiv, who was busy removing his skysuit. The silvery garment had seams which opened readily when a toggle was drawn along them, an intriguing feature which enabled Divivvidiv to shed the suit in only a few seconds, revealing a frail-looking body of humanoid form and proportions. The alien's thin frame was clad in a one-piece suit made up of dozens of sections of black material which overlapped like birds' feathers.

The outlandishness of the costume; the bald grey cranium; the virtually noseless, corpselike face—all of these combined to inspire in Toller a powerful xenophobia which was augmented by the discovery that the alien had a smell. The odour was not unpleasant in itself—it was sweet and soupy, like a rich beef broth—but the incongruity of the source rendered it highly distasteful to Toller. He glanced at Steenameert and wrinkled his nose. Steenameert, who had been surveying the strange room, did likewise.

You may be interested to learn that you also have an objectionable smell, Divivvidiv commented. *Though I suspect*

144

*that yours is much to do with inadequate hygiene and would
draw complaints from members of your own species.*

Toller smiled coldly. "Recovering from your little bout of
the shakes, are you? Backbone beginning to stiffen again?
Let me remind you that I can still end your life at any second
and am quite prepared to do so."

*You are a blusterer, Toller Maraquine. At heart you doubt
your ability to fulfil the role you have assumed in society, and
you try to disguise that fact in various ways—one of which is
the issuing of flamboyant threats.*

"Take care, greyface!" Toller was disconcerted at having
a ghoulish figure from some distant region of the universe so
casually penetrate the innermost recesses of his mind and
then blurt out its findings, revealing secrets which he scarcely
ever admitted to himself. He glanced at Steenameert, but
the younger man had resumed his scanning of the room,
almost certainly being diplomatic.

*I advise you to divest yourselves of those clumsy insulated
suits,* Divivvidiv replied unconcernedly. *Crude though they
look, they are probably quite efficient and will soon make you
highly uncomfortable at these temperatures.*

Toller, who was already sweating, gazed suspiciously at
Divivvidiv. "If you are hoping to surprise me while I am
entangled with—"

Nothing could be further from my thoughts. Divivvidiv was
now free of his silver suit and was standing close to Toller,
swaying slightly above anchored feet. *You know that.*

The multiplex levels of communication inherent in mental
contact left Toller with no doubt about the alien's truthful-
ness. But, he wondered, could that be a telepathic technique?
Could super-speech be a vehicle for a super-lie, one which
carried total conviction for the listener?

"Keep the pistol on him while I get out of this suit," he
said to Steenameert. "If he moves . . . if he even blinks . . .
put a ball in him."

Your thought processes are unusually complicated for a

145

Primitive. Divivvidiv seemed increasingly at his ease, and his silent words might have been shaded with amusement.

"I'm glad you realise you are not dealing with simpletons," Toller said as he struggled out of his skysuit. "And why are you becoming so satisfied with yourself, greyface? What reason is there for it?"

Reason is the reason. An incongruously human chuckle escaped Divivvidiv's black-rimmed mouth. *Now that I have had the opportunity to appraise your mental structure more thoroughly—and find you fairly amenable to reason—I realise that I can protect myself and my interests simply by making your position clear to you. The more information I impart to you, the more stable our relationship will be. That is why I suggested moving to these more comfortable surroundings, where we can converse without so many distractions.*

"Nothing can distract me in this matter," Toller said, wondering if the full extent of the lie would be apparent to Divivvidiv. The mode of communication alone was enough to swamp his mind with wonder, and when the outlandish nature and appearance of the alien—to say nothing of the bizarre circumstances of the meeting—were taken into consideration it was a matter of some surprise to him that his brain was able to function at all. He would have to keep Vantara in the forefront of his thoughts at all times. Nothing else mattered but the need to find and rescue her, and return her to the safety of Overland. . . .

There is no need to keep pointing that barbaric weapon at me, Divivvidiv said as Toller got free of his skysuit and took the pistol from Steenameert to enable him to strip down as well. *I told you that logic will prevail over force.*

"In that case you have nothing to be alarmed about," Toller replied comfortably. "If it comes to a falling out, you can fire syllogisms at me and I will have to make do with firing mere bullets at you."

You grow complacent.

"And you grow tiresome, greyface. Tell me how you plan

to retrieve the women and thus preserve your own life."

Divivvidiv projected feelings of exasperation. *I have a question for you, Toller Maraquine. It may seem irrelevant to our circumstances, but if you will control your impatience for a short time understanding will come. Is that reasonable?*

Toller nodded reluctantly, with an uneasy suspicion that he was being manipulated.

Good! Now, how many worlds are in your planetary system?

"Three," Toller said. "Land, Overland and Farland. My paternal grandfather—whose name I am proud to bear—died on Farland."

Your knowledge of astronomy is deficient. Has it not come to your attention that there are now four worlds in the local system?

"*Four* worlds?" Toller stared at Divivvidiv, frowning, as he half-remembered someone having spoken to him in recent days about a blue planet. "*Now* four worlds? You speak as if a new world had been added to our little flock by magic."

That is exactly what has happened—although no magic was involved. Divivvidiv leaned forward. *My people have transported their home planet—which is called Dussarra—across hundreds of light years. They plucked it from its ancient orbit about a distant sun, and they placed it in a new orbit about your sun. Does that suggest anything to you about their powers?*

"Yes—powers of imagination," Toller said with a show of scorn in spite of a dreadful conviction that the alien was presenting the unvarnished truth. "Even if you could move an entire world, how could its inhabitants survive in the coldness and darkness between the stars? How long would such a journey take?"

No time at all! Interstellar travel has to be accomplished instantaneously. The concepts are far beyond your grasp—through no fault of your own—but I will try to implant analogies which will give you some measure of understanding.

Divivvidiv's inhuman eyes closed for a second. Toller felt a wrenching sensation within his head, disturbing and yet curiously pleasurable, and he gasped as—like a slewing beam from a lighthouse—a flaring intellectual luminance swept through his mind. For one tantalising instant he seemed on the verge of knowing everything that a complete being ought to know, then there came a wavering, an accelerating slippage, followed by an aching sense of loss as the light moved away from him. The philosophical darkness which rolled in to take its place was, however, less oppressive, less monolithic than before. There were twilight areas. Toller had a fleeting glimpse of vacuums within vacuums; of interstellar space as a spongy nothingness riddled with tubes and tunnels of a greater nothingness; of insubstantial galactic highways whose entrances coincided with their exits. . . .

"I believe, I *believe*," he breathed. "But—between us—nothing has changed."

You disappoint me, Toller Maraquine. Divivvidiv stepped over his discarded suit, which had been drawn to the floor by air currents, and moved closer to Toller. *Where is your curiosity? Where is your spirit of scientific enquiry? Do you not wish to know why my people embarked upon such a mammoth venture? Do you think it is a commonplace thing for the members of an intelligent species to transport their home world from one part of a galaxy to another?*

"I have already told you—those things are no concern of mine."

Oh, but they are! They are also the concern of every living creature on every planet of this system. Divivvidiv's mouth underwent further asymmetrical changes, tugged by the invisible tides of emotion. *You see, my people are fleeing for their lives. We are fugitives from the greatest catastrophe in the recent history of the universe. Does that fact not make you the least bit inquisitive?*

Toller glanced at Steenameert, who appeared to have frozen halfway through the task of removing his skysuit, and for the first time in days his preoccupation with Vantara and her fate began to loosen its hold on his mind.

"Catastrophe!" he said. "But the stars are billions upon billions of miles apart! Are you talking about some manner of great explosion? If it ever happens I cannot see how—"

It has already happened, Divivvidiv cut in. *And it matters little that stars are billions of miles apart—the scale of the explosion was such that upwards of a hundred* galaxies *will be destroyed by it!*

Toller tried to conjure up a mental image to go with the alien's words, but his imagination baulked. "What could cause such an explo. . . ? And if it has already happened why are we still here? How can you know about it?"

Divivvidiv was now very close to Toller, and his sweet body odour was thick in Toller's nostrils. *Again, the concepts are beyond you, but. . . .*

The slewing beam from the lighthouse was fiercer this time, and Toller's instinct was to shrink away from it, but there was nothing he could do to protect himself. He shuddered as, within a tiny fraction of a second, his inner model of reality was torn apart and rebuilt, and he found that his newly vouchsafed vision of space as an emptiness riddled with transient wormholes of greater emptiness was a simplification. The cosmos—he now knew, or almost knew—was born in an explosion which was inconceivable in its ferocity, and within a minute its entire volume was permeated by seething masses of *ropes*. The ropes—comparatively ancient and decaying relics of a period of cosmic history which had spanned a length of time equal to one human breath—had a diameter approximating one millionth of that of a human hair, and were so massive that a single inch weighed as much as an average-sized planet. They writhed and twisted and oscillated, and in their blind contortions they decided nothing less than the disposition of matter throughout the universe: the patterns of galaxies, the patterns of clusters of galaxies, the patterns of sheets of clusters of galaxies.

As the universe grew older—and intelligent life made its first appearance—the ropes grew fewer in number. Their incredible stores of energy squandered by their frenzied threshings and twistings, by the propagation of gravitational waves, they became more of a cosmic rarity. As they slowly erased themselves from existence the universe became more stable, a safer place for frail biological constructs such as human beings—but it was not homogenous. There were anomalous regions in which ropes remained plentiful, so plentiful that interactions and collisions were bound to occur, with consequences beyond the descriptive powers of any system of mathematics.

At one location no less than twelve ropes had intersected and yielded up their total energy in an explosion which was destined to annihilate perhaps a hundred galaxies, and to have a profound effect on a further thousand. No living creature would ever *see* the explosion, so close was the speed of its fronts to that of light, but intelligent beings—using data gathered by subspace probes—could deduce its existence. And once the deduction had been made there was only one thing left to do.

Flee!

Flee far and fast. . . .

Toller blinked vigorously, momentarily certain that a watery ripple had passed across his vision, but he realised almost at once that the effect had been subjective and illusory. His internal model of the universe had been torn asunder and rebuilt in drastically different form, and now he, too, was different. A quick glance at Steenameert's pale face and blanked-out eyes confirmed that he also had undergone a similar chastening metamorphosis.

A voice from Toller's distant past whispered a warning: *Your defences have been breached! Should he choose to do so, greyface could overwhelm you in this very instant!*

Responding to the warning, Toller alerted himself. He triangulated his gaze on the alien's face and saw nothing there but a growing display of relaxation and satisfaction. There was no sense of physical threat, but that in itself might have constituted another kind of menace. They were in Divivvidiv's stronghold and there was no telling what semimagical forces the alien might be able to summon to do his bidding without so much as having to raise a finger.

Striving to assimilate all that he had learned, Toller shook his head as though recovering from a blow. His mind had been swamped in the influx of pure knowledge—to the extent that all normal thought processes were being prorogued— but, even so, he had a dim awareness that one great question remained unanswered. What could it be? He had been told too much in too short a time, and yet he was troubled by a nagging conviction that he had been told too little. And, all the while, the hideous alien in his costume of wafting black rags gave the impression of being more and more content with the situation. . . .

"Why do you seem so pleased with yourself, greyface?" Toller growled. "After all, nothing has changed between us."

Oh, but it has, Divivvidiv assured him, shading his words with a kind of glee. *You are not immune to reason, and therefore in this situation logic has to work for me and against you. Without admitting as much to yourself, you have already begun to realise how pointless it would be for you to pit yourself against representatives of the greatest civilisation in the galaxy.*

"I refuse to. . . ."

And now that you have come so far, Divivvidiv went on relentlessly, *I will complete the edifice of logic which to me is an impregnable defence and to you an insurmountable barrier. You were on the verge of asking why your insignificant pair of little worlds had to become involved with Dussarra's flight from annihilation.*

The answer is that binary planets sharing a common atmosphere are extremely rare. Dussarran astronomers are aware

*of only three other examples in this galaxy—all of them very
distant and less well matched than Land and Overland. As
you already know, we can move our home world instantaneously from star to star, but energy limitations prevent us
from leaping more than a few light years at a time. That fact
means that the annihilation front, which even now is roiling
outwards through this region of the galaxy, would always have
been at our heels . . . unless . . . unless, Toller Maraquine
. . . we found the way to make the leap to another galaxy.*

Toller became aware of his own breathing, a regular and
impersonal sound, like waves subsiding on a distant beach.

*We designed a machine which was capable of transporting
the home world across the required distance, but for its construction the machine required a very special physical environment. There had, of course, to be freedom from gravity to
prevent the machine from distorting under its own weight—a
factor which posed us no problems. There also had to be a
limitless supply of oxygen and helium to facilitate accretive
growth of the machine—and that is why we chose to position
the Xa at the barycentre of your two worlds.*

*In addition to all the other knowledge which I have im-
pressed on your mind, Toller Maraquine, it is necessary for
you to appreciate that the Xa is almost complete. It will be
activated in approximately six days from now, and when that
happens the planet Dussarra will simply vanish from your
sight. It will have been instantaneously relocated in another
galaxy—one which is nine million light years from here.*

*Absorb what I am telling you, Toller Maraquine—for your
own sake, for your own peace of mind.*

*There is nothing you can do to retrieve your females. The
massed resources of a thousand civilisations like yours would
be powerless in this situation. I urge you—accept what I say
and return to your home world in peace and with no qualms of
conscience, knowing that you have done all that any individual
could possibly do. . . .*

Toller stared into the black-drilled orbs of the alien's eyes, tranced, communing with himself and with another—that heroic figure from heroic times past whose example and counsel, although inferred, he prized above all else. "What would the real Toller have done?" he asked himself, silently moving his lips to frame the words. He remained immobile for several seconds, half-seduced by the blandishments of the alien logic, then he recoiled, eyes widening, like a man evading the jaws of a steel trap.

"Take this pistol from me," he said to Steenameert. "And give me my sword."

I have lost you again. Divivvidiv cowered back from him. *You are acting without thinking. What are you going to do?*

Toller accepted the weapon from Steenameert, closing his fingers around the familiar mouldings of the haft, and pressed the tip of the blade to the alien's throat. Crimson stars sparkled across his vision.

"What am I going to do, greyface?" he whispered. "Why, I am going to part your head from your foul body unless you stop telling me what *you* want me to hear and start telling me what *I* want to hear. Has your wonderful intellect absorbed that message? Tell me—*now!*—how I can rescue our women." He bored with the steel blade into Divivvidiv's throat.

The alien's black-rimmed mouth distorted and his frail body began its convulsive trembling, but this time the threat of instant death did not entirely destroy his self-control. *I have told you all there is to tell. You have to understand the situation—there is nothing you can do.*

"I could kill you!"

Yes, but what would that achieve? Nothing! Nothing!

"I. . . ." Toller refused to be diverted. "You said the women were transported to your world . . . instantaneously . . . by one of your machines. . . ."

Yes?

"In that case, we will pursue them by the same mode of transport," Toller ground out, shocked by his own words.

The quaking of Divivvidiv's body grew less severe. *Is there no end to your obtuseness, Toller Maraquine? You ask to be transported to the heart of a Dussarran mega-city, the population of which is in excess of thirty millions! What do you think you and your companion could achieve there?*

"I would have you as a hostage. I will bargain with your miserable life."

The tremors in Divivvidiv's frame ceased altogether. *This is quite incredible, but there is just a chance—infinitesimal though it may be—that in your blind and primitive stubbornness you could succeed where vastly superior beings would have been doomed to failure. What an intriguing concept! This could even form a major topic for discussion at the next meeting of the. . . .*

"Enough!" Still gripping the alien's shoulder with his left hand, Toller lowered his sword slightly. "You will do as I command? You will take us to Dussarra?"

You leave me no choice. We will go immediately.

"This is more to my liking." Toller released his grip on Divivvidiv's shoulder, then tightened his fingers again, so fiercely that the alien winced. "Or is it less to my liking?"

I do not understand you! What has happened?

"You ceased your shivering, greyface. You ceased being afraid."

But that was a natural reaction to your new proposal.

"Was it? I don't trust you, greyface." Toller produced a cold smile. "This is the way we Primitives conduct ourselves when negotiating with an enemy. We rely to a great extent on our brute instincts—the instincts which are so despised by an advanced being like you—and mine are telling me that you would *like* us to proceed to Dussarra by way of your magical machine. I suspect that were we to do so I would be immediately overwhelmed, or rendered unconscious, or disadvantaged in some other way which would put me at your mercy."

There would be no point in my pitting reason against your

wild and uninformed imaginings. A note of challenge had begun to insinuate itself into Divivvidiv's manner. *May I therefore be informed as to what fresh proposals you are going to put forward under the aegis of your treasured primitive instincts?*

"Certainly!" Toller thought of his grandfather and smiled again. "I am taking you to Dussarra as my hostage—exactly as planned—but the journey will be completed without resort to geometrical sorceries. Two good Kolcorronian spaceships —built of the finest wood and fully provisioned—are waiting close by.

"One of them will carry the three of us to Dussarra."

Chapter 11

The Primitive's words, coming at Divivvidiv out of shifting and formless blurs of emotional activity, were so unexpected —so ludicrous in their content—that at first he felt little sense of shock or alarm. It had been disconcerting to find that the Primitives were capable of coordinated, purposeful action while their neural systems were emitting no coherent signals, but he had put that down as a transient condition brought about by rage or fear. Surely an accidental sequence of words, with only a superficial resemblance to a rational sentence, would be abandoned by the larger Primitive as soon as the storms subsided in his mind.

"What do you think of that idea?" the Primitive said, his disgustingly pink and thick-lipped mouth widening.

Divivvidiv gazed at him for a moment and felt the beginnings of terror as he observed alien mental processes slowly taking place. The Primitive had heard his own words as if they were being uttered by another being. He had been almost as surprised as Divivvidiv by their content, but now he was returning to what passed for his rational mode of cerebration and was actually assuming responsibility for the words and the preposterous notion they embodied.

The idea is insane, Divivvidiv projected. *You do not have to try putting it into practice merely because you verbalised it in a moment of stress. Be sensible, Toller Maraquine—protect your modern self from your ancient self!*

Divivvidiv forced an understanding of his thoughts into the Primitive's mind, fully expecting the odiferous giant to modify his mental stance. To Divivvidiv's dismay the Primitive reacted with a blend of contempt, amusement, pride and sheerest blind obstinacy.

"Stiffen your backbone, greyface," he boomed. "And try to show proper gratitude to me! You have tested my patience with your boasts about your kind's space-faring prowess—if that word can be applied to your geometrical sorceries—but now I am going to acquaint you with the *realities* of going into the black.

"My paternal grandfather—whose name I am proud to bear—was the first man to take one of our spaceships to another world, and I feel privileged that destiny has called upon me to emulate his exploits. Get back into your silver fineries, greyface—we have work ahead of us."

But this is suicidal! It is madness! Divivvidiv felt himself begin to quiver at the prospect of having to risk his life in one of the barbaric wooden shells he had examined so briefly in the preliminary phase of the Xa's development. He had preserved the flimsy artifacts on the chance that the Director might show some interest in their origins. Why had he not had the foresight to destroy them? And why had the designers of the station—those autocrats in the high levels of the Palace of Numbers—not allowed for the possibility of alien intruders?

"Suicidal, you say? Not as suicidal as allowing you to . . . teleport . . . me into the centre of one of your cities." The larger Primitive slackened his grip on Divivvidiv's shoulder a little, lessening the pain.

The giant was swelling in confidence with every second, but Divivvidiv was aware of a growing disquiet in the mind of his companion. He could not analyse the feeling for the present, because too much of his mental capacity was being taken up in dealing with his predicament, but he hoped that Steenameert was going to put forward a rational argument against using one of the wooden spaceships. At the low-brain level of communication, Divivvidiv could hear the Xa calling to him, a distracting undertone which added to an already dangerous degree of stress.

You have no astrogational instruments of any kind, therefore the journey you contemplate is impossible. A new thought

157

occurred to Divivvidiv. *I know you actually believe that your grandfather flew one of your ships to another world, but without a precise knowledge of the vessel's speed and. . . .*

"He had help with the various computations." The giant pressed harder with the tip of his sword, the weapon with which he appeared to compensate for his mental inadequacies. "You will provide me with the same assistance. You are equal to the task, aren't you, greyface? I mean, you have already spoken at length about your immeasurable superiority in all the sciences."

I still say the risks are unjustifiable. Your so-called spaceship could have deteriorated beyond. . . . Divivvidiv left the thought uncompleted as the second barbarian suddenly gave voice to his anxieties.

"Can I have a word, sir?" His worried gaze was fixed on the giant's face. "Just a brief word?"

"What is it, Baten?"

Divivvidiv gained access to what was coming and was disappointed when he realised that Steenameert's concern was less with immediate practicalities than with the cosmological overview he had been given earlier. Nevertheless, his intervention diverted most of the giant's crude mindforce away from Divivvidiv and gave him a welcome opportunity to take stock of his situation.

What is happening, Beloved Creator? The Xa found its way into Divivvidiv's mind on the instant. *I have repaired the damage to my body, but I still feel some pain. I wish I had sense organs capable of seeing and hearing within the station. Are the Primitives with you?*

That is no concern of yours.

But there has been talk of ropes, Beloved Creator! From you? Are you capable of issuing words which do not correspond to reality?

No ethical being has that capability, Divivvidiv replied irritably. *Be calm!*

Are you an ethical being, Beloved Creator?

158

Be calm, I tell you! Divivvidiv closed all his low-brain channels in an effort to end the Xa's pestering.

"The scarecrow told us of a vast explosion, sir," Steenameert said to the giant. "We have to take note of what he said. Entire galaxies will be annihilated! According to him Overland and Land will soon be destroyed in one great flash!"

"Baten, why do you plague me with all this talk of galaxies and explosions at this time?"

The smaller Primitive's repulsive features showed signs of agitation. "He said it would happen *soon*, sir."

"Soon? How soon is soon?"

"That is what we must find out."

Beloved Creator! Divivvidiv was shocked to find that the Xa had regained access to his mind, apparently with little effort. *Did you say to the Primitives that I am to be killed only six days from now?*

The way in which the question was framed revealed to Divivvidiv that a communications leakage had developed somewhere in the station's heavy shielding, enabling the Xa to pick up wisps of mental interactions which should have been denied to it. Useful though the discovery would have been at another time, it now served only to aggravate his feelings of anger and alarm.

I command you! He projected the words at the Xa with all the force he could gather. *Go into general quiescence and remain in that condition until I recall you.*

". . . asking you, greyface," the giant was shouting, "how long will it be until my home world is affected by the explosion of which you spoke?"

I cannot be precise—but two hundred of your years is a likely figure.

"Two hundred years." The giant glanced at his companion. "It seems a short span for a world, but for me—at this very moment—it seems an eternity. There is much to do, Baten, and we must act quickly."

159

More quickly than you realise, Divivvidiv added, encircling the thought with all the defences of his high-brain so that not even the Xa could gain a hint of what was going on in his mind. The guilt which had formerly troubled him each time he remembered the fate his kind was planning for the inhabitants of the twin worlds had been erased, for the present anyway. The raw emotions of contempt, disgust and fear engendered in him by his gigantic captor had seen to that.

In only ten days, Toller Maraquine, he thought, *your insignificant little home world will cease to exist.*

Chapter 12

When Cassyll Maraquine emerged from the palace he was perspiring freely. Regardless of the impropriety for one of his station, he immediately took off his formal tabard and opened his blouse at the neck, allowing heat to escape from his body. He breathed deeply of the fresh morning air and looked around for Bartan Drumme.

"You look like a boiled lobster," Bartan commented jovially, emerging from behind the base of the heroic statue of King Chakkell which dominated the forecourt as Chakkell had once dominated the entire planet.

"It was like a baker's oven in there." Cassyll dabbed his brow with a handkerchief. "Daseene is killing herself, living in conditions like that, but when I try to advise her to take the air. . . ."

"What is the point of being the ruler if you can't make death the subject of royal edicts?"

"This is not a fit topic for jests," Cassyll said. "I fear that Daseene has only a little time left to her—and this astonishing business of the barrier, plus her worries about the well-being of Countess Vantara, can only make matters worse."

"You must be concerned for Toller's safety. Is there a scale upon which such emotions are balanced? Upon which your feelings weigh less heavily on the pan than those of Daseene?"

"Toller can take care of himself."

Bartan nodded. "Yes, but he isn't his grandfather."

"What does that mean? What manner of convoluted family tree would I have if my father and my son were one and the same?" Cassyll demanded, not hiding his vexation.

"I'm sorry, old friend. I love young Toller almost as much

161

as. . . ." Bartan raised his shoulders to a level with his ears, a way of agreeing that they should talk about other things. "Shall we find a comfortable seat?"

"It would be preferable to an uncomfortable seat."

The two men, forcibly nudging each other to show that their friendship was still intact, walked in the direction of the Lain River. They reached it near the Lord Glo Bridge, turned east along the embankment and sat down on a marble bench. The air was quiet and balmy, pervaded by the kind of privileged mid-morning calmness which is typical of administrative districts in capital cities. Ptertha were plentiful that morning, glistening like glass spheres as they followed the course of the river, darting and swooping a few feet above the surface of the breeze-ruffled water.

Bartan waited only a few seconds and said, "What is the verdict?"

"She wants to send a fleet."

"Did you tell her there aren't any ships available?"

"She told me not to vex her with minor details." Cassyll gave a humourless laugh. "Details!"

"What are you going to do?"

"I have promised to find out exactly how many ships can be made airworthy, by cannibalising others if necessary, and report the situation to her. Many engine parts will need to be repaired or replaced, and there is a dearth of balloon fabric. It could take as long as twenty days before we can send anybody aloft, and. . . ." Cassyll fell silent, twisting the gold ring he wore on the sixth finger of his left hand.

"And you were hoping Toller would have returned long before then," Bartan said sympathetically. "He probably *will* be back . . . with that countess hanging around his neck . . . It takes a lot to deflect that young man from his course."

"Excellent choice of words—I took some fresh readings early this foreday and I'd say that the barrier is now almost a hundred miles across. It means that no ship could possibly fly around it."

"There you are then!" Bartan said with a display of cheerfulness. "Toller *has* to come back soon!"

"You're a good friend," Cassyll replied, trying to smile. "I love you, Bartan, but I would love you even more if you could tell me why that blue world appeared in our system and caused a crystal wall to be built between us and our ancestral planet."

"You think the two are related?"

"I'm *sure* they are related." Cassyll glanced up at the sky, at the enigmatic disk of white light which hovered at the zenith. "Just as I'm sure that neither bodes us any good."

Chapter 13

"I am going to have much to occupy my mind in the hours to come," Toller said to Divivvidiv, omitting the now-ritual insult about the colour of the alien's face as a sign that he was speaking unemotionally, dealing in cold facts.

"Therefore I take this opportunity to make your position absolutely clear to you," he went on. "It is incumbent on *you* to preserve your own life, and you can best do that by giving me your full support in our venture. If I find you lying to me, or giving me tricky answers to questions, or allowing me to blunder into a danger of which you could have given me a warning—I will kill you. Your execution may not be instantaneous—because you are valuable to me—but, if I believe that you have gone against me in any of the ways I have just mentioned . . . and if subsequently there is a move against us from any quarter . . . you will die immediately.

"You know how readily I act in such matters. At all times I will keep myself prepared to lop your head from your shoulders, and may be so keyed up to do so that any sudden disturbance—even as little as a sneeze from you—could precipitate your demise. I know how great the odds are against me. As far as I am concerned I am practically dead already, so do not delude yourself that you can exert leverage on me in any circumstance. If you want to remain alive you must make yourself an unquestioning instrument of my will.

"Have I made myself clear?"

Very clear, Divivvidiv replied. *Your tendency to belabour the point shows no sign of fading.*

Toller frowned at the alien, wondering if such a craven creature could summon up the nerve to be insolent while in a position of extreme danger. He finished tying all the thongs

164

on his own skysuit, then took the pistol from Steenameert to allow him to do likewise. Divivvidiv had already encased himself in his silver garment, making his general appearance more acceptable to human eyes, and now there was nothing to prevent the small group setting out on the journey to the alien's home planet. Toller tried not to think about what lay ahead. The future he had engineered for himself was filled with inconceivable menace, but he dared not try to anticipate the dangers in case he should become prey to self-doubts which might weaken his hold over Divivvidiv.

"A question before we leave, and before you reply think of the warnings I gave you," he said to the alien, glancing around the strange and inhospitable room. "Will the very fact of your quitting this place alert or in any way give advantage to those who will oppose us?"

It is most unlikely, the alien replied. *The entire facility is operating automatically. It is most unlikely, at this stage, that anybody on Dussarra will try to communicate with me in person.*

"Most unlikely? Is that all the assurance you can give?"
You demanded the truth.

"Fair enough." Toller nodded to Steenameert and the trio moved towards the door by which they had entered the room. The alien progressed confidently, sliding his feet on the perforated floor, while Toller and Steenameert walked with a top-heavy roll as though balancing on narrow beams. When they reached the pressure lock Divivvidiv unclipped the grey metallic box of his personal propulsion unit from the wall. He began to fasten it to his waist with gleaming clamps.

"Leave that," Toller ordered.

But you have seen it before. Divivvidiv spread his hands in an oddly human gesture. *It is only my transporter.*

"A device which gives you the speed of an arrow—I seem to remember that you approached with uncanny speed when Baten and I were trapped in your glass cage." Toller prodded the box with his sword, sending it drifting away from the alien. "It would be quite pointless for you to burden yourself with the temptation to try escaping—especially as I intend to escort you to my ship in regal style."

Toller unfastened a coil of thin rope from his belt, passed the free end around Divivvidiv's body and tied it with a hard-drawn knot. He pulled Divivvidiv into the pressure lock with him and Steenameert, and signalled the alien to operate the controls, which resembled blue tablets set in the seamless grey wall. The inner door slid shut in magical silence, and a few seconds later the outer hatch opened to give a view of the metallic grey plain and glittering crystal sea beyond it. Icy air billowed inwards. Toller drew his scarf up over his mouth and nose, glad to be escaping from the oppressive architecture of the station's interior, and went forward into the familiar skyscapes of the weightless zone.

The sun had moved closer to Overland, and in doing so had crossed the datum plane, rising above the artificial horizon created by the vast disk which Toller now knew to be an incomprehensible machine. Rays of sunlight, striking billions of crystals at a shallow angle, created barricades of prismatic fire which dazzled the eye. So great was the brilliance that even Overland, a hemicircle of luminance which spanned the sky directly above, was dim and ghostly in comparison.

Toller paid out his line a short distance, activated his propulsion unit and set off for the Inner Defence Group with Divivvidiv being dragged in an undignified slow spin in his wake. The trio flew out over the rim of the alien station, the sound of their exhausts greedily absorbed by the surrounding void. Toller kept silent during the flight and concentrated on remembering all the steps involved in taking a spaceship outside the air bridge. During his two obligatory training sessions everything had seemed very simple and obvious, but that had been years in the past and now the complexities appeared enormous.

The group of wooden vessels eventually showed up in the

brilliance ahead as small yellow, orange and tan silhouettes which did not assume any proper colouration until Toller had swung in a curve past them and got the sun behind him. Close by was the skyship in which he had made the ascent, its balloon beginning to look puffy and wrinkled as the gas inside it contracted through loss of heat. At the planetary surface the weight of the collapsing envelope would have expelled the gas, but in the absence of gravity the balloon simply puckered like the skin of some moribund creature of the deeps.

Toller shut down his microjet and coasted to rest, twitching the line to bring his silent prisoner into place beside him. Steenameert expertly drifted himself to a halt nearby, a few yards above the fantastic conglomeration of huge crystals. Two miles away across the burning sea the alien station was outlined like a castle against the darkest part of the sky, where occasional meteors made furtive dashes to oblivion.

"A rare sight, Baten," Toller said. "One that not many can claim to have seen. One that you will no doubt remember."

"I expect I will, sir," Baten replied, a puzzled expression appearing in his eyes.

"I want you to take two messages back with you—one for my father and one for Queen Daseene. I have no time to write them out, so I want you to listen carefully and—" Toller broke off as Steenameert violently crossed and uncrossed his arms in a gesture of disagreement.

"What are you saying to me?" the younger man cried out. "Have I not served you well?"

It was Toller's turn to be puzzled. "Nobody could have done better. I intend to include a citation in my message to the Queen so that you. . . ."

"Then why are you dismissing me at this most crucial moment in the venture?"

Toller pulled down his scarf and smiled. "I am moved by your loyalty, Baten, but things have reached a pass at which I have no right to expect anything further from you. The voyage to the intruders' home world will almost certainly result in my death—I am not deluding myself on that score —but that is an acceptable prospect to me because it is a matter of my personal honour. Having set out with the avowed intention of rescuing the Countess Vantara, I could never return to Prad and admit that I had abandoned the attempt simply because—"

"And what about *my* personal honour?" Steenameert demanded, his voice trembling with emotion. "Do you think that honour is a prerogative of the aristocracy? Do you imagine that I could ever hold my head up again, knowing that I had cravenly forsaken my duty at the first whiff of danger?"

"Baten, this goes beyond duty."

"Not for me." Steenameert's voice had a new edge of hardness which made it almost unrecognisable. "Not for *me*!"

Toller paused for a few seconds, his eyes prickling painfully. "You may accompany me to Dussarra on one condition."

"You have but to name it, sir!"

"The condition is that you cease addressing me as 'sir'. We will go into this thing as private citizens, leaving the Sky Service and all its ways behind us. We will undertake the venture as friends and equals—is that understood?"

"I . . ." Steenameert's new-found assertiveness seemed to have deserted him. "That would be difficult for me . . . for one of my upbringing. . . ."

"Your upbringing counted for little a moment ago," Toller interrupted, grinning. "It is a long time since I have been chastised so vigorously."

Steenameert gave a sheepish grin. "I fear I may have lost my temper."

"Keep hold of it until we reach Dussarra—then you may say good riddance to it for ever." Toller turned his attention to his alien captive. "What do you say, greyface?"

I say it is not too late for you to abandon this pointless exercise, Divivvidiv replied, breaking a long silence. *Why don't you try to use what little intelligence you have?*

"He hasn't understood a word of our discourse," Toller said to Steenameert. "And *he* calls *us* Primitives!"

Without speaking further Toller activated his propulsion unit and manoeuvred himself and the alien close to the nearer of the spaceships. The varnished, straight-grained timbers of the hull glowed in the sunlight with warm shades of brown. The ship had been assembled in the weightless zone from five cylindrical sections hauled up from Overland by skyship. It was four yards in diameter—and in the past had been regarded by Toller as a massive structure—but now, in comparison with the alien station, it seemed totally inadequate for its purpose. Reminding himself that his grandfather had successfully crossed the interplanetary void in a similar vessel, Toller thrust his doubts aside.

He examined the circlet of crystal which bound the ship to the glassy plain, and turned again to Divivvidiv. "Is there any strength in that manacle? Is there likely to be any damage to the ship if I simply blast off?"

The crystal will fracture easily.

"Are you sure? Perhaps it would be better if you were to instruct the being in the machine to release its hold."

It is best if I do not communicate with the Xa at this time. The alien's face was hidden behind a reflective visor, but to Toller his words carried conviction. *Remember that I will be with you inside that barbaric contraption—it is in my interests to see that no harm befalls it.*

"Very well," Toller said, unfastening from his belt the coil of rope which tethered the alien and allowing the end to drift free. "My fellow Primitive and I have certain chores to carry out which demand our uninterrupted attention. I am going to leave you here for a short time—with a request that you do not stray. You will comply?"

I promise not to move an inch.

Toller had made his request with mock courtesy, knowing that the alien was incapable of changing his position, and had not expected a reply which seemed to match his own style of humour. It occurred to him, fleetingly, that the little exchange might have had some significance for the future if there had been any prospect of normal contact between the Dussarran and Kolcorronian cultures. As it was, he had more pressing concerns on his mind.

The rear section of the vessel was actually a specially designed skyship in which the customary square gondola had been replaced by a cylindrical spaceship section. Folded within it was a full-size balloon which gave crewmen the capability of taking the section down to a planetary surface and of rejoining the mother ship while it waited aloft. Toller had no use for the detachable module in the forthcoming mission because descent by balloon was both conspicuous and painfully slow.

"What do you think, Baten?" he said as they drifted in the thin cold air. "Is it worth trying to rid ourselves of the tail section? We have plenty of jacks, and I have no relish for the idea of lugging an extra engine and all those extra control mechanisms."

"The sealing mastic has been there a long time," Steenameert said doubtfully. "It will have worked its way into the leather seals, the wood, the pegs, the lashings . . . It will be like basalt. Even with jacks it could take four or five men to separate the section from the main hull, and there's no telling what damage would be done in the process. On top of that, we would have to shorten all the control rods and reconnect them to the permanent engine. . . ."

"To cut a long story short," Toller put in, "we should take the ship as it is. Very well! If you will be so kind as to retrieve our supply of parachutes and fallbags, I will inspect the ship —and then we will be on our way."

*

170

The flight to Dussarra produced little in the way of surprises for Toller.

Practically all that was known about the business of travelling to destinations beyond the Land/Overland pair came from notes made by Ilven Zavotle, who had been a member of the single historic expedition to Farland. Toller had studied abstracts from the notes during his training and was relieved to find them corresponding well with practical experience. He had enough to occupy his thoughts without any waywardness on the part of the ship or the cosmic environment.

The surrounding sky became black, exactly as predicted, and a short time later the ship warmed up, making it necessary for those on board to remove their insulated suits. According to the long-dead Zavotle, the bitter coldness of the weightless zone between the twin worlds was caused by atmospheric convection, and when a ship escaped into vacuum it was free to accept the sun's bountiful heat. Also as predicted, the meteor display—a permanent feature of the home worlds' night skies—could no longer be seen. Zavotle's explanation was that the meteors were still present, hurtling through space at unimaginable velocities, and that they only became visible on encountering a planet's atmosphere. The possibility of the ship being destroyed between heartbeats by an unseen rocky projectile was one that Toller did not care to dwell on.

He discovered that the steering of the spaceship was the single most demanding task, somewhat akin to balancing a pole on the end of a finger. The pilot's station on the topmost deck was equipped with a low-power telescope mounted parallel to the ship's longitudinal axis. It was necessary to keep the instrument's crosshairs fixed on a reference star, and doing so required close concentration and skilful balancing with the lateral jets.

Steenameert, in spite of his lack of experience, soon proved himself better at the job than Toller and, furthermore, claimed to enjoy long spells at the controls. That arrangement suited Toller quite well, giving him what he needed most—time in which to try assimilating all that had happened in a few crowded hours. He would lounge for lengthy periods in a restraint net on the circular top deck, sometimes half-asleep, sometimes watching Steenameert and Divivvidiv.

The latter had been highly apprehensive during the first hours of the flight, but had gradually regained his composure as it became evident that the ship was not going to explode. He, too, spent much of his time in a restraint net, but not in repose. Dussarra, he had explained, was only eight million miles away from the twin worlds and preceding them in a closely matching orbit. Those facts simplified the parameters of the flight, but nevertheless the relevant calculations were arduous for one who was not a professional mathematician and working without computational aids.

At times Divivvidiv, using a pencil held oddly in slim grey fingers, made notes on a pad supplied to him by Toller. He gave frequent instructions to Steenameert about firing or closing down the main engine, or centring the astrogational crosshairs on a new target. Intermittently he went into a trance-like condition in which, Toller assumed, he was using telepathy or unknown senses to monitor the ship's spatial relationship with its destination. Another necessary assumption was that the alien was not communing with others of his species and setting up a trap for his captors.

It was in the interests of all concerned to complete the flight as quickly as possible, but Toller had been astonished when Divivvidiv—after less than an hour of assessing the ship's performance—had predicted a transit time of three to four days, with an allowance for certain variables. When Toller tried analysing the figures he found himself having to accept the notion of travelling at speeds of well over 100,000 miles an hour, and he promptly abandoned the calculations. The bars of sunlight coming into the ship through the portholes seemed unmoving; the whorled and spangled universe outside was as serene and changeless as ever—so it was

172

better to forget about the chilling dreamworld of mathematics and imagine himself gently drifting from one island to another in a glassy black sea.

One of the traits Toller shared with his grandfather was impatience—even a few days of forced inactivity being enough to unsettle him. He had read Ilven Zavotle's log of the Farland flight in its entirety and could recall a related passage word for word. *Our captain has taken to quitting the control deck for long periods. He spends hours at a time in the middle sections, wedged in place at a porthole, and seems to find some kind of solace in these reveries in which he does nothing but stare into the depths of the universe.*

Feeling oddly furtive and self-conscious, Toller occasionally emulated his grandfather, going down into the strange netherworld of the ship where the narrow rays of light from the ports created confusing patterns of shadow among the internal struts and the bins which housed supplies of power crystals, firesalt, food and water. He would position himself in a narrow space between two storage lockers, and simply allow his thoughts to drift while he gazed through the nearby porthole. The sound of the main engine was stronger there, the smell of the hull's tarred canvas lining more noticeable, but he could think better in the solitude.

Inevitably, his thoughts often turned to the mysteries and dangers of the near future. It seemed incredible that not very long ago he had bemoaned the dearth of adventure in his life, the lack of any opportunity to prove himself worthy of his illustrious name. Now he was engaged in a venture which, although honourable, was so desperate that even the old Toller Maraquine might have counselled against it, one for which—try though he might—it was almost impossible to foresee a successful outcome.

The idea had come to him in an instant of total despair and he had seized on it gratefully and with manic certitude, seeing a clear-cut way through all the barriers and pitfalls of circumstance. It had all seemed so perfect. He could not be

teleported to the alien planet in pursuit of his loved one—
therefore he would fly there in a Kolcorronian ship and take
the whole of Dussarra by surprise. Divivvidiv averred he was
an unimportant member of his society and consequently
without value as a hostage, but his claim was belied by his
being in sole command of the great midpoint station. The
stage was all set for a hero—armed with nought but daring,
imagination and a trusty blade—to astound and confound
the might of an alien world. There would be the swift, unseen
descent by failbag and parachute to a point near the enemy
capital . . . the clandestine penetration of the alien leader's
citadel . . . the bargaining sessions in which Toller held the
upper hand . . . the reunion with Vantara . . . the return to
Overland by way of teleporter and skyship or parachute . . .
the idyllic, aureate future with Vantara by his side. . . .

You *fool*! The recriminations would sometimes come with
the same devastating psychic force as the original preposterous idea, and in those moments Toller would writhe and
almost moan aloud with self-loathing. Only one element of
the bizarre situation remained changeless amidst the turmoil
of his thoughts, giving him the resolve he needed to see the
matter through. He had vowed to himself and to others that
he would make his way to Vantara's side, and—that being
the case—he had no option but to press forward, regardless
of how slight the chances of success might be, even if it
transpired that certain death lay ahead. . . .

Viewed from a height of more than four thousand miles, the
home world of the alien intruders looked remarkably similar
to Land and Overland. The cloud cover consisted of the
same patterns of broad flowing rivers breaking up into vortex
streams or isolated whirlpools. It was only when Toller made
his eyes refocus that he saw through the filigrees of shining
vapour to the planetary surface and realised that the proportion of land masses to oceans was lower than he would
have expected. The predominant colour was blue, with only

occasional patches of subdued ochres to indicate land.

"It looks as though we could all end up with wet arses," he said sombrely, gazing down through a porthole at the great convex shield of the planet.

It is not too late to abandon your insane scheme. Divivvidiv turned his black-drilled eyes towards Toller. *There is nothing at all to prevent you from going home and living out your life in security and comfort.*

"Are you trying to undermine our resolve?"

I am doing what you told me I must do in order to preserve my life—giving you sound information and advice.

"Do not become over-zealous," Toller said. "The only information I require from you at this stage concerns the drop to the surface. Are you positive you have made the due allowance for crosswinds? While I have no wish to descend in the sea, I have an equally strong aversion to the idea of landing in the heart of the city."

You can trust me—all relevant factors have been taken into consideration.

Divivvidiv had scarcely left his restraint net since the ship had been turned over at the midpoint of the flight, his time being spent in hushed meditation and the issuing of numerous demands for course and speed adjustments. Toller had formed the opinion that the alien, even with his awesome talents, had found it much more taxing to guide the ship while it was travelling "backwards" and he was referring to marker stars which were opposed to the direction of flight.

Now, however, with the ship in orbit at the fringes of Dussarra's atmosphere Divivvidiv was in a much more re-laxed and accessible mood. It was obvious that he feared the descent through the planet's atmosphere, but—for some reason peculiar to his kind—the fact that it involved no hand-to-hand *killing* enabled him to face the ordeal with much the same fortitude as a reasonably courageous human.

He had already donned his silver skysuit in preparation

for quitting the ship—an event due in less than one hour—and was concerning himself with his food supplies. When told that Kolcorronian rations consisted largely of strips of desiccated beef and fish, augmented by disks of compressed grain and dried fruit, he had insisted on bringing provisions of his own. The alien food seemed to consist mainly of varicoloured cubes of tough jelly which had been wrapped in gold foil. Divivvidiv had taken a number of them from a pocket and was carefully scrutinising the gleaming blocks, possibly in search of a tidbit.

Toller was again struck by his composure and, doing his utmost to foresee adverse factors, wondered if Divivvidiv was in possession of whole realms of knowledge of a kind which had not even been hinted at in all their telepathic exchanges. As an exercise in practical strategics, Toller tried to project his mind thousands of years into the future of the Kolcorronian civilisation, with emphasis on the technology of warfare, and on the instant an alarming vision blossomed behind his eyes.

"Tell me something, greyface," he said. "That *thing* you call the Xa . . . It *is* a mere machine, isn't it?"

Basically—yes.

"And you have endowed it with the ability to see, with utmost clarity, objects which are thousands of miles away?"

Yes.

"It therefore seems eminently logical to me that your home world, the cradle of your civilisation, would be plentifully provided with similar machines." Toller paused to let his words have effect and the alien was able to follow his line of thought unaided by speech.

You are quite wrong! Divivvidiv injected amusement into his reply. *There are no devices detecting this ship and giving warning of its presence. We do not keep a watch on our skies. Why should we?*

"To warn you of invading armies . . . enemy forces."

But where would such invaders come from? And why

should another culture act in a hostile manner towards Dussarra?

"Conquest," Toller said, beginning to wish he had never started the exchange. "The desire to conquer and rule. . . ."

That is tribal thinking, Toller Maraquine—it has no place among civilised communities. Divivvidiv returned his attention to the sorting of his food cubes.

"Complacency is the enemy of. . . ." Toller, to his annoyance, found himself unable to complete what he had hoped would be an aphorism. Becoming restless, he operated the handle of the air machine, mixing a fresh charge of firesalt with the water in its wire mesh reservoir. Divivvidiv had shown an interest in the device at the start of the flight, and had explained that air was made up of a mixture of gases, one of which—oxygen—supported life, fed fires and led to the rusting of iron. When firesalt came into contact with water it gave off copious quantities of oxygen, thus enabling the ship's crew to survive long journeys through interplanetary vacuum. Toller had made a written note of the new scientific knowledge for the benefit of interested parties back in Prad, even though he did not care to speculate on their chances of receiving it.

It would have been a simple matter to bring the ship down to a level where the surrounding air was breathable, shut down the main engine and bail out. That way they would have been quitting a vessel which appeared to be at rest, and the whole business of getting into the fallbags and linking them together would have been comparatively easy. However, Divivvidiv had objected that the inert ship would then follow roughly the same path down through the atmosphere as the three parachutists, arriving at the surface like a bomb which could possibly claim Dussarran lives.

Toller had not been unduly alarmed at that prospect—he regarded the entire alien population as sworn enemies—but he had accepted the argument that his bargaining position could be compromised by the unnecessary loss of life. There was also the consideration that he wanted to land stealthily, and not to the accompaniment of a huge explosion.

For those reasons the ship had been turned on its side after being brought into the atmosphere and had been aimed in a direction which, according to Divivvidiv, would allow it to fall harmlessly into the sea. The main engine was still firing, with the controls lashed at the minimum thrust setting, and now Toller and Steenameert were faced with the problem of keeping hold of their prisoner while abandoning a ship which was building up a respectable speed. Divivvidiv, being much lighter than the other two, would fall through the air at a lesser rate. He had only to get free once and the laws of physics would see to it that his escape was made good as the vertical separation between him and the humans increased.

Toller had been very much aware of the problem and had insisted on all three being connected by a single strong line before emerging from the ship. There was only one exit, which was located in the middle section, and it had been kept as small as possible to preserve the structural integrity of the hull. In consequence, the three had been forced to cling to one another in a kind of distasteful intimacy while Toller pulled back the greased bolts. The door was a truncated cone, so that interior pressure would force it tighter into the seals of the frame, and it took all the power of his free arm to wrench the crafted wooden disk backwards into the ship.

A howling blast of icy air battered at Toller's skysuit. Tightening his grip on Divivvidiv's slight figure and Steenameert's encircling arm, he launched all of them out into cold white sunlight. They tumbled in the ship's slipstream. An instant later their ears were assailed by a stuttering roar and the universe turned a blinding white as they were engulfed in the choking gases of the condensation trail.

The roiling dazzlement went on for a matter of seconds, and then they were adrift in the sterile sunlit air, hundreds of miles above the surface of Dussarra. All about them was a panoply of stars, galaxies and frozen comets in which the ship's exhaust formed a glowing cloud as, holding to a freakishly steady course, the vessel dwindled from their perceptions. The only way now in which Toller could return to his home world was by using the alien magic of a matter transmitter, but he had little time at that stage to ruminate over the situation.

Being adrift in a planet's upper atmosphere, with nothing but thousands of miles of empty air yawning below, was a harrowing experience even for a veteran Kolcorronian skyman, and Toller knew it had to be correspondingly worse for Divivvidiv. The alien was not quaking, but the movements of his arms and legs seemed aimless, and there were no wisps of mental communication from him.

"Let's get him into his fallbag before we all freeze to death," Toller said. Steenameert nodded and they drew themselves close to Divivvidiv on the common line. The alien's bulky parachute hampered them in the task of drawing the fleece-lined sack up over his head and adjusting the various closures and ventilation ring.

This is more comfortable than I had expected, Divivvidiv told them. *I may be able to sleep and dream during the fall —but what will happen if I have difficulty in getting out of the bag when it is time to use the parachutes?*

"Put your mind at ease," Toller called into the neck of the bag. "We will not allow you to bounce."

The scarf covering most of his face was already stiff with frozen exhalations and in spite of the protection of his skysuit he was beginning to shiver. He separated from the alien and struggled into his own fallbag, a job he accomplished slowly because of the awkward presence of his sword. He began to feel oddly guilty as he realised he was in a way looking forward to a spell in the bag's snug and undemanding warmth.

As soon as he had cocooned himself he closed his eyes and

179

prepared to doze. He was falling towards the planet, but it was going to be quite some time before his speed built up enough to produce slipstream sounds. For the present all was quiet, and he was very tired, and nothing was required of him. . . .

Toller awoke an indeterminate time later and knew at once that there was darkness outside. Dussarra's shadow had swung round to encompass the three specks of life which, having surrendered themselves to the planet's gravity, were making the long pilgrimage from the fringes of space. Suddenly curious about how the alien world would look at night, Toller roused himself, opened the neck of the fallbag and peered out.

He could see the featureless shapes representing Steenameert and Divivvidiv close by, outlined against the silver blazes of the universe, but his gaze was captured and held by the spectacle of the enigmatic planet laid out below him. The visible hemisphere was mostly in darkness, with only a slim line of blue-white radiance adorning its eastern edge. Toller had seen Land and Overland in similar conditions many times, but there the areas where night held sway had always been dominated by a slumbrous blackness which was only relieved by astronomical reflection. He was unprepared for his first glimpse of the nightside of a world which was the home of an advanced technical civilisation.

The major land masses, which had appeared insignificant in daytime, were glittering networks of yellow light. Islands appeared brighter in contrast to the surrounding darkness, but even the oceans were plentifully speckled with points of brilliance which conjured in Toller's mind visions of gargantuan ships, as large as cities, engaged in global commerce. The planet might have been a vast metal sphere pierced in a million places to emit light from an interior source.

Toller gazed down at it for a long time and then, feeling subdued and chastened, pulled the neck of the fallbag up over his head and closed it to shut out the intrusive cold.

He knew he had been deceived and trapped the instant his feet touched the ground.

The three parachutes had opened almost in unison above a night-black landscape in which the only sign of habitation was a thin line of lights, several miles away to the west. There had been no wind to complicate the touchdown for the inexperienced Divivvidiv, and Toller had felt a resurgence of his old optimism as the trio sank into a starlit expanse of grassland. He had prepared himself for a gentle impact, the sensation of his boots going into yielding turf, the feel and smell of grass. . . .

All visual indicators had remained unchanged. As far as the evidence of his eyes was concerned, Toller had touched down in what could have been the rolling savannahs of his home world. Steenameert and Divivvidiv were not far away to his left. They too were standing in grass—and yet Toller could feel flat masonry beneath his feet. He and his two companions were alone in an open stretch of empty pasture —and yet he could hear movement all around, sense the pressure of minds.

"Defend yourself, Baten," he shouted, drawing his sword. "We are betrayed!"

He turned towards Divivvidiv, snorting in his rage, but the swaddled figure of the alien was nowhere to be seen. It was as if he had ceased to exist.

Put the weapon down, Toller Maraquine. Divivvidiv's tone was both kindly and contemptuous. *You are surrounded by more than a thousand stability officers—many of them armed —and any hostile action on your part will most surely result in your death.*

Toller shook his head and spoke in a growl. "I can take many of them with me."

Possibly, but if that were the way of it you would never see

181

your female again. She is only a few miles from here and within a matter of minutes you could be in her company. Alive you might, possibly, be of some comfort or service to her; but if you are dead. . . .

Toller allowed his sword to fall, heard it ringing on stone pavement, and his eyes filled with tears of frustration.

Chapter 14

It was not until Toller and Steenameert had submitted to the pressure of many hands, and to having their wrists bound together behind their backs, that the alien scales were lifted from their eyes. Retinal communications were permitted to pass to the brain, unaffected by external forces, and suddenly the two Kolcorronians could see normally again.

Night still reigned, but the perceived starlit meadows had been replaced by a complex diorama of dimly lit buildings in the middle distance and ranks of shadowy Dussarran figures in the foreground. Toller guessed he was near the centre of an enormous plaza. The surrounding buildings were delineated by gentle curves, in contrast to the rectangular architecture of his home world, and their outlines were punctuated by slim trees which swayed continuously although the humid night air was perfectly still. The only familiar element Toller could find was the face of Steenameert, turned towards him above a sea of industrious, seething, black-clad alien figures.

"It seems that you have won," Toller said, fighting to keep his voice steady. "Sorcery prevails over strength."

Divivvidiv moved a little closer through the crush of odorous bodies. *For your own good, Toller Maraquine, put behind you all your primitive ideas about sorcery. There are no unfair advantages in nature. What is commonplace to my people seems magical to yours, but that is simply because we are more advanced in every branch of learning.*

"It is as good as magic when men are deceived by their own eyes."

That was simply done. When I was close enough to the ground I was able to enlist the telepathic aid of some of my fellow Dussarrans. As soon as you and your companion were sufficiently outnumbered we were able to dictate what you could see, in the same way that a crowd can drown out a single voice. Nothing magical about it!

"But you cannot deny that luck was on your side," Toller grumbled, feeling himself being pushed towards a vehicle which had arrived in the vicinity. "For us to land where we did—so close to a city, in the midst of your lackeys . . . That had to be magic or blind luck."

Neither! Divivvidiv and Toller were losing sight of each other in the press of bodies, but the alien's silent words were clear. *As soon as I had given warning of what was happening my people took control of the local wind cells and guided us to this spot. I told you at the outset, Toller Maraquine—your mission had NO chance of succeeding.*

I am now returning to my post, so it is unlikely that we will ever see each other again, but you have no need to fear for your life. Unlike you Primitives, we Dussarrans do not. . . .

Uncharacteristically for Divivvidiv, the incisive quality of his thought processes faded. There was a moment of woolliness, shadings of what Toller half-identified as guilt, and then the psychic contact was broken. The concept of telepathy was so new to Toller that he felt a dull amazement at even being able to think in such terms, but he was left with the conviction that the alien had suffered an unexpected crisis of conscience, perhaps triggered by the stresses of the fall from the edge of space.

Guilt! The word was a spiteful mosquito hovering and dipping in Toller's confused consciousness. *Is greyface lying to me? Are Baten and I being tricked? Are we being led meekly to our deaths?*

Clumsily and inexpertly, he tried to reach out with his mind to the one Dussarran he knew, but there was only an echoing mental silence. Divivvidiv had withdrawn, was lost behind the palisades of his previous existence, and there was no time for retrospection. The vehicle which had nuzzled through the nocturnal ferment of the alien cityscape looked like nothing so much as a huge black egg. It floated a hand's breadth above the seamless pavement. An opening appeared in its side with no apparent aid from mechanisms that Toller could visualise—in one instant the shell was complete, in the next there was a circular entrance to a redly glowing interior. Dozens of hands were pushing him and Steenameert towards it.

Toller's first instinct was to resist with all the power he could muster, but one part of him had somehow come to hope that Divivvidiv was not entirely his enemy. It was a slim hope—based on little more than certain nuances of thought and the notion that the alien might have a sense of humour—but it was the only dim guide star remaining to him.

With Steenameert jostling against him he clambered into the vehicle, feeling it rock slightly under the shifting of their weight. The door flowed itself out of existence, like molten metal closing in response to surface tension, and a sudden pressure under foot told them the vehicle was rising into the night sky. There were no seats, but that was of no importance in the cramped interior because the thickly quilted skysuits of the two Kolcorronians largely filled the available space. It was easier to remain standing. Toller had been too hot for some time, but was only becoming aware of it as stealthy rivulets of sweat darted down his back.

"Well, Baten," he said dispiritedly, "I gave you ample warning about what might happen."

Steenameert mustered a smile. "I have no complaints. I am going to see sights the like of which I had never imagined, and my life is in no danger."

"That's if we can believe what greyface said—he has already lied to us."

"For a reason! This time he has nothing to gain by telling us an untruth."

"I suppose you are right." Toller was reminded of the odd wavering, the telepathic stains of guilt and self-reproach in Divivvidiv's last communication, but he had no time to pursue the line of thought. He and Steenameert swayed against each other as the direction of their weight shifted. There was a barely perceptible jolt as the vehicle came to rest. A small hole appeared in the side and rippled outwards in the dull metal to become a circular doorway.

Beyond it was a kind of short corridor which seemed to be fashioned from a mottled glassy tube of elliptical cross-section. The material was blurrily streaked with grey, yellow and orange, and was either lit from behind or was giving off an even glow of its own. Toller looked to his left and right and saw that the near end of the tube met the outer shell of the transporter in a curved seam so neat that it would have been impossible to slide a strip of finest paper into it. He transferred his attention to the far end of the corridor. It terminated in an ovoidal wall at the centre of which was a small circular aperture which continuously opened and shrank in a manner which for Toller, exhausted and emotionally drained though he was, had to have biological implications.

"Is somebody trying to make us feel welcome?" he said to Steenameert as he started forward, moving clumsily in his voluminous skysuit, hands still tied behind his back. As he and Steenameert reached the end of the corridor the aperture in the wall rolled back to give them clear access to a large and complicated enclosed space, a circular hall rimmed with stairs and galleries. Imposing though the alien cathedral might have been to Toller in his normal state of mind, its architectural vistas now flowed outwards in his vision, centring all of his attention on the small group of women who were running in his direction.

And foremost among them was the Countess Vantara!

"Toller!" she screamed, her beautiful features transformed into a mask of inhumanly enhanced desire. "Toller, my love!

186

You came, you came, you came . . . I should have known it would be you!"

She hurled herself against him with such force that he was almost driven backwards. Her arms went around his neck and she kissed him with wet lips and urgently probing tongue. Toller was both thrilled and gratified, senses overwhelmed to the extent that he scarcely noticed the stockier form of Lieutenant Pertree moving behind him. The lieutenant began to untie his hands, while the three remaining members of the crew converged on Steenameert with similar intent. Vantara pushed Toller back to arm's length, still clasping his neck, and it was only then that her eyes began to take stock of the true situation.

"You're a prisoner!" she accused. "You have been captured, just like us!" She recoiled from Toller, her expression changing to one of disappointment and anger. "Did your ship also blunder into that strange reef?"

"No. I approached it in daylight and managed to get by. On reaching Prad and being told that your ship had failed to arrive, I immediately set out to find you."

"Where are your forces?"

Toller rubbed his newly freed wrists. "There are no forces —Baten is my only companion."

Vantara's jaw sagged as she shot an incredulous glance to her lieutenant. "You set out—a general commanding an army of one—to challenge an invader!"

"At that time I had no way of knowing there was an enemy presence," Toller said stiffly. "My only thought was of your safety. Besides, two men or a thousand—what difference would it have made?"

"Can this be the *real* Toller Maraquine who preaches defeatism, or is it an impostor conjured up by those foul beings who deny us our freedom?" Vantara turned away before Toller could protest and walked quickly towards the nearest stair.

First I'm too foolhardy—then I'm too timid, Toller thought, feeling both wounded and baffled. In his confusion he stared at the three young women in ranker uniforms who were attending to Steenameert. They were helping him out of his cumbersome skysuit, and at the same time—their welcome to him apparently undiminished—were smiling and plying him with questions. Steenameert looked embarrassed but gratified.

"You must excuse my aristocratic commander," Lieutenant Pertree said, gazing up at Toller with a wry glint in her eye. "The terms of our detention here could hardly be described as onerous, but the countess—being of royal blood, and therefore possessing an exquisite degree of sensitivity—finds the life much more harrowing than would a commoner."

Toller was almost grateful for the flicker of anger which brought reality into sharp focus. "I remember you, lieutenant, and I see that you are as insubordinate and disloyal as ever."

Pertree sighed. "I remember you, captain, and I see that you are as besotted and calf-eyed as ever."

"Lieutenant, I will not tolerate that kind of. . . ." Toller allowed the sentence to die, suddenly recalling that he had only permitted Steenameert to accompany him into the unknown on condition that they discard all the stultifying appurtenances of rank and class. He smiled apologetically and began ridding himself of the stifling swaddles of his skysuit.

"I'm sorry," he said. "The old ways die hard. I have heard your given name more than once, but confess to having forgotten it. . . ."

"Jerene."

He smiled. "My name is Toller. May we pledge friendship and in consequence present a united front against the common enemy?" He had expected the sturdy lieutenant to appear mollified to some extent, and therefore he was surprised when a look of alarm manifested itself on her rounded features.

"It must be true," she breathed, suddenly losing her air of case-hardened composure. "You would never have spoken that way in normal circumstances. Tell me, *Toller*, have we been transported to another world? Are we lost forever? Is this prison on a strange planet millions of miles from Overland?"

"Yes." Toller saw that the three other women had begun listening intently to his words. "How could you fail to know such things?"

"Night came upon us when we were two hours below the datum plane," Jerene said in a small, reflective voice. "It was decided that we would continue at reduced speed through the hours of darkness and carry out the inversion manoeuvre at first light. . . ."

She went on to describe how the crew, most of them sleeping, had been thrown into a panic by a great shuddering groan from the balloon. It had been accompanied by the sound of the four acceleration struts breaking and ripping into the material of the envelope. Almost at once choking billows of miglign gas had spewed downwards around the crew from the balloon mouth as the flimsy structure collapsed inwards. Finally, to add to the terror and confusion, the gondola had coasted into the writhing folds of the ruined envelope and had been swallowed by them.

It had taken fear-protracted minutes for the bewildered astronauts to fight clear of the wreckage. Enough light was being reflected from Land for them to make the incredible discovery that their ship had collided with a crystalline barricade which appeared to span the horizons like a dull-glowing frozen sea. And only furlongs away—wonder piled upon wonder—had been the outline of a fantastic castle, exotic and enigmatic, silhouetted against the silvered cosmos.

Somehow they had managed to retrieve enough personal propulsion units to enable them to fly to the castle. Somehow they had managed to locate a door in its metallic surface. They had entered, and—*somehow*—had found themselves, with no perceptible lapse of time, prisoners in a grey-and-yellow cathedral. . . .

"It is much as I suspected," Toller said when the lieutenant had finished. "Something told me that she . . . that all of you were still alive."

"But what *happened* to us?"

"The Dussarrans employ a gas which quickly renders those who breathe it insensible. It must have——"

"We deduced that much for ourselves," Jerene interrupted, "but what happened after that? We have been told that we were magically transported to another world, but we have only the monsters' word for that. We believe we are somewhere inside the castle. It is true that we have normal weight—as though standing on solid ground—but that could be more magic."

Toller shook his head. "I'm sorry, but what you have been told is true. Our captors have the ability to travel through the space between the stars at the speed of thought. You have indeed been transported, in the blink of an eye, to their home world of Dussarra."

His words drew cries of mingled concern and disbelief from the listening women. A tall, snub-nosed blonde in the uniform of a skycorporal laughed and whispered something to the woman next to her. It came to Toller that the lessons in cosmology and galactic history that he and Steenameert had received from Divivvidiv had brought about fundamental changes in their inner selves, separating them from the rest of their kind. He got a slight but uncomfortable insight into how he, while steeped in ignorance, must have appeared to Divivvidiv.

"How do *you* know that all the humbug about being magicked through the heavens is true?" Jerene challenged. "You have to go by what you have been told, just like the rest of us."

"Far from it!" Toller replied, beginning to divest himself of his own skysuit. "When Baten and I entered the castle, as you call it, we took its corpse-faced master prisoner at swordpoint. And we brought him here as a hostage in a good Kolcorronian ship—therefore we can testify that all of us, at this very moment, are millions of miles away from Overland. We are on the home planet of the invaders."

Jerene's eyes widened and as she gazed up at Toller her face became tinged with pink. "You did all that for. . . ." She glanced towards the stair by which Vantara had departed the company. "You took one of those ancient ships from the Defence Group . . . and flew it to another world . . . all because. . . ."

"We bagged and parachuted all the way to the ground with our prisoner," Steenameert put in, breaking a lengthy silence. "It was only then that the cursed scarecrows overwhelmed our senses and blinded us to the forces which lay in ambush. Had it been a fair and honorable contest things would have been very different. We would have walked in here with our hostage—who would have been quaking and in fear of his life because of the blade that lay across his throat—and then we would have bartered him for your freedom."

"I must report this to the captain." Jerene had become slightly breathless, and the pupils of her eyes seemed to have distended as they hunted over Toller's face. "She should be apprised of all the facts."

"She believes us still to be in our own weightless zone!" Toller sighed with relief and smiled as he realised why Vantara's attitude towards him had shifted so rapidly. "It was only natural that she should have expected me to arrive at the head of an armada. It was only natural that she should have felt a certain disappointment."

"Yes, but had she been a little less impatient. . . ." Steenameert abandoned his comment and lowered his head.

Toller glared at him. "What are you saying, Baten?"

"Nothing! Nothing at all!"

"Sir?" The tall blonde stepped forward as she addressed

Toller. "Can you tell us how long we have been here?"

"Why? Can't you count the days?"

"There is no day or night within this dome. The light never changes."

Toller, who had been trying to reconcile himself to the idea of being imprisoned for a long time, found the prospect of living in continuous even light strangely depressing. "I would say you have been here some twenty-five days. But what about your meals? Do they not mark the days?"

"*Meals!*" the blonde gave a wry smile. "Each cell has a basket which the monsters constantly replenish with cubes of . . . Well, each of us has a different opinion about what we are forced to eat."

"Spiced bluehorn hoof," another tall woman—a swarthy, brown-eyed skyprivate—suggested in aggrieved tones.

"Spiced bluehorn *shit*," the remaining flier put in with an exaggerated scowl, bringing snorts of amusement from her companions. She had cropped brown hair which made an ill match for her conventionally pretty face.

"These are Tradlo, Mistekka and Arvand," Jerene said, indicating the three rankers in turn. "And, as you will have noticed, they have already forgotten how to conduct themselves in the presence of an officer."

"Rank no longer means anything to me." Toller nodded an informal greeting to the women. "Speak as you will; do as you will."

"In that case. . . ." Arvand shimmied to Steenameert's side, clasped his arm and gave him a warm smile. "It is difficult to sleep in a lonely bed—don't you agree?"

"Not fair!" the blonde Tradlo cried, disconcerting Steenameert further by gripping his other arm. "All rations must be shared equally!"

Toller had an urge to move off in pursuit of Vantara, but it was obvious from Jerene's manner that she was eager to go on speaking to him. He acquiesced when she turned away from the others, implicitly creating a space in which they could converse discreetly about matters of consequence.

"Toller, I am sorry that I have shown a tendency to make little of you," she began hesitantly. "You always seemed to bluster so much . . . and there was that sword . . . You made it so obvious that you longed to emulate your grandfather that—the logic of it now escapes me—all who met you assumed your ambitions to be in vain.

"But for anyone to do what you have done . . . for you to have flown one of those antiquated wooden barrels through the black deeps of space to another world . . . for you simply to *be* here. . . .

"All I can say is that Vantara is the luckiest woman in all of history, and that you will have no need, *ever again*, to stand in the shadow of your grandfather. There can never be any doubt that you and he were peers."

Toller blinked to ease a sudden smarting in his eyes. "I value what you say, but all I did. . . ."

"Tell me something." Jerene switched to a tone of practicality rather sooner than Toller might have liked. "Have the monsters cast a spell over us? How is it that we can hear what they say, even when they are not in our presence, even when there is no sound? Is it magic?"

"There is no magic," Toller explained, again aware of the gulf which had opened between him and his kind. "It is the Dussarran way. They have progressed far beyond the need for shaping words with their mouths. They speak mind-to-mind, no matter how great the distance involved. Have these things not been explained to you?"

"Not a word. We are animals in a zoo as far as they are concerned."

"I suppose I received my education because the scarecrow I dealt with was buying time, preserving his life." Toller looked around the galleried dome with distaste. "When do the Dussarrans communicate with you?"

"There is one who seems to be known as the Director," Jerene replied. "He will speak to us for hours at a time—

always asking questions about our lives on Overland, about our families, about our food, farming methods, the differences between men's clothing and women's clothing . . . Nothing is too trivial for him.

"Then there is another one—possibly a female—who gives us our orders."

"What manner of orders?"

Jerene shrugged. "When to leave our cells and come down here to the main floor . . . that sort of thing. We stay here while the food and water is being replenished up there by one of the monsters."

"Does this so-called Director ever visit you in person? Do you ever get Dussarrans who seem to be important figures in their own society making close inspections?"

"It is difficult for us to tell. We sometimes see groups of the monsters behind that partition, but. . . ." Jerene indicated a glazed, box-like structure which enclosed one of the entrances to the dome, then she gave Toller a thoughtful look. "Why do you enquire of such things, Toller?"

He gave her a thin smile. "I have lost one perfectly good hostage—now I am in the market for another."

"But after what you have told us . . . It is impossible to escape from here."

"You are wrong on that point," Toller said quietly, his expression becoming sombre. "It is possible to escape from *any* stronghold . . . provided that one's heart is sufficiently set on it . . . provided that one is prepared to risk making the ultimate escape. . . ."

Toller and Steenameert were arguing about traditional and modern methods of constructing furniture, with emphasis on the design of chairs.

"Don't forget that we have had iron for only fifty years or so," Toller said. "The design of brackets and angle braces will improve; the design of woodscrews will improve."

"That is of little import," Steenameert countered. "Furniture should be regarded as a form of art. A chair should be regarded as a sculpture as much as a contrivance for supporting fat arses. Any artist will tell you that wood should only be mated to wood. Tenons and dovetails are *natural*, Toller, and not only are they much stronger than your wood-and-metal hybrids, they have a *rightness* which. . . ."

He continued speaking as Toller knelt and tested the gallery flooring with a heavy webbing-repair needle taken from his emergency pouch. Toller looked up at him and shook his head, signifying that the floor construction was too strong to be ripped upwards in a surprise raid on anybody who happened to be underneath. They were in the part of the first gallery directly above the enclosure where, according to Lieutenant Pertree, groups of Dussarrans sometimes gathered to observe their captives.

"Yes, but ever since the Migration only the rich have been able to employ the services of competent joiners," Toller said as he straightened up. "Surely it is better for the ordinary citizen and his family to have *something* to plank their arses on—and I doubt if many of the said arses are fat—than for them to squat on the floor."

Toller and Steenameert were openly talking about furniture design—a subject which evoked mental images of joints and frames—and at the same time were searching for weak points in the structure of their prison. They continued the contrived discussion as they made their way downstairs to the enclosure itself. They were novices, true primitives, in the darkly glimmering and bottomless world of telepathic communication, but they had gleaned enough from their encounter with Divivvidiv to believe that the aliens were fallible and could be deceived. It was likely that attempts were being made to eavesdrop on their innermost thought processes, but Kolcorronians were warriors by instinct and had a talent for misleading enemies.

"You can't deny that doors have been improved by the addition of iron hinges and fittings," Toller said as he reached the enclosure. In general it was surprisingly similar to what an artisan from Land or Overland would have built for the same purpose. It was a rectangular three-element structure with one edge attached to the wall on each side of an entrance to the dome. The three faces ran from the floor to the underside of the first gallery, and were glazed from waist-level upwards.

Still arguing about historical developments in his home world's carpentry, Toller casually leaned against a corner of the enclosure and felt it shift slightly. He stood head and shoulders above all the aliens he had seen, and furthermore was built in much bulkier proportions, from which facts he estimated that his body weight was at least three times that of the average Dussarran. His physical power could be factorised upwards again, because of differences in muscle density, making him a force that Divivvidiv and his kind were unaccustomed to dealing with. There was a good possibility that a structure which a Dussarran saw as a formidable barrier could be breached by a single charge from Toller and Steenameert.

The alien captors had many undeniable advantages over the handful of Kolcorronians, but—Toller hoped—they were too sure of themselves, too complacent. Their best thinkers seemed to be expending their energies on remote abstracts, such as the dissolution of galaxies, while dismissing more immediate threats from close at hand. They were like high kings preparing defences against global enemies, and all the while ignoring the body servant with the phial of poison or the smiling concubine with the slim dagger. . . .

"I concede the point about doors and door furniture, but that is a special case," Steenameert said, nodding significantly as he tested a panel with his foot. "Metal has a natural function there, but it will always be out of place when you come to chairs and tables."

"We shall see what we shall see," Toller replied as they continued their leisurely circuit of the dome.

They had been imprisoned for an indeterminate time, only a few hours, but already Toller's impatient and turbulent nature was rebelling against the monotony of confinement. A telepathic voice with indefinable female undertones had directed him and Steenameert to particular cells on the first gallery. Toller had inspected his briefly and then, being uncooperative on principle, had announced that he did not like it and was going to use another. As the cells were identical, and did not even have doors, there was no reason to prefer one above any other, but the reaction he had hoped to provoke did not occur.

He had lain for a while on the spongy oblong that was his bed, but had quickly become bored and had tried to visit Vantara in her cell. His hope had been that her attitude towards him would have improved once she had learned from Jerene that it had been impossible for him to have arrived at the head of an army of rescuers. She had, however, remained aloof and uncommunicative in her little enclave— her cell was flanked by those of the other women. Trying to be philosophical about it, Toller had decided that being informed she was a prisoner millions of miles from home— instead of only a few thousand—was good enough grounds for any woman to lapse into a spell of depression.

Becoming even more restless, he had explored every gallery of the dome. It was big enough to accommodate twenty times as many captives as at present, but none of the feature-less compartments showed any sign of previous occupation. Had the place been designed as a prison? Did the Dussarrans have such things as prisons? Or was the dome, with its sterile shadowless illumination, more the equivalent of a zoo? A birdcage?

The torrent of questions caused a stirring in Toller's memory. Just before he and Divivvidiv had parted company, possibly for ever, the little alien's mental presence seemed to have been disturbed by a dark emotion. Toller had intuitively recognised it as guilt—and in retrospect that identification appeared more and more accurate. At the time Toller had wondered if he and Steenameert were being led away to be slaughtered, but his suspicions had been ill founded—so what had been causing the turmoil in Divivvidiv's alien soul?

There was also the matter of the Xa—that fantastic sea of living crystal—and the reason for its presence in the weightless zone between Land and Overland. Now that Toller's consciousness had been saturated with exotic concepts, now that strangeness had in a way become the norm, he could accept the notion that the Xa's function was to hurl an entire world into the heart of a galaxy which was millions of light years distant.

When he had first encountered the proposition it had been remote from the realities of life on the sister planets. It had been a conceptual soap bubble; a gossamer palace constructed from pale-tinted abstracts—*but now everything was different!*

He and Vantara and some loyal companions were imprisoned on that ill-fated world, and . . . and. . . .

Toller's brow wrinkled as other pertinent memories began to flicker behind his eyes. During his first antagonistic meeting with Divivvidiv the alien had told him that the intergalactic leap was due to take place in about six days' time. Had it been *six* days? Yes, that memory held true . . . and the flight to Dussarra had taken roughly four days . . . and more precious time had slipped away during the long fall from the edge of space. . . .

Icy sweat prickled through Toller's skin as he realised that the time available to the small band of lost Kolcorronians could conveniently be reckoned in hours.

Or perhaps only minutes. . . .

Chapter 15

The sight of black-clad, corpse-faced figures assembling behind the metal-and-glass screen came like the answer to a prayer.

Toller froze in mid-stride—trying to control the tumult in his mind, trying to think and at the same time not to think. His realisation that the stupendous leap to a remote part of the universe had to take place in the very near future had filled him with pessimism. He needed a new hostage to give him even the faintest hope of escaping from Dussarra, but his off-hand way of mentioning the subject to Jerene had been a disguise for despair. His own society had faced its fair share of crises, and, although there were no real parallels, he could not imagine any official or scientific group on Overland deciding to visit a zoo at a comparable time.

And yet—in the aseptic and cheerless luminance of the dome—a few of the enemy were gathering, perhaps incautiously, perhaps making themselves vulnerable to a determined assault. The odds against a Kolcorronian success were vanishingly small, but the mere existence of odds—no matter how infinitesimal—was the only spur that Toller needed. . . .

He strode across the open floor to where Steenameert and two of the rankers—Mistekka and Arvand—were sitting cross-legged and engaged in discussion. The women looked up at him without moving, but Baten hurriedly got his feet as soon as he saw Toller's expression.

"Come on, Baten," Toller said in a low voice. "Keep your mind on whatever it was, but follow me—this may be our only chance." He looked down at the women. "Go at once and tell Vantara and Jerene to make ready to leave. We may have to move quickly."

He turned and walked towards the enclosure, which now held about ten Dussarrans, with Steenameert at his side. "We will take the right hand edge of the box . . . yes, the Kailian black grape does make the most distinctive wine . . . I think we can hit hardest coming from the right . . . but it contains too much acid for my taste. . . ."

Blanking all structured thought from his mind, surrendering himself to a crimson rage, Toller broke into a fast, loping run. The side of the enclosure expanded in his vision and he saw white-orbed, grey faces turning in his direction. He was moving at high speed now and could hear Steenameert snorting as he strove to keep pace. The metal-and-glass structure filled his view, and the voice of instinct was screaming at him to halt or risk terrible injury.

Snarling like an animal, Toller hit the enclosure with his shoulder and felt the edge of it tear free from the wall of the dome. Steenameert impacted with it at almost the same instant, having chosen to launch himself feet first at a lower panel. The side of the enclosure crumpled and was driven inwards, trapping several Dussarrans in the narrowing angle between it and the front wall. A huge pane of glass fell on Steenameert as he was scrambling to his feet, chilling Toller with images of brittle daggers, but the sheet remained intact and bounced harmlessly to the floor. Some of the Dussarrans were emitting thin mewing cries—the first sounds Toller had heard these aliens make with their mouths—as they backed away in obvious panic.

"Do not be in such haste about leaving," Toller shouted, his shoulder hard against the metal panel, keeping pressure on the trapped Dussarrans. "We have three of your number here and they may require medical attention."

He examined the haphazardly acquired captives. Two of them were still on their feet, held upright and immobile by the compressive force that he was exerting, their livid faces regarding him from a distance of inches. The third alien had dropped down to a crouching position inside the metal sandwich, possibly unconscious or dead. As Toller glared ferociously at the pair who were standing, he made no attempt to disguise the revulsion inspired in him by their noseless faces and tremulous, black-lipped mouths. They maintained a petrified silence, but Toller's head was filled with a confused telepathic yammering. It was a mental distillation of pure fear—an exhilarating reminder that the Dussarrans were not a warrior breed—and therefore Toller saw it as a favourable omen as far as the hopes of his compatriots were concerned.

"See if the women are ready to proceed," he called out to Steenameert. "In the meantime I will persuade the scarecrows to listen to reason."

Steenameert nodded and darted away to where the female astronauts—Vantara among them—were clustered at the foot of a stair. Toller returned his attention to the scene within the enclosure. The aliens, all of them identical to his gaze in their scrappy dark garments, were poised near the doorway which led out of the dome. Their soupy body odour pervaded the confined space.

"Which of you is the leader?" Toller demanded. "Which of you nightmares can speak for the others?"

The aliens made no response. Seconds dragged by in which they did nothing but stare at Toller with eyes which were like black-holed chips of white porcelain. Although no telepathic voices were ranging words in his mind, he had no doubt that silent alarms were being transmitted to other Dussarrans— a thought which prompted him to reinforce his words with action.

"I see that a little firmness is called for," he said giving the aliens the peaceful smile with which he often prefaced an act of violence. It was a trait he had inherited from his grandfather, he had been told, and he had half-consciously cultivated it since his youth. Without further warning he changed his stance and abruptly redoubled the force he was exerting on the wall panel. The aliens caught between it and the front of the enclosure gasped aloud, their ashen faces contorting with pain, and Toller was almost sure he heard the fracturing of a fragile bone.

Stop that, you savage! One of the group by the exit took a step forward. *There can be no excuse for such barbarism!*

"Perhaps not," Toller replied, giving a slight bow, "but if you and your loathsome kin had not abducted my friends and penned them like beasts—which is *your* kind of barbarism—you would never have been exposed to *my* kind of barbarism. Do you see the principle involved? Or is the concept of natural justice cherished only by untutored Primitives?"

Primitive is an appropriate word for you, Toller Maraquine, came the alien's voiceless reply. *Can you not understand that it is impossible for you to leave this world?*

"And can you not understand that I *will* leave this world —one way or another? And if it should transpire that death is my only escape, I will take some of your kind along the same road." Toller glanced to his left and saw that the rest of the humans had reached the enclosure. To his surprise, Vantara was at the rear of the group and was looking at him with uncertain, troubled eyes.

"We are with you, Toller," Steenameert called out.

"Excellent!" Toller returned his attention to the alien speaker. "You were elected spokesman, so I am going to assume that you possess some degree of some importance. You therefore will have the honour of being my principal hostage. Come to my side!"

What if I refuse?

"I have scarcely begun to squeeze these fine specimens of Dussarran manhood, and already their puny bones are beginning to crack." Toller's two upright captives moved their heads anxiously as he shifted his weight.

If you kill my deputies you will lose what little advantage you have at this moment.

"That would only be the start of the killing," Toller said, longing for the reassurance of his sword. He had judged the

Dussarrans to be lacking in physical courage, but to his growing unease the alien confronting him was proving to be unexpectedly stubborn. In appearance he was not distinguished from his fellows—the multiplex costume of pendant dark-hued scraps seemed to be universal among the aliens—but this individual conveyed the impression of being much more resolute than Divivvidiv.

Perhaps . . . An incredible idea began to flicker far back in Toller's consciousness. *Can it be that fortune has delivered into my hands the best hostage of all? Could this unremarkable and unprepossessing figure be the King of all the Dussarrans? What was the title Divivvidiv had accorded him? Director! And what name? Zunnunun!*

"Tell me, scarecrow," he said in a gentle voice, "what is your name?"

My name is of no relevance, the alien replied. *I shall make one last appeal to your powers of reason. Your plan—if such an insane vision can be dignified with that word—is to force us to send you back whence you came by way of an instantaneous relocation unit. You and your followers would then return to one of your home planets, either by balloon or parachute. Is that a fair summation of your ambitions?*

"I congratulate you, corpse-face!" The alien's refusal to divulge his name was a fresh inspiration and encouragement for Toller.

The plan can never succeed! The more rational members of your group have severe doubts about attempting it, and in that respect they display considerable wisdom.

Toller's eyes were again drawn to Vantara, but she lowered her head, refusing to meet his gaze.

I am not at liberty to go into details at this time, Toller Maraquine, the alien went on, *but the fact is that all of you are very fortunate to be here on Dussarra. You must believe what I. . . .*

"I believe that you are the King of all the Dussarrans," Toller shouted, giving way to a rage which was fuelled by subtle new fears. "This thing is going on far too long! Tell me your name right now, or—and I swear by my honour—I will crush these three until the blood spurts from their eyes!"

The alien figure brought a hand up to its concave chest. *My name is Zunnunun.*

"I thought so!" Toller glanced triumphantly at Vantara, Steenameert and the others. "I will now give. . . ."

You will do precisely nothing, Zunnunun cut in, silencing Toller with a curious ease. *I had planned to study the psychological relationship between you and your chosen female, but I have come to realise that in an unmodified state you will either kill yourself or continue to cause more trouble than you are worth. Accordingly, I have made the decision to bring your existence to an end.*

Toller shook his head and his voice was no longer human. "It would take more than you and the likes of you to kill me."

Oh, I have no intention of killing you. The Dussarran's psychic tone was now light, amused and confident. *Your body will remain in perfect health—and will be useful to me in breeding experiments—but it will be inhabited by a different and more docile personality.*

"You cannot do that!"

But I can! In fact, the process has already begun—as you will realise if you try to move. Zunnunun's mouth flowed into a ghastly parody of a smile. *You were right when you began to suspect that our confrontation was going on too long. I was then assembling sufficient of my people to form a telepathic lens. That lens is now focused on your brain, and in a few seconds you will cease to exist.*

Goodbye, Toller Maraquine!

Toller tried to hurl himself at the alien, but—as had been predicted—he found himself unable to move. And something was happening within his mind. There was an invasion, a loosening, a shameful but joyous sense of yielding, an acceptance of the fact that life as Toller Maraquine II had always been wearisome, and the time had come when he could—gladly—lay that burden down. . . .

Chapter 16

"Twelve ships! Is that all?" Daseene gave Cassyll Maraquine a reproving stare. "I was sure we could have done much better than that."

"I am sorry, Majesty, but the factory is hard-pressed even to prepare that number," Cassyll said, concealing his impatience over being required to repeat the same statements for the third time in an hour. "One of the major problems is the lack of reliable engines and parts."

"But I have seen hundreds of engines stacked in the old parade ground at Kandell. With my own eyes I have seen them. *Stacked*!"

"Yes, but they are the old-style brakka wood units, and they have been replaced by steel engines."

"Well, *un*-replace them in that case!" Daseene snapped, adjusting her coif of pearls.

"They won't fit into the new mountings." A veteran of many similar interviews with the Queen, Cassyll spoke in tones which were the embodiment of cool reasonableness. "It would take an excessive time to adapt one to the other, and many auxiliary components of the old engines are missing."

Daseene narrowed her eyes and leaned forward in her high-backed chair. "Sometimes, my dear Maraquine, you remind me of your father."

Cassyll smiled in spite of the oppressive heat in the audience room. "I appreciate the compliment, Majesty."

"It wasn't meant as a compliment, and well you know it," Daseene said. "Your father performed some small service for my husband during the Migration, and—"

"If I may jog your Majesty's memory to just the slightest

extent," Cassyll put in drily, "he saved the lives of your entire family."

"I'm not sure if it was as dramatic as all that—but, no matter . . . He made himself useful on *one* occasion, and then proceeded to spend the rest of his life reminding my husband of the incident and demanding royal favours."

"I am honoured to serve your Majesty at all times," Cassyll said, easily negotiating familiar territory, "and would never dream of asking for indulgence in return."

"No, you have no need—you simply go ahead and arrange everything to suit yourself—and that is precisely my point! Your father had a way of pretending to do what the King wanted and all the time he was doing what *he* wanted. You have exactly the same way with you, Cassyll Maraquine. Sometimes I suspect that it is you, and not I, who rules this. . . ."

Daseene leaned forward again, her rheumy eyes intent. "You do not look at all well, my dear fellow. Your face is quite crimson and your brow glistens with sweat. Are you suffering from an ague?"

"No, Majesty."

"Well, *something* ails you. You do not look well. It is my opinion that you should consult your physician."

"I shall do so without delay," Cassyll said. He was yearning for the moment he could escape the intolerable heat of the room, but he had not yet achieved the purpose of his visit. Contrary to what Daseene had just said, he was not the complete master of his own affairs. He gazed into her fragile face, wondering if she was playing games with him. Perhaps she knew perfectly well that he was being tortured by the excessive warmth, and was waiting for him either to faint or give in and plead for respite.

"Why are you occupying so much of my time anyway?" she said. "You must want something."

"As it so happens, Majesty, there is one—"

"Hah!"

"It is quite a routine matter . . . well within my normal areas of jurisdiction . . . but I thought, more or less in passing, that I should mention it to your Majesty . . . not that there is any. . . ."

"Out with it, Maraquine!" Daseene glanced at the ceiling in exasperation. "What are you up to?"

Cassyll swallowed, trying to relieve the dryness in his throat. "The barrier which has appeared between Land and Overland is a matter of great scientific interest. I and Bartan Drumme have the privilege of serving as your Majesty's principal scientific advisers, and—after sober consideration of all the facts—we feel that we should accompany the fleet which is to—"

"Never!" Suddenly Daseene's face was an alabaster mask upon which a skilled artist had painted a likeness of the woman who used to be. "You will stay where I need you, Maraquine—right here on the ground! The same goes for your bosom friend, the eternal stripling, Bartan Drumme. Do I make myself clear?"

"Very clear, Majesty."

"I am well aware that you are concerned for your son— just as I fear for the safety of my granddaughter—but there are times when one must turn a deaf ear to all appeals from the heart," Daseene said in a voice which surprised Cassyll with its vigour.

"I understand, Majesty." Cassyll bowed, and was turning to leave when Daseene halted him by raising one hand.

"And before you depart," she said, "let me remind you of what I said earlier—be sure to see a doctor."

Chapter 17

The startled cry from Steenameert reached Toller across dark distances of the soul, shadowy distances, where unseen worlds prowled their orbital paths. Each world was the embodiment of a new personality, one of which was destined to be his, and he had little concern for the trivialities of his old existence. Aloof and vaguely irritated, he asked himself why the young man was calling his name. What in all the black reaches of the cosmos could be important enough to justify distracting him at a time like this, just when momentous decisions were being made about his destiny?

But something else was happening! A battle was beginning in the stygian landscapes which surrounded him. Powerful external forces were being brought to bear on the psychic lens whose curvatures governed every aspect of his future. . . .

The lens shattered! Released from his mental and physical paralysis, Toller was reborn into a world of tumult. Dozens of black-clad and ragged-edged Dussarran figures were running across the floor of the dome towards the enclosure. A woman was screaming. The aliens Toller had been crushing behind the panel were now free and were staggering towards their leader. Other aliens who had been clustered behind Zunnunun were fleeing through the exit to unknown parts of the building.

Come with us! A Dussarran appeared at Toller's side and tugged his arm. *We are your friends!*

Toller shook himself free of the grey-fingered hand. The alien seemed no different from any of those he had already encountered, except that the ubiquitous piecemeal costume dangling around his spindly form featured a few diamond-shapes of drab green.

"Friends?" Toller made as if to thrust the newcomer away, then—accepting urgent telepathic guidance—realised the alien was one of a group which had recalled him to his own existence with no time to spare. The choice was not a difficult one in any case—stay and face the quietly invincible Director Zunnunun, or seize the unexpected offer of salvation.

"Baten!" Toller saw that Steenameert was staring at him with concern. "We have to trust these people!"

Steenameert nodded, as did some of the women behind him. The entire group of humans began to run in the company of their alien rescuers, but their escape route was being blocked by other Dussarrans who were spilling through the dome's multiple entrances. The opposing forces converged and the scene quickly became chaotic as black-clad bodies locked with each other in all the grotesqueries of spontaneous physical combat.

Toller's perception of the scene underwent rapid shifts as he saw that the Dussarrans' idea of hand-to-hand struggle was to throw themselves at each other, lock arms and legs with opponents and bring them to the ground. Once that had happened they lay in ineffectual pairs, like copulating insects, each cancelling the other's contribution to the battle. The advantage from the humans' point of view was that no weapons were being used—the aliens fought like angry children, and although hostile enough were manifestly lacking in the ability to incapacitate an enemy. Toller was comforted when he realised that he and his new allies would not be annihilated in a few bloody seconds; but then the negative aspect of the situation came to him. The struggle was too democratic, too much like casting votes. In this style of combat the numerically superior force was bound to win.

Again longing for his sword, Toller turned on one of the group of unfriendly aliens who were closing on him with arms outspread. Toller clubbed him to the ground with one diagonal blow of his fist, and then—with murder in his heart

—drove his heel down on the alien's neck, while at the same time hurling away two more attackers.

The feeling of living firmness crunching into inert mush told him immediately that the Dussarran was dead, but a more dramatic confirmation came from the surrounding mêlée. The mass of black-ragged aliens—friend and foe alike—underwent a convulsive spasm as though some powerful unseen force had torn through them. Their various pairings were dissolved and the air was filled with wordless keenings of anguish. All at once Toller and the other humans were the only mobile and concerted force on the bizarre battle ground.

"What happened?" Jerene shouted, her round face and clear eyes beaconing at Toller from the confusion.

"The scarecrows all suffer when one of their number dies near at hand," Toller replied, remembering what Divivvidiv had told him about the strange telepathic backlash which accompanied the death of a Dussarran. "The trouble is that those who are favourably disposed to us are not spared. Get them on their feet and keep them moving—otherwise we are lost."

The other six Kolcorronians responded at once, snatching suitably emblazoned aliens to their feet and urging them to run. They had to be dragged or pushed for some yards before their limbs began to pick up the motive rhythms. The ill-sorted band passed through an archway, entered a corridor and continued their awkward progress towards double-leafed doors at its far end. Other Dussarrans, shown to be friendly by their green-dappled clothing, were waiting at the door and making urgent beckoning signals.

My name is Greturk. The alien that Toller was propelling forwards looked up at him and his silent words were charged with fear and loathing. *You deliberately ended a life! You behaved like a Vadavak! Have you no feelings?*

"Yes—I have a powerful feeling that I want to get out of this place."

211

That is not what I meant.

"I know! You were talking about the reflux." Toller pushed the alien harder to emphasise his words. "You had better understand that I would quite happily break a *thousand* Dussarran necks to obtain my goal—so prepare yourself for a few more refluxes if we are attacked again."

The chances of a new attack grew less, however, as the group reached the double door and were ushered through it by urgent hands. Livid alien faces danced around Toller, advancing and receding in the confusion, as he escaped from the confines of the corridor into a night which was shot through with artificial light. In part the light came from the façades of rectangular buildings, but there seemed to be free-floating blocks of radiance and a profusion of vari-coloured rays among which drifted vivid lines of intense red and yellow.

Toller had no time to fathom the exotic scene, because an egg-shaped vehicle—a larger version of the one which had earlier transported Steenameert and him to the dome—was waiting only a few paces away. He had the impression that its lower surface was not quite touching the ground. Its circular entrance revealed a dim-lit interior from which other Dussarrans beckoned. Toller halted by the entrance and helped cram his own people plus some of their alien rescuers into the vehicle. At the innermost end of the corridor more aliens were appearing, their mobility almost fully restored, and were running towards him like flapping black birds striving to take to the air.

Toller had no fear of pursuers who could be laid low by the death of only one of their number, but he was hounded by a conviction that Zunnunun was too resourceful to remain off balance for long, that other enemy forces were being ranged against him at that very moment. He threw himself into the oval vehicle, adding to the press of bodies inside, and the entrance flowed out of existence behind him. There came a giddy shifting of weight which signalled that the vehicle was moving and silently becoming airborne. It came to him that he had not seen a pilot or anything like a station from which a pilot could operate, and the eerie thought occurred that the Dussarran craft could control its own movements.

He was straining to see about him, trying to verify the idea, when he realised that Vantara was quite close by in the airless compression of alien and human forms. Her face was pale, distraught and immobile—rather like a tragic mask of the real woman—and, although her eyes were turned in his direction, he was not sure that she was looking at him. Feeling oddly self-conscious, he tried to produce a reassuring smile.

"Take heart, Vantara," he said in a directed whisper, "I vow to you that no matter what befalls us I will be at your side."

There followed an odd and timeless moment in which her gaze hunted over his face, and then—to Toller it was like a perfect sunrise—she answered his smile. "Toller, my dear Toller! I'm sorry if I have not been—"

Do not speak! Greturk, the alien at Toller's side, cut in with an urgent telepathic warning. *Do not think about what is happening—otherwise we will be easily followed. Try to forget who and what you are. Try to believe that you are nothing more than bubbles of air rising in a huge cauldron of boiling water . . . going this way and that way . . . swirling and spiralling in unpredictable paths. . . .*

Toller nodded and closed his eyes. He was a bubble rising in a huge cauldron . . . going this way and that . . . following a dangerous and unpredictable path. . . .

Toller had become so deeply absorbed in the mental discipline, the negation of coherent thought, that he was scarcely aware of the vehicle coming to a halt. At one moment he was jammed upright, barely able to move because of the pressure of human and alien bodies; and at the next he was staggering slightly in a comparatively generous amount of floor space and Dussarrans were vanishing through the circular exit which had appeared in the vehicle's side. He was receiving no structured telepathic communications, but his head was filled with a pulsing urgency. The very air seemed tremulous, agitated by a pervasive sense of panic.

You must disembark quickly. The silent message came from Greturk, the only alien to have remained inside the egg-shaped craft. *There is very little time to spare.*

"What is going on here?" Jerene put in before Toller could voice the same question.

Greturk's black lips twitched. *We are in the midst of a civil conflict—a war you might call it—the first in many thousands of years.*

"A civil war!" Toller said. "In that case why are you so concerned about a few outsiders like us?"

This will come as a surprise—but you and the rest of your kind are at the centre of the controversy which divides Dussarran society.

Toller blinked down at the alien. "I don't understand."

I know that the Decisioner responsible for the Xa project has explained to you the basic reasons for our presence in this part of the galaxy. How much of that information have you retained?

"There was something about Ropes," Toller replied, frowning. "An explosion which will destroy dozens of galaxies. . . ."

Steenameert cleared his throat and moved closer. "We were told that the crystal sea . . . the Xa . . . is a machine which will hurl your home world into a distant galaxy, where you will be safe from the explosion."

I am quite impressed, Greturk answered, glancing from Toller to Steenameert while at the same time gesturing towards the vehicle's exit. *It is unusual for a species at your early stage of development to be able to accommodate concepts which are so far from primitive myth-based visions of. . . .*

"We have no relish for being styled as Primitives," Toller growled. "Divivvidiv learned that to his cost."

Perhaps that is why he withheld a piece of information which he knew would provoke an extreme reaction from you.

"Out with it!" Toller scowled into the alien's livid face. "Out with it at once, or I may be. . . ."

There is no need to bluster against me, Toller Maraquine, Greturk replied. *I was opposed to the Xa project from the day of its inception. I am not culpable in any way, and therefore have no compunction about informing you that on the instant in which Dussarra is projected into the target galaxy your home world . . . and its neighbour . . . will cease to exist.*

Chapter 18

In common with the rest of his companions, Toller was so stunned by Greturk's words that—in spite of the alien's diminutive stature—he meekly allowed himself to be pushed and prodded out of the vehicle. The darkness outside was as copiously shot through with glowing colour as before, and in addition there were curved, tapering columns at the focus of which hovered a sheet of green luminance. Paying little heed to his surroundings, Toller brought Greturk to a halt by grasping his shoulders, and the rest of the humans crowded around him.

"What was that?" he demanded, using the form of words through force of habit—the telepathic communication had been perfectly clear, each word loaded with associated and corroborative layers of meaning. The Kolcorronians knew that a death sentence had been passed on their home worlds, but their minds were unable to accept the concept.

Greturk vainly tried to squirm free of Toller's grip. *It is vital that we should keep moving.*

"It is even more vital that you explain yourself," Toller countered, refusing to leave the spot. "Why is Overland to be destroyed?"

Greturk's black-drilled eyes swept around the group, and Toller knew at once that all of them were about to be subjected to that disconcerting form of telepathy in which many facts were implanted in the mind forcibly and simultaneously. As had been the case with Divivvidiv, he felt a cerebral beam of lighthouse intensity begin to slew across his consciousness. . . .

As the sister worlds rotate about their common centre of gravity the disk-shaped instrument known as the Xa turns with them. Twice in the course of each revolution the Xa's axis points directly at the Dussarran home world—once when it is projected through Land, once when it is projected through Overland. It is at one of these instants of perfect alignment that the Xa will be activated, making Dussarra the focus of supra-geometrical energies which will cause the planet to be relocated in the target galaxy. In that same instant Land and Overland will cease to exist in this continuum. Because Overland is the less massive of the pair, the relocation pulse will be directed through it during the forthcoming alignment. That alignment is due to occur less than ten minutes from now. If we are to prevent the relocation taking place—and thus save your home worlds from annihilation—we must proceed with all possible speed. The Director is almost certain to unleash the Vadavaks upon us. RELEASE ME AT ONCE —AND FOLLOW ME CLOSELY!

The moment of communion ended and Toller found himself—totally convinced that what he had learned was true— running behind the little alien. They were heading towards the circle of inward-leaning columns whose tips were immersed in greenish fire. Vantara was holding Toller's left hand and Steenameert was running by his right, in step with Jerene. The three female rankers—Tradlo, Mistekka and Arvand—were keeping pace, and it was obvious from the grimly urgent set of their faces that they had absorbed Greturk's message to the full. It was impossible to see far into the ambient darkness because of the profusion of glowing blocks and criss-crossing lines of radiance, but Toller was somehow persuaded that silent battles were taking place over a wide area. Hundreds, perhaps thousands, of black-clad Dussarrans were locked together in their strange form of hand-to-hand combat, clogging and coagulating, each individual content to do no more than immobilise one of his counterparts on the enemy side.

"Why are you doing this?" Toller shouted at Greturk's back, giving voice to the queries which had been accumulating in sheltered bywaters of his mind ever since the escape from the dome. "What is it to you if others perish?"

Again the swinging beam of mental radiance . . . but faster this time . . . a flaring whiplash of knowledge. . . .

Dussarran society has long been divided over the issue of relocating the planet. Despite various pronouncements from the Palace of Numbers about Ropes, many citizens have always doubted that they exist in actuality. We believe that other interpretations of the sub-space probe data could be just as valid. In any case, it is our opinion that intergalactic relocation is an intemperate response to the situation. We had, however, failed to bring Director Zunnunun round to our point of view, or to rally a majority of the public behind us.

The relocation seemed destined to take place without any concrete opposition—and then came the rumours that one of the sacrificial worlds was inhabited by a humanoid species. It was in an attempt to prevent the spread of that knowledge that Director Zunnunun insisted on the Xa station being designed in such a way that it could be governed by a single Decisioner.

His plan could well have succeeded had it not been for one unforeseen development. The Xa, of necessity, had to have some degree of consciousness to enable it to control its own growth, but the technologists had never before produced such an instrument on that scale. They were taken by surprise when, on reaching a certain level of complexity, the Xa developed self-awareness—a personality—and began to fear its own dissolution. It was during imperfectly screened exchanges between the Xa and Decisioner Divivvidiv that adepts here on Dussarra established beyond doubt that a burgeoning civilisation would be annihilated as a result of the relocation —and that was sufficient to unite and mobilise the opposition parties.

The telepathic communication, as well as lodging a store of hard facts like pebbles in the forefront of Toller's mind, was luridly stained with anxiety and urgency. There was a despairing sense of time slipping away too quickly, of great invisible doors of opportunity being slammed in his face. Toller tried to run faster to draw abreast of Greturk, but the alien was fleet of foot and easily kept ahead. They were now only forty or so paces from the tapering columns, and Toller saw that other green-dappled aliens were waiting at the centre of the circle. There were at least six of them, some beckoning to the runners, others struggling to move a white box which was about the size of a small desk.

"Why are we running?" Corporal Tradlo called out from close behind Toller, her words punctuated with gasps. "What is to be gained by . . . wearing ourselves out . . . if nought can be achieved?"

Good question, Toller thought. It had just occurred to him that there was little point in escaping by means of the alien matter transmitter to a world which was about to be obliterated.

There is much that can be done, came Greturk's reply. *The problem lies in doing it quickly enough.*

"What can be done?" The question came from several of the humans simultaneously.

The white object you see being dragged on to the transfer plate by my brothers is a simplified version of the machine which was used to transport this world to its present location. The plan is to take it to Overland and use it to displace the planet by a short distance. A few tens of miles would be sufficient to destabilise the Xa and start its axis wandering. Under those conditions the relocation of Dussarra could not be attempted.

Toller stumbled to a halt at the edge of the green-lit circle, his gaze fixed on the white box. "How could *that* move an entire planet?" he said in tones of wonder. "It is much too small."

Even in a moment of crushing urgency there was a note of ironic amusement in Greturk's reply. *How large must a fulcrum be, Toller Maraquine?*

Before Toller could speak further there came a vast humming sound from directly above and curved rows of lights appeared far up in the gaudy darkness. The lights were in fixed positions with regard to each other, giving the impression they belonged to a huge skyship which was taking up its station overhead. The oppressive humming rose and fell at an increasing tempo, creating a sonic bludgeoning effect which numbed mind and body.

Run to the centre of the plate! Greturk fussed and fluttered like a protective bird around the group of humans, goading them into motion. *We have no more time!*

Still holding Vantara's hand, Toller moved on to a circular area of coppery metal some ten paces in diameter. Steenameert and the three rankers crowded on to the disk with him, and the group coalesced with the knot of aliens who were gathered around the white box. . . .

And suddenly—without any physical sensation—the interplanetary leap took place.

The sights of the garish, light-fractured night of the Dussarran home planet vanished on the instant, and a mellow darkness closed in around the travellers. *This is impossible*, Toller thought, momentarily paralysed with wonder, only then realising that, although he had been forced to accept the idea of teleportation intellectually, in his heart there had lurked a conviction that it could not be done. There had not been so much as a twinge or a tingle anywhere in his body to inform him that he was being transported across millions of miles of space, and yet . . . A single glance at the richly emblazoned age-old sky of the sister planets told Toller that he was standing in the peaceful grasslands of his home world.

Having grown up on Overland and spent his adult life navigating across its surface, Toller had the almost instinctive ability to use the companion world as a clock and compass. His brief look at Land, which was almost perfectly centred in the dome of the sky, established that he was on Overland's equator and possibly as little as fifty miles east of the capital city of Prad. The fact that the great disk of Land was divided just about evenly into night and day sides showed that dawn would soon break—which confirmed what Greturk had said about the timing of the Dussarran relocation.

When he returned his attention to earthly matters he saw by the half-light that several of the aliens were kneeling by the white box. They had opened a small door in its side and one of them was making rapid adjustments to something in the interior. A moment later that alien slammed the door shut and sprang to his feet.

The impeller is now alive and will activate itself in four minutes! He spread his arms and made violent scooping movements with his hands, a signal which—even without telepathic aid—the humans readily understood. *Withdraw to the safety line!*

There was a general movement away from the machine. Toller felt slim hands urging him to hurry, and it came to him that these Dussarrans—in spite of their nightmarish appearance—were altruists of the highest order. They had gone to great lengths and exposed themselves to unguessable dangers with no motivation other than the desire to preserve the existence of a totally unknown culture. Toller was reasonably certain that he would not have behaved as well in parallel circumstances, and all at once he felt a rush of mingled emotions—respect and affection—towards the Dussarrans. He ran with the others, losing contact with Vantara on the way, and slowed to a halt when they did, some sixty yards away from the enigmatic white rectangle.

"Is this far enough?" he said to Greturk, trying to visualise the unleashing of forces of sufficient magnitude to disturb a world lumbering through space and time, massively complacent in its shadowy orbit.

This is a safe distance, Greturk replied. *Had the impeller not been built illegally, and in great haste, it could have been shielded in such a way that there would have been no need to move away from it. Ideally, it would also have been con-*

221

structed with widespread anchor points, in such a way that it could not be overturned. Director Zunnunun, by advancing the time of relocation, has forced us to fall back on exigency plans.

Toller frowned, his mind still overwhelmed by partially absorbed ideas and concepts. "What would happen to a man who was too close to the impeller when it . . . when it did what is required of it?"

There would be a conflict of geometries. Greturk's eyes swam like twin moons in the grey twilight. *The constituent atoms of the man's body would be sliced into a billion times a billion layers. . . ."*

"I was told my grandfather died in such a manner," Toller said in a low voice. "It must have been instantaneous . . . and painless . . . but I don't think I want to emulate him to that extent."

We are safe while we stay at this distance from the machine, Greturk replied, looking all about him. *Safe from the effects of the machine, anyway.*

"How much time remains until the Xa is triggered?"

Greturk did not consult any kind of chronometer, but his response was immediate. *Almost seven minutes.*

"And only about three minutes remain until that thing . . . the impeller . . . does its work." Toller took a deep breath of satisfaction and glanced at the other humans. "It seems to me that we are quite safe. What do you say, my fellow Kolcorronians? Shall we prepare to celebrate our deliverance?"

"I'm ready for a few beakers of good Kailian black when you are," Steenameert cried out heartily, and the other humans—watched by silent aliens—cheered and waved their arms in agreement.

Toller was gratified beyond measure when Vantara moved through the gloaming to his side and put her hand in his. Seen in the nascent light of pre-dawn, her face was impossibly beautiful, and suddenly he felt that his entire life had been nothing more than a prelude to this moment of supreme justification. He had been faced with a challenge worthy of the real Toller Maraquine, he had met every demand made of him without flinching, and now a time of reward lay ahead. . . .

"I have been so busy congratulating myself on my good fortune that I have given little thought to you and all your companions, to whom we owe so much," he said to Greturk. "Can you return safely to Dussarra?"

Returning home poses some problems for the present, but I have more serious worries at this time. Greturk continued to scan his surroundings as though every dimly-seen tuft of grass might conceal a deadly enemy. *My principal fear is that Director Zunnunun will have set the Vadavaks upon us. We have, of course, done what we could to make pursuit difficult, but Zunnunun's resources are far greater than ours. . . .*

"What are these Vadavaks?" Toller said. "Are they ferocious hunting beasts which cannot be eluded?"

No. Greturk's thoughts were shaded with something akin to embarrassment. *They are Dussarrans who were born with a major defect in the areas of their brains which are concerned with perception and communication. They are incapable of direct communication with other Dussarrans. We regard the condition in much the same way as you regard deafness.*

"But why should they be feared?"

They do not experience the reflux. They are capable of killing.

"You mean," Toller said, suddenly understanding Greturk's embarrassment, "they are something like me?"

To the ordinary Dussarran the taking of a life is the ultimate abhorrence.

"That may be less due to ethics than dread of the backlash." Toller knew he was in danger of offending the alien who had done so much for the group of fugitives, but he was unable to hold back his words. "After all, you noble Dussarrans were quite prepared to annihilate the entire population of my home world. Did that not offend your delicate sensibilities? Is killing all right as long as it is done at a remove?"

Many of us have put our own lives at risk to preserve your people, Greturk countered. *We make no claim to be perfect, but. . . .*

"I apologise for my ingratitude and shoddy manners," Toller cut in. "Look, if you are so worried about these Vadavaks appearing out of nowhere, can you not adjust the impeller's controls and cause it to act sooner? Four minutes seems an irksome length of time to wait."

We chose four minutes to allow for variables such as having to withdraw across difficult terrain. Now that the machine has been activated, its internal processes cannot be advanced or retarded. Neither can it be switched off and returned to an inert condition.

Steenameert, who had been paying close attention to the dialogue, raised a hand. "If the machine is immune to interference . . . if it cannot be switched off . . . are we not already in an inviolable position? Is it not too late for the enemy to try to thwart us?"

Given sufficient time we could *have rendered the impeller virtually immune to interference.* Greturk's eyes flickered closed for a moment. *As it is, it could be neutralised merely by turning it on its side. . . .*

"What?" Steenameert shot Toller a perplexed glance. "Is that all it would take to stop it working?"

Greturk shook his head in a surprisingly human manner. *The impeller would not be affected internally in any way, but unless it is in a horizontal attitude—with its line of action passing through or close to the centre of the planet—its motive energies will be squandered.*

"I—" Toller broke off as the faintest breath of coolness entered his mind, a feather-flick of unease so tiny and fleeting that it could have been a product of his imagination. He raised his head, separating himself from the discussion, and took stock of his surroundings. Nothing seemed to have changed. The grassy plain reached out to a horizon which was made irregular by low hills to the north; a short distance away the white casing of the impeller glowed placidly through the pewter-coloured light of early dawn; the incongruous group of Dussarrans and humans looked exactly as before —and yet Toller was vaguely alarmed.

On impulse he glanced up at the sky and there, centred on Land and almost touching the terminator on the planet's dark side, was a pulsing yellow star. He knew at once that he was looking at the Xa, thousands of miles above.

No sooner had he made the identification than a faint telepathic voice reached him—strained, enfeebled, tortured —wisping downwards from the zenith. *Why are you doing this to me, Beloved Creator? Please, please do not kill me.*

Feeling oddly like an intruder, Toller spoke quietly to Greturk. "The Xa is . . . unhappy."

It was fortunate for all of us that the Xa's increasing complexity allowed it to. . . . Greturk suddenly flinched, as if experiencing a spasm of pain, and spun to face the east. The other Dussarrans did likewise. Toller followed their concerted gazes and his heart lurched as he saw that the previously bare plain was now the setting for a party of about fifty figures clad in white. They were perhaps two furlongs distant, and above them was a fast-fading ellipse of greenish illumination.

The Vadavaks are upon us! Greturk took one futile step backwards. *And so close!*

Toller glared down at Greturk. "Are they armed?"

Armed?

"Yes! *Armed!* Do they carry weapons?"

Greturk had begun to shiver, but his telepathic response was clear and well controlled. *The Vadavaks are equipped with enervators—instruments of social correction specially designed by Director Zunnunun. The enervators are black rods with glowing red tips. The slightest contact with one of the*

225

tips will cause intense pain and paralysis for several minutes.

"I have heard of more fearsome weapons," Toller sneered, squeezing Vantara's hand before releasing it and putting an encouraging arm around Steenameert's shoulder. "What do you say, Baten? Shall we teach these bumptious pygmies a lesson or two?"

Contact with one enervator rod causes pain and paralysis, Greturk added. *The Vadavaks carry an enervator in each hand—and simultaneous contact with two rods causes pain and death.*

"That is a more serious matter," Toller said soberly, staring at the blurred smear of white on a drab grey-green background which was the enemy's sole manifestation thus far. "How long does it take for death to occur?"

Five seconds. Perhaps ten. Much depends on the size and strength of the individual.

"Much could be achieved in ten seconds," Toller replied, a dryness developing in his mouth as he saw that the Vadavaks had already begun to advance at speed. "If only. . . ."

Your sword is in the possession of Director Zunnunun and can never be retrieved—but one of our number holoviewed it well enough for copying. Greturk nodded to one of the other Dussarrans who moved forward dragging a sack made of a seamless grey material. *We had hoped that the Vadavaks would not make contact with us—in which case we would have destroyed these weapons without ever showing them to you—but now we have no alternative.*

The Dussarran opened the sack and Toller felt a surge of fierce gladness as he saw that it contained seven swords of the distinctive late Kolcorronian pattern. He dropped to his knees and eagerly reached for the familiar weapons.

Be careful! Greturk warned. *In particular, do not touch the blades with your bare hands—they now have monomolecular edges which can never be blunted, and they will penetrate your flesh as easily as they would sink into fresh snow.*

"Swords!" Jerene's rounded features bore an angry expression as she stepped forward. "What do we want with a collection of antiques? Could you not have copied our pistols?"

Greturk shook his head again. *There was no time . . . their interior mechanisms were not readily visible to us . . . all we could do in the limited time available was to produce five scaled-down versions of the sword for use by the smaller and weaker females of your race.*

"That was most considerate of you," Jerene exclaimed sarcastically, "but you may be interested to learn that any woman here could. . . ."

"The enemy has taken to the field!" Toller put all the power of his lungs into the shout. "Are we to squabble among ourselves or go out and do battle?"

He pointed to where the gleaming white motes which represented the Vadavaks were spreading across the field of view, becoming larger collectively and individually, each advancing speck developing arms and legs, a face, the capability of inflicting death. On the horizon behind the Vadavaks the sun was appearing as a needle-spray of blinding fire, casting a fateful and melodramatic glow over the natural arena in which the fates of three worlds were to be decided.

Toller took the sword of his fancy from the sack and tried it in his hand to make sure that the balance had not been disturbed by alien machinations. The feel of the familiar weapon was comforting—the spirit of his grandfather was with him again—but it was less reassuring than he had hoped and expected. Seven humans, only one of whom was trained with the sword, were going against at least fifty well-armed aliens. By all accounts, his fabled namesake would have gloried in such a situation—but, no matter how many versions of the forthcoming battle the present-day Toller conjured up in his mind, he could not find one in which there were no deaths among his companions. Some of them, if not all, were bound to die—and Toller could see no glory in that fact. It was degrading, brutal, depressing, obscene, terrifying. . . .

But, even as the adjectives paraded through his mind, he was forced to acknowledge another diamond-hard fact. Unless the Dussarran machine was successfully defended for another three to four minutes, until it performed its vital task, every man, woman and child on Overland would be annihilated in an unimaginable pulse of energy. *That*—above all else—had to be the single truth which governed his actions in the trial which lay ahead.

He looked around his little group of warriors, wondering if his face was as pale as theirs. They had taken their swords in hand and were gazing at him with expressions which seemed to convey complete faith in his leadership. Their trust was probably a legacy from all those times when he had swaggered and boasted of his prowess in combat—and now he was appalled by the responsibility he had taken upon himself. These people knew they were facing death, and they were afraid, and in the moment of ultimate tribulation they were turning to the only source of hope they could find. It was quite likely that they now regarded Toller as a pillar of strength, and he was numbed with guilt and regret as he realised the extent of his unworthiness to play that role.

"If we advance too far to meet the enemy they will be able to outflank us and overturn the machine," he heard himself say in a firm, clear voice. "We must form a defensive line outside the radius of safety—and take a solemn vow that *none* of the Vadavaks shall pass.

"There are many more things I would like to say—" Toller's eyes locked fleetingly with Vantara's and he repressed an urge to reach out and touch her face—"but now is not the time. We have important work to do first."

Toller turned and ran on a curving path to a point which placed him exactly between the impeller and the oncoming force of Vadavaks. Within a few seconds the other humans had taken up stations on either side of him, at spacings which they instinctively felt could be protected by the sword. The Vadavaks were now only a hundred yards or so away, running fast, and the sound of their feet swishing through the grass could easily be heard by the defenders. Pinpoints of red light danced before them in a horizontal swarm.

Toller tightened his grip on his sword as he saw that the Vadavaks, in place of the rag-like garments of the ordinary Dussarran citizen, wore white helmets and armour. The latter was of a glistening material which seemed to have no effect on the wearer's mobility in spite of covering torso and limbs. The livid, black-holed faces glaring from under the rims of the alien helmets gave the attackers the semblance of an army of corpses, indefatigable because they were already dead.

Toller raised his sword to the first readiness position and waited. *I beg of you, Beloved Creator*, the Xa's words threaded down from the remoteness of the sky, *do not kill me.*

One of the Vadavaks outdistanced the others, nominating himself as Toller's first individual opponent, and dived forward with twin black rods outstretched like stings. The alien must have been totally accustomed to routing docile and unarmed civilians, because he came at Toller with head and torso quite unprotected. Toller struck down into his thin neck and the alien went down and backwards in a fountain of blood, his head connected to his body by only a narrow strip of tissue. The rods he had been holding fell close beside each other at Toller's feet.

Toller stamped on them, extinguishing the crimson glow at their tips, and his momentum took him into immediate conflict with two more Vadavaks. The pair apparently had not enough time to learn anything from the fate of their companion, because they remained close together and lunged at Toller with enervator rods held only a few inches apart. He took their arms off below the elbows with two transverse strokes which sheared the white armour as if it were paper.

The aliens dropped to their knees, their mouths black circles of silent agony, and doubled over the stumps of their forearms.

Toller paid them no further attention—they had ceased to be combatants—and ran his gaze along the line of battle. The Vadavaks were throwing themselves into the fray with undiminished vigour and ferocity, but Toller was heartened to notice that not one Kolcorronian had been laid low. Their lack of experience in handling swords was being more than compensated for by the incredible sharpness of the blades, and the Vadavaks were being cut down as quickly as they advanced. The defence line had lost its regularity, but it was remaining intact, and the white wave of alien attackers was now liberally stained with red as its members collided with and stumbled over their wounded.

Can it be possible? Toller wondered. *Are we all to be spared, after all? There can be very little time left before the impeller does its work, and if the Vadavaks are stupid enough not to change their tactics. . . .*

From the corner of his eye Toller saw a flicker of white as an alien appeared beyond one end of the battle line and ran towards the rectangular shape of the impeller. Toller broke free and ran on a course which enabled him to intercept the Vadavak about halfway across the margin of safety. The alien slid to a halt in the grass and turned on Toller, the milky marbles of his eyes gleaming beneath the rim of his helmet. He was holding one of his enervator rods as though it were a sword, darting and slicing with the glowing tip, striving to make contact with the skin of Toller's sword arm.

Toller dealt with him by making a sideways flick of his blade which lopped the end off the menacing rod. The alien threw it down, transferred his remaining rod into his right hand and resumed the duel, apparently quite unafraid. Toller —acutely aware that he was within the impeller's radius of death—decided to end the matter speedily in a rain of unstoppable blows. He was on the point of lunging forward when he heard a sound close behind him. He spun around just in time to see a second Vadavak thrusting an enervator rod into his midriff. Toller did his utmost to twist clear of the spitefully gleaming tip, but it made contact with him and pain fountained up through his chest. He fell to his knees, gasping for breath, and his two opponents—now moving at a much more leisurely pace, apparently relishing their moment of victory—closed in on him with black rods upraised.

A second touch from one of the red tips would bring about his death, Toller had been warned, and it was obvious that the Vadavaks intended to make sure of him by administering multiple contacts. But he had no intention of accepting death so easily, not with so much at stake. In spite of the debilitating pain which was washing through his body, he made a despairing effort to raise his sword to fend off the descending rods —and was thrilled to find his arms responding with close to normal speed and control.

The Vadavaks, abruptly realising their peril, stabbed at him with their enervators, but his sword was now moving swiftly in a near-visible defensive arc. The black rods were destroyed and scattered in an instant as Toller rose to his feet. One of the aliens got away from him by sprinting off to safety; the other was transfixed as he turned to flee. Toller withdrew his sword from the twitching body and ran back to rejoin the main battle. He noticed a soreness in his legs for the first few paces, but it quickly faded and he deduced that a Dussarran enervator was a fairly inadequate weapon when used against a large and healthy human.

That seemed a favourable omen, but when Toller reappraised the continuing struggle he saw the situation had altered for the worse in the brief time that he had been sidetracked. One of the women was on the ground and surrounded by Vadavaks who were jabbing at her with red-glowing enervators. Fearing that the inert figure might be Vantara, Toller pounded his way towards her attackers with a hoarse cry of rage. He reached them simultaneously with Steenameert, taking them unawares, and in an imposs-ibly short space of time—a time of raging red mists speckled with seething bright-rimmed corpuscles—the two humans had reduced at least five of the enemy to a bloody mass of carrion.

The woman on the ground was revealed as Corporal Tradlo. An enervator had been driven down her throat, her blonde hair was matted with blood, and it was obvious that she was dead.

Toller raised his eyes from her and saw that the remaining four women had split into pairs, each of which was busily engaged in close combat. To his left, Jerene and Mistekka had taken on four Vadavaks and were giving every appear-ance of being able to deal with the threat; to his right, Vantara and Arvand were almost hidden by a larger group of aliens who were pressing in on them from all sides.

Marvelling at the aliens' carelessness over the essential matter of guarding their flanks, Toller nodded to Steena-meert and they flung themselves at the milling group of white-clad figures. Again they wrought a fearful slaughter in the space of a few heartbeats, inflicting terrible gouting wounds which either levelled the recipients at once or sent them staggering blindly away to sink down and expire in pools of blood.

Other aliens were coming forward to take their places, but Toller was beginning to sense a change in the overall situation. The Vadavaks, possessing not even a rudimentary battle sense, were pressing their attack with undiminished fervour in spite of conspicuous lack of success—and their forces were rapidly being depleted. Snatching a quick glance around the complex scene, Toller guessed that less than half of the Vadavaks were still on their feet, and a proportion of those were becoming slow and uncertain in their movements.

It had to be less than a minute until the impeller unleashed the energies which would displace the planet, and from that time onward Director Zunnunun's warriors would—

presumably—have no reason to continue the struggle. They should be well content to withdraw at that stage and limit the number of their dead. Feeling a resurgence of optimism, Toller risked looking in the direction of Greturk and his fellow Dussarrans, hoping for an indication that the machine was about to function. He felt a dull shock when he saw that his allies had disappeared—the only sign that they had ever been present being a fast-fading tinge of green in the morning air.

An instant later Toller paid the price for allowing himself to be distracted from the deadly conflict all about him. Pain exploded through him as something touched his left shoulder, and an instant later the sensation was repeated again in the region of his left hip. He had twice been hit from behind by enervators, but this time—miraculously—the effect was less devastating than before and he was able to remain on his feet. His attacker, who had clearly expected a quick and easy kill, was still gaping at him in astonishment when Toller swung an ill-controlled blow which was intended to sever the alien's neck. The strike was slightly lacking in reach, because of Toller's partial immobility, and the sword tip reached no further than the Vadavak's throat, slicing cleanly through his windpipe. He clapped a hand to his throat and backed rapidly away, only to be impaled from behind by a sword held by the tall, dark-haired figure of Mistekka.

"These large bodkins are quite fun," she called out to Toller, her brown eyes glinting as she casually pushed the dying alien away. "I'm beginning to see why you always carried one."

"Just don't get careless!" No sooner had Toller spoken than he heard Steenameert give a bellow of pain. He turned and saw that his friend was surrounded by four Vadavaks who were jabbing at him with their enervators, at least one of which had found its mark.

"Stay on your feet, Baten!" Toller shouted. He threw himself forward, closely followed by Mistekka and the stockier figure of Jerene. They descended on Steenameert's attackers in a murderous swoop which, again in what seemed the blink of an eye, had a significant effect on the balance of forces. Steenameert had been hit with enervators several times and was sinking to the ground in spite of Arvand's attempts to hold him up. But when Toller took a broader view he was uplifted to see that the humans were running out of live opponents. Of the original attacking force only two were on their feet in the immediate vicinity, and they were being competently dealt with by Jerene and Mistekka.

Three other Vadavaks, having faced strong and well-armed enemies for the first time, were withdrawing in dismay, fleeing across the plain towards the point where they had materialised. The only other movements among the aliens, Toller noted with an exultant feeling of relief, came from the white-and-crimson carpet of the wounded. It was a tragedy that even one of the Kolcorronians had been lost, but. . . .

"Behind you, Toller!"

Jerene's warning shriek came too late. Toller heard the sudden movement shockingly close behind him, and realised at once that he had become too complacent, too certain that the diminutive Vadavaks had none of the tenacity of a genuine warrior. Now he felt a curious, unmanning sensation in the calf of his left leg. There was no pain to speak of, and yet he had just received the most serious injury of his life. He looked down and saw that a Kolcorronian sword, almost certainly Tradlo's, had gone to the bone in his leg. He struck backwards at the wounded Vadavak who had been lying on the ground, feigning death and awaiting his chance to strike. The alien sighed and rolled away to meet the point of Jerene's sword.

"We must finish the lot of them," Jerene shouted. "Show no mercy!"

"Keep everybody well away from the machine," Toller said to her, wondering why Vantara was not more in evidence in her capacity as Jerene's commander. "It is bound to detonate, or whatever it does, any second now."

Jerene nodded and signalled for the combatants to move farther away from the box, which was now glowing like fresh snow in the light of the rising sun. "And we had better take a look at that leg of yours."

"I'll be. . . ." Toller glanced down at his leg and felt a moment of giddiness as he saw that a grinning red mouth had opened right across the calf. It was spewing blood down his ankle on to the grass, and in its depths he could see the gleam of bone. When he tried to move the leg his foot remained obstinately on the ground.

"That has to be stitched here and now," Jerene said in a hard and unemotional voice. "Somebody give me a field kit."

Toller allowed himself to be lowered to the ground beside Steenameert, who was beginning to show signs of regaining consciousness. He felt nauseated, and was glad to surrender all responsibility to another for a period, even when the pain of the stitching began. With his chin resting on folded hands, Toller clenched his teeth and distracted himself from the pain by thinking about the impeller. What would the crucial moment be like? Would they hear great explosions or be blinded by flashes of lightning? And why was the cursed box taking so long to unleash its power?

"Surely more than four minutes have passed since we arrived in this place," he said to those who had clustered around to watch his leg being repaired. "What say you? Can you see anything happening?"

Steenameert, who was lying with his face towards the sky, startled Toller by answering his question as though he had never been unconscious. "I don't know about our wonderful white box, Toller—but I think something very strange is happening up there."

He pointed straight up to the zenith and others followed his example. Toller twisted his upper body around, grunting as he involuntarily disturbed the work being done on his leg, and looked into the centre of the sky. The vast disk of Land was divided equally by the terminator, and mounted exactly on the central line was the pulsing yellow star the watchers knew to be the Xa. But changes had taken place since Toller had first looked at it.

The Xa had grown much brighter—it now resembled a miniature sun—and its pulsations had become so rapid that they were almost merging into each other. It came to Toller that he had been so preoccupied with Greturk's impeller, and the events surrounding it, that he had practically forgotten about that infinitely greater impeller which had spread itself across the weightless zone. The collective attention focused on the distant Xa seemed to throw a telepathic gateway wide open. . . .

I cannot believe you are doing this to me, Beloved Creator! The anguish-laden message washed down out of an aureate sky. *After all I have done for you, you are bringing forward the time of my death! I implore you, Beloved Creator, do not deny me a last few minutes in your treasured company. . . .*

"What's going on here?" Toller growled, tearing the needle and suture from Jerene's fingers as he raised himself to a sitting position. "Greturk told us that his cursed box of tricks would do its job long before the Xa . . . long before Dussarra was hurled into another galaxy . . . but the way things are going. . . ." He fell silent, a chill perspiration gathering on his brow as he realised that he, and everybody he knew, and his entire home world could be on the point of instantaneous destruction.

Steenameert raised himself on one elbow. "It may be that Greturk's device is imperfect. He told us it was built in too much haste. Dussarrans can make mistakes, also, and it may be that the delay mechanism he spoke of is not. . . ." Steenameert's voice faded and his eyes grew wide as he pointed with one trembling finger at something beyond Toller's shoulder.

Toller followed his gaze and swore savagely as he saw

something which had the power to dismay him, even in this time of astonishing and momentous events. The gleaming white figure of a Vadavak, one who must have concealed himself during the closing chaotic moments of battle, had appeared by the boxy shape of the impeller. Professional training must have made him much stronger than the average Dussarran because, as the petrified humans watched, he squatted and put his hands under one edge of the impeller, then slowly but steadily straightened up.

The impeller tilted in unison with his movements and fell on its side. An instant later, almost as though triggered by impact, something in the white box began to emit a mechanical scream.

Toller tried to scramble to his feet, but his left leg refused to take his weight and he lurched painfully to the ground. "That's the final warning," he shouted, undergoing a unique kind of torment because of his inability to move. "The machine must be uprighted—*otherwise all is lost!*"

He looked to the three women who were standing in his field of view, willing them to undertake what he could not. Mistekka and Arvand continued to stare down at him, frozen to the spot by a new kind of fear. Vantara dropped to her knees, covered her face and began to sob.

"I expect promotion for this," Jerene exclaimed as she leapt to her feet, took her sword in hand and began to run towards the impeller. The strength inherent in her solid limbs, sprinter's strength, drove her through the impeding grass at a speed Toller doubted he could have matched even had he not been wounded.

The lone Vadavak, showing vastly greater courage and obduracy than his vanquished comrades, chose not to retreat. He ran towards Jerene and, when separated from her by several paces, dived at her ankles. She partially thwarted him with a scything blow of her sword—a touch of crimson was abruptly added to the bleached palette of the scene—but the alien succeeded in clamping his hands around one of

Jerene's shins, bringing her to the ground. There followed a moment in which it was impossible to see what was happening, a moment in which Toller was struck dumb with anxiety, and then Jerene was up and running again.

The shrieking of the white rectangle seemed to intensify as she reached it. She grasped its nearer top edge and tried to pull it downwards, but it resisted her efforts. She ran around to the farther side and disappeared from view as she stooped to gain a more effective hold on the massive cabinet. And then, with nerve-destroying slowness, the impeller rotated into its normal attitude.

In less than one heartbeat, Jerene had reappeared from behind the impeller and was sprinting—head thrown back and limbs blurring—towards the fear-stricken watchers. She had covered perhaps a third of the distance to safety when the impeller suddenly fell silent. In the absence of its frenetic screaming another message of hysteria was perceived with silent and dreadful clarity, beating down from the remote apex of the heavens.

Do not kill me, Beloved Creator! Do not. . . .

Toller, his face contorted into an inhuman mask of dread, looked beyond Jerene and saw the lustrous cabinet of the impeller begin to change its appearance. It glimmered and threw off expanding pale images of itself, layered versions of reality which flowed outwards to encompass all that could be seen of space and time.

Jerene was running through that shimmering matrix of what was and what might be, and Toller fancied she was calling his name. In one agonising thrust of his limbs he forced himself into an upright position and tried to move towards her.

But above Jerene the entire dome of the sky had begun to convulse and contort. Concentric rings of eye-searing brilliance were pulsing and flooding outwards from the Xa, and they were clashing in intolerable discords with the emanations from the white box. . . .

Too much is happening at once, Toller thought in the wildest extremities of terror.

EVERYTHING IS HAPPENING AT ONCE. . . .

Chapter 19

A deep, velvety and infinite darkness—a kind of night which was outside of Toller's previous experience—suddenly pervaded the scene. It was as though an opaque cover had been clamped over the entire planet. The blackness above was made even more intense by the fact that the impeller, after its display of dimensional sorcery, was now glowing like a huge block of fluorescent ice, casting a shallow pool of illumination over the silenced battle field.

Toller was still, blinking, trying to force his eyes to adapt to the strange new conditions, when Jerene reached him and allowed herself to be brought to a halt by his arms. She clung to him for a brief period, trembling and breathing harshly, then straightened up and stepped back a pace. For an instant Toller half-expected her to give him a formal salute, as though making amends for the breach of some rigorous discipline. Vantara, who had been standing close by, moved to Toller's side and gently enfolded his arm with hers.

Toller was scarcely aware of her presence as he gazed into the awesome emptiness of the heavens. At first he had thought the dark celestial canopy was completely featureless, but as his eyes continued to adjust he began to pick out coldly remote points of light which could be identified as stars. They were faint and sparse compared to those he had known all his life, so meagre with their output of light that an appreciable time went by before he seized on the strangest and most disconcerting factor of all.

Overland's sister world had vanished from its place directly above.

In its place, in the crown of the heavens, there was nothing more than a handful of chilly flecks of light arranged in alien configurations.

Steenameert, overcoming his paralysis, rose to his feet behind Toller and spoke with the rapt voice of a child. "It was all to no avail, Toller. We have been cast out. This place is not home to us."

Toller nodded, not trusting himself to reply, still yielding up his mind and soul to the black void which spanned his vision. *We have indeed been cast out*, he told himself. *This is how the universe will look when it has grown old. . . .*

"Such darkness," Vantara whispered, pressing herself closer to Toller. "It pleases me not at all—and I'm *cold*."

"In that case," Toller said, firmly disentangling his arm from hers, "I suggest that you begin gathering materials to build a fire. It may be a long time until dawn—if dawn ever comes."

"Of course dawn will come!" Vantara, angered by his symbolic rejection, was instantly on the offensive. "How can dawn fail to come? What a foolish thing to say!"

Toller realised with a surge of pity that she had no inkling, no glimmer of understanding of the momentous series of events the group had survived. His own insight, derived from telepathic exchanges with Divivvidiv and Greturk, was nebulous and patchy, but he knew in his bones that Overland—instead of being annihilated—had been projected into an inconceivably remote region of the universe.

And the "universe" he was thinking about was not even the limited and well-defined entity which came to mind when Kolcorronian scientists used the word. It was that woolly, intangible and maddeningly elusive philosophical concept which Divivvidiv had referred to as the *space-time continuum*. Toller had grasped the notion at the time of his telepathic tuition, but in spite of all his efforts his understanding of it had been fading ever since, like the wistful memory of a dream.

Now it was all but gone, the only lingering remnant being

241

its effect on his modes of thinking. Without being able to justify the idea in any form of words, he was quite prepared to believe that the incomprehensible forces unleashed by the Xa in its death throes could have displaced Overland in time as well as in space, perhaps far into the future of some parallel cosmos.

He was finding it hard to remember why he had ever been enamoured of Vantara in the first place—and now, gazing at her beautiful but petulant face, he sensed an unbridgeable gulf opening between them. She had closed her mind, and as a consequence had no way of sharing Toller's principal worry of the moment. Once, during the long hours of the flight to Dussarra, he had asked Divivvidiv how he knew the relocation device would not deposit the planet in the depths of interstellar space, too far from a sun for "minor" adjustments to be made in its position. Divivvidiv, possibly lost for a good answer, had slipped away from the question with some comments about *probability coalescence* and *abstruse self-generating design features of the Xa* which in the final outcome were to cope with *biological viability zones* and *orbital dynamics*.

Now Toller had to ask himself if there was a sun hidden behind the passive bulk of the planet. Either there would be a normal sunrise some hours from now, or Overland would grow colder and colder, and all its inhabitants would perish in never-ending blackness. There was only one way to obtain the answer, Toller realised, and that was by waiting. And there was no point in waiting in the dark. . . .

"Why is everyone not gathering wood?" he shouted jovially, turning away from Vantara. "Let us find an agreeable place—away from these miserable alien corpses—and light a good fire to comfort us through the night."

Cheered by having been presented with a homely objective, Steenameert, Mistekka and Arvand darted away towards a clump of wryberry bushes, the rounded outlines of which had gradually become visible in the starlight. Vantara gave Toller a prolonged stare, which he guessed to be one of disdain, then turned and slowly walked after the others, leaving him in the sole company of Jerene.

"Your leg needs many more stitches, but there is not enough light." She glanced at the impeller, which had now faded into a rectangular patch of grey. "I will bind the wound now and finish the job properly in the morning."

"Thank you," Toller said, suddenly realising that he was quite incapable of walking unaided. The wound, while serious enough, seemed insignificant in comparison to his size, and he was chastened to find that he felt cold, ill and weak. He stood patiently while Jerene bound his calf tightly with a bandage from the field kit.

"This is where my farm upbringing comes in useful," she said, securing the dressing with an expert knot.

"Thank you again!" Toller spoke in mock indignation, grateful to be distracted from his haunting worry about the sun. "You may nail new shoes to my hooves in the morning, but in the meantime will you assist me to join the others by the fire?"

Jerene stood up, put an arm around his waist and helped him walk towards the flicker of orange light which was already beckoning through the darkness. He found it more difficult and painful than he had expected to make progress through the long grass, and he was relieved when Jerene stopped to rest.

"Now I *doubly* deserve promotion," she said breathlessly. "You weigh nearly as much as my pet greyhorn."

"I'll see to your promotion as soon as. . . ." Toller paused, hesitating to make any promises for a future which might not exist. "You were very courageous when you ran to the machine. My blood froze for fear that you would not get clear of it in time."

"Why were you so concerned?" Jerene murmured. "After all, I had achieved what I set out to do."

"It may have been because. . . ." Toller smiled, realising

243

that Jerene was playing an ancient game with him, and all at once as they stood together in the darkness that game became more important to him than all his fear for the future of the planet. He drew her closer to him and they kissed with a kind of gentle fervour.

"The countess can see what we are doing," Jerene said, still being provocative as the kiss ended, and her breath was warm in his mouth. "The countess will not be pleased."

"What countess?" Toller said, and he and Jerene began to laugh as they clung together in the dark, dark night.

Toller had not expected to sleep. His wounded leg had begun throbbing like a busy machine, and in any case it had been inconceivable to him that he could lay down the burden of consciousness while wondering if his world was lost in a starless void. But the warmth of the fire had been pleasant, and it had felt good to have Jerene lying at his side with one arm draped across his chest, and he had been more tired than he knew. . . .

He opened his eyes with a start, trying to solve the urgent problem of deciding where he was. The fire had been reduced to white-coated embers, but it gave enough light for him to see the sleeping forms of his tiny band of warriors—and suddenly the great question was again hammering between his temples. He abruptly raised his head, causing Jerene to sigh in her sleep, and scanned the edges of the world.

There was a faint but unmistakable feathering of pearly light above one section of the horizon.

Toller's vision blurred with gratification as he took in the full, wondrous meaning of the tentative glow, then he sank back down to rest.

Chapter 20

Queen Daseene had suffered a major stroke, one which was almost certain to prove fatal.

As news of the impending tragedy raced out from Prad to the towns and lesser communities of Overland, the common people—already chastened by inexplicable events in the sky—became even more morose and subdued. Those of a religious or superstitious turn of mind saw the Queen's illness as having been foretold by the spate of omens which had so radically transformed the appearance of the heavens. And even those who had no time for the supernatural were affected by their awareness that something *very* strange had happened at dawn three days previously.

The early risers who had been out of doors at the crucial time were extremely graphic in their reports. They had spoken of the initial awe-inspiring moment during which a fierce source of yellow light, like a miniature sun, had appeared at the zenith, centred on the great disk of Land. Hardly had the eye become accustomed to the cosmic intruder when multiple shells of luminance, concentric to different sources, had exploded into pulsing conflict across the dawn sky.

And then—a final incredible act in the cosmic drama—the sky had . . . *died*.

The same word—died—had been employed over and over again. It sprang spontaneously to the lips of untutored observers who had spent their lives under heavens which were extravagantly patterned with light, spilling over with astronomical jewels of every kind.

The sky had appeared to die when Land simply blinked out of existence—along with the Great Wheel and a myriad of lesser silver spirals; countless thousands of stars, the most brilliant of which had formed the constellation of the Tree; the irregular streamers of misty radiance strewn like delicate tresses among the galaxies; the comets whose glowing and tapering fans partitioned the universe; the darting meteors which had enlivened the dome of night, briefly linking star to star.

All of these had disappeared in an instant, and now the sky seemed dead—all the more so because of the cold, aloof and infinitely remote points of light which, instead of illuminating the sky, served only to emphasise its lack of light.

Toller Maraquine, supported by his crutches, was watching the sunset from the south-facing balcony of his family's home. He had a hot drink positioned within reach on the wide stone balustrade, but it was forgotten for the time being as he saw the sky assume deeper and more sombre colours. He repressed a shiver as the alienness of the darkening celestial dome made itself more and more apparent, and it was not merely the aching absence of the sister world from its ordained station directly overhead which disturbed him. He had spent a fair amount of time on the "outside" of Overland —where most of the inhabitants could not even visualise having the detailed convexity of another planet suspended above them—and had quickly become accustomed to the changed environment.

His present sense of alienation, he had to admit to himself, was caused by the stark *emptiness* of the night sky. Doing his utmost to be pragmatic, calm and reasonable he had tried to shrug the whole thing off. What did it matter, he had asked himself, if the irrelevant and uncaring night sky contained a billion stars or only a scattered handful? Would either condition affect the yield of a harvest by so much as a single grain?

The trouble was that the reassuring negative answer failed to provide sufficient reassurance. He had no idea of what fate had overtaken Land or Dussarra—for all he knew those worlds no longer existed *anywhere*—but he understood with a bleak and sterile exactitude that Overland had been, to use Steenameert's phrase, cast out. This was an *alien* region of the space-time continuum. It had a heart-sinking quality to it. Somehow, within the blink of an eye, Overland had been flung into a decayed universe which had grown old and cold . . . *old and cold* . . . and the paramount question was posed: Could human life—individually and collectively—go on just as it had always done?

Physically, there appeared to be no obstacle to prevent the men and women of Kolcorron living out their lives in the same manner as their forebears had done since the beginnings of history. But was it possible that the drear sense of isolation, of inhabiting an outpost in the black wastes of infinity, could alter the racial outlook?

Land and Overland—sister worlds, so close that they were linked by a bridge of air—might have been designed by some cosmic Planner to coax and lure their inhabitants into becoming interplanetary travellers. And, once that critical first step had been taken, there had beckoned a universe laden with astronomical treasures—so obviously charged with the forces of life—that it would have been impossible for the adventurer to turn back. Toller's people had been predisposed by their spatial environment to look outwards, to believe that their future lay in *moving* outwards into a fertile and welcoming universe—but how would they feel now? Would there ever appear a hero with sufficient vision and courage, sufficient *stature*, to gaze at the remote and icy stars of Overland's bleak new sky and vow to make them his own?

Unwilling to confront abstracts any longer, Toller turned his back on the red-gold sunset and took a sip of his mulled brandy. As well as being heated, the liquor had been spiced and buttered to offset the coolness of the twilight air. He found its calorific familiarity deeply comforting as he watched his father and Bartan Drumme fuss over the telescopes which had been set up on the balcony. In his eyes the two older men had become granite pillars of intellectual fortitude and good sense in a quicksand universe, and his respect for them had been enhanced beyond measure. They were discussing a strange scientific anomaly, a quirky lesion in the fabric of the new reality, which thus far had been noticed by relatively few people.

"It is quite ironic," Cassyll Maraquine was saying. "It would be no exaggeration to say that, taking the state factories as a whole, there are at least a gross of highly qualified engineers and technicians who are directly answerable to me. They spend much of their time peering at the most accurate measuring instruments we can devise—but none of them saw *anything*!"

"Be fair," Bartan murmured. "There is no change in the way in which circles relate to circles, and most of your—"

Cassyll shook his greying head. "No excuse, old friend! It took a humble employee of the Cardapin brewery—a cooper!—to fight his way to me through all the cursed barriers that bureaucracies insist on erecting in spite of one's doughtiest efforts to prevent them. I have since plucked the man out of his lowly occupation and appointed him to my personal staff, where—"

"Tell me, father," Toller cut in, his curiosity aroused. "What *is* this to-do concerning rings and circles and wheels and the like which perplexes you so? What can be so strange and intriguing about an ordinary circle?"

"A circle has always had certain fixed properties, just like any other geometrical figure, and now those properties have suffered a sudden change," Cassyll said in solemn tones. "Until now, as you very well know, the circumference of a circle has been *exactly* equal to three times its diameter. Now, however—if you care to put the matter to the test— you will find that the ratio of circumference to diameter is slightly *more* than three."

"But. . . ." Toller tried to assimilate the idea, but his mind baulked at the task. "What does it mean?"

"It means we are a long way from home," Drumme put in, with a twist of the lips which hinted that he had said something very profound.

"Yes, but will it make any difference to our lives?"

Cassyll snorted as he took the lens cap off a telescope. "There speaks a man who has never had to earn his crusts in commerce or industry! The re-design and re-calibration of certain classes of machinery is going to cost the state a veritable fortune. And then there will be clerical costs, and accountancy costs, and—"

"Clerical?"

"Just think of it, Toller. We have twelve fingers, so we naturally count to the base of twelve. That, coupled with the fact that the circumference of a circle used to be precisely three times the diameter, made whole areas of computation absurdly easy. From now on, however, everything in that line is going to be more difficult—and I am not talking about matters as rudimentary as a cooper having to learn to make longer straps for his barrels. Take, for example, the—"

"Tell me," Toller said quickly, anxious to forestall one of his father's rambling discourses, "what *is* the new ratio? I ought to know that much, at least."

Cassyll glanced significantly at Bartan. "There has been a certain amount of discussion on that point. I have been too busy—what with the distressing events at the palace and so forth—to take measurements in person. Some of my staff are claiming that the new ratio is three-and-a-seventh— which, of course, is nonsense."

"Why is it nonsense?" Bartan said with some heat.

"Because, my old friend, there has to be a natural harmony in the world of numbers. Three-and-a-seventh would work in with nothing. I have no doubt at all that when the measurements are made with proper accuracy we will find that the new ratio is amenable to. . . ."

Toller allowed his attention to wander away from what promised to be a lengthy argument of the type from which his father and Bartan Drumme had always derived great satisfaction. He wished that Jerene was by his side, but she had gone to visit her family in the village of Divarl and was not expected back until the morrow. Tired of standing by the balustrade, he made his way to a couch, lowered himself on to it and set his crutches aside. His leg, now that the process of healing was well under way, had become stiff and capable of producing excruciating pain when subjected to any degree of stress. Simply living with such a leg, continually devising strategies to prevent it unleashing bolts of agony, was an experience which Toller found enervating and exhausting, and he was glad to lie down.

"Son, perhaps you should go off to your room and take your night's sleep," Cassyll Maraquine said gently, coming to stand by the couch. "The wound was more severe than you seem to think."

"Not yet—I'd rather stay here for a while." Toller smiled up at his father. "I seem to remember us exchanging similar words many times in the past, when I was a child. Are you about to pack me off to bed whether I like it or not?"

"You are too big for that kind of treatment. Besides, I am busy and I do not want to be plagued with calls for glasses of water."

"And honey straws," Bartan Drumme bantered from farther along the balcony. "Don't forget the honey straws."

"Honey straws!" Toller rose on one elbow. "Is that what I . . . ?"

"Yes, even though it might seem a strange weaning for the one they have begun to call the Godslayer," Cassyll said to Toller. "You didn't know that, did you? One can only guess at what kind of stories your friend Steenameert is noising abroad, but I'm told that every tavern in the realm is ringing with tales of how you flew to a land far beyond the heavens and slew a thousand gods . . . or demons . . . or a promiscuous mixture of both in order to save Overland from being swallowed by a great crystal dragon."

Cassyll paused, looking rueful. "Now that I weigh the matter up, I suspect that the average ale-fuddled plough-man's understanding of what happened is equal to or better than mine. Toller, all those things that were explained to you when mind addressed mind without recourse to speech . . . Have you no recollection at all, not even a trace, of what was meant by the term 'space-time'? I would dearly love to know why two words which can have no logical connection came to be joined together in that particular way."

"I am unable to help you," Toller said with a sigh. "When Divivvidiv was speaking within my head I seemed to have a full understanding of what he meant, but the messages were written in smoke. Everything has faded. I reach for meanings, only to find emptiness. Not a true emptiness—but one which is haunted by echoes, a poignant feeling of massive doors having just closed for ever, of my being too slow and too late. I am sorry, father—I wish it were otherwise."

"Never mind—we will make the journey unaided." Cassyll brought a thick blanket to the couch and draped it over Toller. "The nights are colder here."

Toller nodded and made himself comfortable, yielding to the luxurious feeling of being well cared for and of having no immediate responsibilities. His leg was throbbing warmly, and the physicians had predicted that he would henceforth walk with a limp, but that gave him even more entitlement to bask like a child in snug warmth, secure like a child beneath a blanket which—better than the stoutest armour —gave protection against all those elements of the outside world which might bring harm.

Safely cocooned, his mind misting with drowsiness, Toller tried to define his position in an unfamiliar universe. So much had been *lost*. The Queen was dying, unable to face or even comprehend a reality in which the planet of her birth—to which she had longed to return—no longer existed. Her dream of a single nation encompassing two worlds had been shattered in an instant. It had been a good dream, one with which Toller had instinctively sympathised, but now there would be no mile-high columns of skyships, commercially and culturally laden, plying the invisible trade lanes between Land and Overland. Instead, there would be . . . what?

More tired than he had realised, Toller found himself quite unable to deal with the sly and shifting enigmas of the future. He began slipping in and out of consciousness, and with each return to lucidity the sky was darker and the stars were more numerous, looking brighter than he had expected. The balcony was dark also, because his father and Bartan Drumme were using the telescopes, busily making and comparing notes.

Toller listened to the murmurous activity for an indeterminate time . . . dozing and drifting . . . half-comprehending the stray wisps of conversation that came his way . . . and gradually his mood began to change. He could see now that he had allowed himself, possibly through battle shock and extreme weariness, to be intimidated by the new sky, to become downcast and despondent in the face of it. He had asked if Kolcorron would ever find champions worthy of challenging that inimical black void, and at the very time of posing the question had been too blinkered by pessimism to realise that he was already in the company of such heroes.

Cassyll and Bartan were two middle-aged men whose investment in the old order of things had been much greater than his, and whose stake in a vexed future had to be correspondingly less—but had they slumped down to indulge in self-pity? No! Their reaction had been to take up their swords—swords of the mind—and at that very moment, quietly and without fanfare, they were engaged in no less an undertaking than laying the foundations of a new astronomy!

Halfway between wakefulness and sleep, Toller smiled.

His father and Bartan Drumme were speaking in low voices to avoid disturbing Toller's rest, but whispers insinuate